SINS OF THE FATHER

Sharon Bairden

RED DOG
UK

Published by RED DOG PRESS 2020

First Edition

Hardback ISBN 978-1-913331-52-8

Paperback ISBN 978-1-913331-50-4

Ebook ISBN 978-1-913331-51-1

www.reddogpress.co.uk

Ohana means family; family means nobody gets left behind or forgotten.

To my mum and dad; Anton, Jess, Ashleigh, Logan and Cooper; Lynn, Ian, David, Louise and Lacie. You are my world.

Prologue

Rebecca, Kirkintilloch 2018

IT BEGAN THE same way as always—a sense that something was lurking in the room, a black shape casting its malevolent shadow over her; the feeling of dark beady eyes feasting on her, sharp fingers pinching gently at first then becoming faster, more furious. Their claws dug into her skin, tearing at her muscles until she was sure they would be ripped apart.

In a bid to escape, she bit down hard on the unknown creatures, feeling their small bones crunch against her teeth but her bites didn't register. They didn't stop the relentless grabbing, crawling over her, touching her body, making her squirm, crawling up onto her chest until her breath almost left her.

Struggling against them, she fought to break free with every nerve in her body, pushing until she felt herself being propelled forward—faster, more furious—the wind sounding a mighty roar, escalating to hurricane force, its violence pulling the skin back from her face as she tried desperately to soar to freedom. The vibrations pounded her head, increasing until the point she felt that every bone in her face would shatter, but still the creatures chased, grabbing at their prize and unwilling to let go.

Her heart pumped so hard in her chest, it felt as though it was about to break free. She was sure she was going to have a heart attack or a stroke right here, right now, until finally she forced herself to stretch out her index finger, pushing it forward, screaming to escape and whoosh, it was gone.

Just like that.

The storm had ended and, as she watched the small black hands still grabbing, they slowly faded away; dimmed in their ferocity. It was quiet again.

Still.

Forcing her eyes to open fully, taking deep breaths, her heartbeat slowing down, she reached out and grabbed the torch lying next to her bed. Turning it on, she slumped back on her pillows as she checked her hands and face for the tell-tale marks of the teeth and claws, although she knew there would be none. In the safety of the light, her breathing slowed as she gradually became aware of the familiar surroundings, the weight lifted from her shoulders and the demons retreated to wherever they came from.

She could feel something warm brush up against her, rough fur as a wet nose burrowed into her palm. It was the dog. She gave a start as the memories filled her head. She turned. The cold, stiff body of the man was lying next to her, curled up on his side, his dead eyes never leaving her. She opened her mouth to scream, but nothing came out as the dog lay down and howled.

PART ONE

Rebecca's Story

1

Rebecca, Glasgow, 2002

MY NAME IS Rebecca, I'm sixteen, and this is my story.

I was six years old when I realised I was different. Up until then I thought everyone was like me. I thought everyone switched places with their other selves; the other ones who lived inside them. When I went to school and the other kids laughed at me, then I knew it was just me. Nobody could understand why I would turn from a wee quiet child to this wild thing, tearing around the class, screaming and shouting before cowering in the corner muttering to myself.

'Weirdo! Freak!' The other kids would yell at me. I didn't care, I didn't need them, I had my others.

But at night, when I was alone, when the truth hit me, I would sit at my bedroom window watching as the sun settled down for the night. Crying, I'd whisper to her, 'Please see me.'

I wanted the sun to see me cry, I needed her to come and take me away with her on her night time adventures, far away from the nightmare that was my life. When the sky grew dark and the moon took her place, I'd wait for the man in the moon to appear. I told myself that if he existed, he would see the evil surrounding me. He'd make the sun take me with her. He'd make her protect me. I waited forever but no one ever came to save me, not until it was too late. One nightmare simply replaced another.

So it's no wonder I find myself here, discharged from hospital—a mental hospital—with their voices mocking me inside my head. It's time for a new start, a new beginning. *You're not going to let him get away with it, are you?* the loudest voice hisses. I smile. I am not stupid, of course I am not going to let him get off scot free.

I shiver, the sky is a silky dark. A chill has settled in the branches and the moon and stars wink at me through the leaves. I tremble as the memories run through my head, and bite back my tears, gazing skyward.

The man in the moon smiles at me. It's my sign. It's time to start over again. It's time to make them pay.

Rebecca, Glasgow, 1996

IT WAS COLD the day they arrived. The kind of cold that seeps deep into your bones and settles there. I crouched in the corner of the room, shivering, like a wounded animal taking shelter. Only there was no shelter, not there.

Pity filled their eyes as they moved towards me. Revulsion peeked out too, noses wrinkling as they grew closer to the stench of dirt, neglect and abuse oozing from my body. It was putrid and the smell clung to me. No matter how many times I washed or scrubbed myself, I couldn't get clean, I couldn't get rid of it. My once blonde mass of curls was reduced to a matted muddy mess. It lay lank against my face. I strained to listen for my other self—my stronger self—but she had become silent. Cowered against the wall. I was ten years old and I was alone.

Four of them had come to get me. The heavy clatter of their feet and their muffled shouts had been a welcome distraction from what lay before me. The neighbours must have heard something and reported it. Finally, I'd thought. How long had they closed their ears to what was going on? How long had they pretended they couldn't hear, or see? If only they'd done something sooner. If only…

I'd tried to wake her up. I'd tried so hard. Her. Stella—the woman they called my mother. But she wouldn't wake up. Her body was still, and the blood trailing from her ear was warm. It had pooled on the greasy kitchen lino, a faint metallic smell bled into my nostrils. There had been something strangely comforting about it, a sign that it was all finally over. I ran my fingers through the blood, smearing it against my grubby skin, wanting to keep her close forever.

As I stared at the horror in front of me, a tormented wail escaped from deep inside. Collapsing to the floor, my cries grew louder and louder until something snapped inside my head and the tears stopped as abruptly as they'd started. A strange feeling engulfed me. Something was growing inside me. I felt a sudden rush of energy, and a strength that came from nowhere. My other self was back, her voice loud amongst the others, telling me what to do, taking control.

I took a deep breath, inhaling the scent of death, before I glanced at the figures standing before me. The four of them had stared right back, looks of horror and disgust washed across their faces. A hysterical laugh escaped from my mouth as I drank in their expressions. My laugh became a growl as I dropped to all fours, ready to pounce. They snapped out of their trance-like state and began moving—busy, active. The silence returned.

Four adults filled our tiny kitchen; a man and a woman I recognised as police officers only because of their uniforms. There was another man and woman too, but they were dressed in ordinary clothes. I didn't know who they were. I should have been scared of the strangers in our kitchen, but I'd already seen much worse in my short life.

The room was blurring at the edges, the noises jarring inside my head, my world was spinning and all I wanted to do was to lie down and let it all go. The constant chattering I'd become used to had faded away. I was floating, watching everything from above. My hands covered my face, clawing at my skin, desperately trying to bring myself back.

The adults broke into action.

'Jesus Christ,' snapped the older man. 'Marie, get that child out of here now.'

Marie swooped me up; away from the bloody mess that was my mother. She held me close. I felt my body relax, the tension melting away as she murmured in my ear.

'It's okay, sweetheart, I've got you.'

I buried my face in her soft hair, breathing in the faint clean scent of her shampoo, trying to inhale the goodness that was her and make it part of me. It was too late though, far too late for me. *Rotten Rebecca, dirty rotten little Rebecca*, the voices started up again, all of them at once this time. I tried to block them out as I clung onto Marie.

As Marie carried me outside, she whispered: 'You're as light as a feather, hen.'

I didn't feel light, I felt heavy, weighed down by life.

We were flanked by the police officers, their radios crackling with disjointed voices. The older man walking behind us.

'We've got her, sarge,' I heard the policeman say, the sound of relief evident in his voice.

'She's in some nick, but we've got her.'

The neighbours had looked on from the safety of their gardens. Their whispers carried across the fences.

'That poor wean, look at the state of her. Fur fuck's sake, what the hell's been goin' on in that house?'

'I said you should have phoned the polis before,' another berated her husband. His eyes dropped to the ground.

He should be ashamed. They all should be ashamed. Every single one of them carried some blame for what had happened to me. By doing nothing they were as guilty as the men who had come into my life and destroyed me.

I lifted my head and looked straight at them, my other self's eyes accusing each one of them. I spat a satisfying great big gob of yellow spit. It landed at their feet, just missing contact. None of them moved, none of them said a word. But they knew, they all knew.

Perhaps if I'd looked a little bit harder, I'd have seen the girl peer out at me from behind the safety of the grown-up's limbs and chatter. I would have seen her watch me, and I'd never have forgotten her stare.

But I didn't look. I didn't see her.

Like me, she was invisible.

2

Things moved pretty fast once we left the house. Hands wrapped me in a blanket and bundled me into a police car. It's funny the things you remember—and I remember that blanket, it was a dirty grey colour; it stank of wet dogs and was rough against my little skinny legs. But it was the most comfort I'd felt for a long time. I pulled it tighter around me, hoping it would shield me from the world outside.

Marie sat on one side of me, with the older man on the other side. He'd said nothing to me other than to ask my name and age.

His eyes widened when I told him I was ten. I knew I was small for my age; I always had been. That had been part of the attraction for the men who visited.

The car was warm inside. Someone had pressed a bag of crisps into my hands and as I crammed them into my mouth, I was aware of soft hands stroking my hair. It was Marie. I'd shrunk back from her touch when I'd remembered how dirty my hair was, but she hadn't seemed to mind. She'd murmured reassuringly to me throughout the journey. I didn't hear her words, only the soothing rumble of her voice. The comforting chatter of strangers cocooned me as the world outside rushed by.

When the car stopped, we got out, and I was led into an old grey building. I had no idea where I was. It wasn't in a part of Glasgow I recognised. Litter was scattered outside, the windows black with dirt, an air of neglect cloaking its walls. A little like myself, really.

Inside, the air felt stuffy. The paint was peeling off the walls and a cluster of desks had been shoved together, the towers of paperwork ready to tumble. A faint smell of fish—someone's lunch perhaps—hung in the air, threatening to hit the back of my throat and make me puke. The sound of hushed whispers and frantic phone calls as a room full of strangers watched my entrance. I could see the looks of pity passing across the desks as I picked my way through the office into a small room at the end.

Marie and the man sat me down on an old battered chair. I pushed myself back into it, wanting it to swallow me up. Anything to escape the attention of the two adults who sat across from me, watching me. Marie broke the silence, 'Have you got any relatives pet? Anyone close by?'

I shook my head, unable to speak.

'What about your dad, pet? Is he about?' I shrugged in response.

'You don't know where he is?' she probed.

'I-I-I don't h-have a d-dad.'

'Rebecca, pet, do you know if there are any aunts or uncles, any family at all, that you could stay with at the moment, just until we get things sorted out for you?' Marie asked me kindly.

Again, I shook my head and the tears rolled down my cheeks. Reality suddenly hit me. My mum was gone, and I was on my own.

The man had left the room, leaving me alone with Marie. She said nothing; she just sat with me, her silence strangely reassuring among all the chaos inside my head. The chattering was back, and it was relentless. I screwed my eyes shut and began to hum in an attempt to drown the voices out.

The voices in my head grew quieter and through the open door, I heard the man's words, 'Aye, we need an emergency placement... A couple of weeks just... Maybe more... Damaged... Her ma's dead... No known family.'

I guessed it was me the man was talking about, but my head was like a washing machine, spinning his words and the voices in my head together. *Nobody wants you Rebecca, nobody cares.*

Glancing around the room—empty other than for me and Marie—I felt safe, nobody could hurt me here. *You'll never be safe, Rebecca.* I wanted to stay here. I didn't want them to send me back home. But I worried that if I didn't tell anyone what had really happened back there, they would send me back. And the men would come back. *You can't tell them, Rebecca. Nobody will believe you. Even your own mum didn't believe you, did she?*

My others were right, Mum hadn't believed me, she hadn't stopped bad things happening to me. *You're disgusting, Rebecca. If you tell them they will be disgusted by you too. It's all your own fault, Rebecca.* I decided to say nothing. *Good girl, Rebecca. We'll look after you, you're safe with us.*

'She was on her own,' I'd heard the man say. Those words and their meaning must have penetrated my brain among all the chaos, but I'd been too caught up in what was going on to think much more about it. 'She was on her own,' had stuck there, though.

I was frightened now; I'd never been on my own before. Not properly on my own. Who would look after me? Where would I live? Would I be safe? Would the men come back? The questions were all babbling in my mind, clamouring for attention. My eyes screwed up, I shook my head, and I couldn't hear myself think. I wanted the voices to stop. I wanted them to be quiet. For once.

'Ssshhh,' I scolded them. They faded away a little. My head quiet, I clenched my fists and dug my nails into the palm of my hand. The pain felt good. The man came back into the room and Marie smiled at him. I'd shrank back a little, the flashbacks of strange men coming to our house running through my head. Was he here to hurt me, or to help me? Marie must have sensed my discomfort and threw me a smile.

'Rebecca, this is Jim Aitken. He's one of the social workers who works here with me. It's okay, pet, he's here to help. He was in the house with us, he came back in the police car with us, do you remember?'

I looked at Marie first, then turned to look at Jim. I nodded, recognising him as the man who had been in the house when they'd come for me. I peered at his eyes. They were smiling back at me—real smiles—the creases and crinkles around them reassuring me. I felt my body relax. I was safe. He must be a good man.

Jim moved over to Marie's desk. He leaned over and spoke so softly that I couldn't hear what was said. I could see Marie nodding her head and smiling faintly. They turned to look at me.

'We've found you somewhere to stay tonight, pet,' said Marie quietly. 'Jim is going to take you to the house and Alex here is going to go with you.'

I looked to the door as a younger woman with the shiniest red hair ever walked in. She had a huge grin plastered across her face. Her smile was genuine, there was no doubt about that.

'Hey, Rebecca, I'm Alex Doherty, and I work here with Jim and Marie. I'm going to come along in the car with you for the ride, is that okay?'

I smiled back at her and nodded, thrusting my hand into hers, but not before I tried to wipe the dirt from my fingers.

The next thing I knew, I was being bundled into the back of another car, this time Alex was in the back with me and Jim was driving. I was glad Alex was there. She'd filled the silence with her endless chatter and didn't seem to mind when I didn't answer any of her questions.

She talked about me staying with some people, just until they sorted out something a little more permanent. I didn't know what she meant. I didn't really care. I just nodded and watched the streets of Glasgow rush by, the street lights a blur, Alex chattering in the background.

A few times I caught Jim watching me in his rear-view mirror. I returned his smile but didn't meet his eyes; his stares were making me uncomfortable. *Why does he keep looking at me?* Although I felt uneasy under his gaze, it didn't feel the same as the men who came to our house. It was just unsettling, as though he was trying to see inside my head, to the parts of me I wanted to keep hidden.

I turned away from him and peered out the car window. I was desperately searching for her—my other self. I was wasting my time though, she wasn't out there. She only existed inside of me, along with the others.

It wasn't long before we pulled up in front of a house in the middle of a small estate. It didn't look that much cleaner than where I'd lived with my mum. There were a few stray dogs roaming around, the kind with tails that curl at the end. The unloved kind. Like me. This didn't feel good.

A woman stood at the door; her face painted with a warm smile. She'd looked like she was waiting. Waiting for me? I couldn't see her eyes properly in the fading light, I couldn't tell if her smile was real.

Alex squeezed my hand, offering me reassurance. This is where my next chapter began. If only things had been different.

3

The sight of the woman at the door triggered memories of my life before it all went wrong.

Mum and I lived in the middle of Crofthouse, a housing scheme in the north-east of Glasgow. It wasn't the nicest place to live but, at six years old, I hadn't known anything different. Mum wouldn't let me out to play on the streets back then.

'It's too dangerous, Rebecca,' she'd tell me. 'Folk selling drugs or fighting on the streets. You stay in here with me hen, it's much safer.'

Mum's name was Stella Cartwright and everyone on the scheme knew her. 'They think I'm a snob, hen,' she'd laugh, 'Just because I don't let you hang around the streets like the rest of the wee toe-rags out there.'

I knew we didn't have much money, but in our house it didn't matter. Mum always made sure I was fed and dressed in clean clothes, even if they were second hand. Even then, I wasn't like the other kids, I was made to speak properly and show my manners.

'Just because we've no money, doesn't mean we can't be polite, does it?'

Mum hated cheeky kids and especially kids who asked too many questions. I found that out the hard way when I'd asked her where my dad was. Mum never spoke about my dad and until I'd went to school, it hadn't really bothered me. Other kids talked about their dads all the time, even the kids whose dads didn't live with them. Our class was making Father's Day cards and I refused to make one, 'I haven't got a dad,' I told my teacher. She smiled and said I must have a dad, everyone had a dad, even if they didn't live with them. She let me make a card for my mum instead, though. I ran home from school that day and gave my mum the card, repeating what my teacher had said. Mum's face went pure white as she looked at me, her eyes blazing.

'You ungrateful little bitch,' she spat, grabbing me by the collar of my school shirt. Her face pushed into mine, she hissed: 'Aye, you had a father, useless bastard that he was. As soon as you came along, he scarpered, leaving me to get on with it. If it hadn't been for you, I'd have been out of this shithole by now. It's your bloody fault we are here, and here *you* are daring to ask *me* about your dad!'

'I'm sorry,' I whimpered. I'd witnessed my mum's temper before when I'd given her cheek but never like this. I was terrified. 'I-i-it's just Miss Ovens s-s-said that everyone had a…'

I didn't get to finish my sentence. The slap across my face silenced me.

'Listen to me. Your dad left because he didn't want you. He didn't bloody care about you. I'm the one who's put food in your belly and a roof over your head, so shut your bloody mouth about your dad and you can tell that bloody teacher to mind her own business.'

I didn't ask about him again.

That night, in my bed, still reeling from my mum's attack on me, was when I first became aware of my others.

Your dad isn't here because he doesn't love you. You're not good enough to have a dad. Bad Rebecca doesn't have a dad. I could hear their voices inside my head, laughing at me.

I cried myself to sleep that night. When I woke up the next morning, three small slashes lined my thigh, the blood dried in little red threads. I had no idea how they got there, not even when I went to the toilet for a pee and saw Mum's razor lying out on the shelf.

Mum must have felt bad about losing her temper with me. A couple of days later, she called me through to her bedroom. She pointed to her bed where a small wooden jewellery box lay. Painted white with tiny blue and yellow flowers printed all over, it was the kind that played music when the lid opened. It had a tiny little dancer who twirled round as the music played. But that wasn't what she'd wanted to show me.

She pushed the box across the bed towards me. As I opened the lid slowly, the dancer spun, and the shimmer of something shiny caught my eye. A necklace with half a heart and the words 'Side by Side or Miles Apart…' inscribed in tiny letters.

'It's from your dad, but don't get your hopes up, hen, that's all he ever left you. I wasn't even going to give it to you, but I guess you've got the right to have something of his. He's gone though, so there's no point in wasting any more of your time thinking about him. You don't need him.' She sunk back on the bed and I knew by the look on her face not to ask her anything else.

Alone at night in my room, I opened the box. Listening to the music, I clutched the pendant close to me and my heart soared, I did have a dad. I knew it. One day, I'd find him.

I painted a picture of my dad in my imagination. Big and strong. He was rich. He lived in a big house in the country, like a castle. In the fantasy world I created, my dad would come and find me, he'd take me on holiday, buy me a pony and I'd be his little princess. As I stroked the jewellery box, my imagination running away with me, my fingers caught on something; a small scrap of paper had been stuck under the felt lining of the jewellery box. Taking it out carefully, I'd smoothed it over. The words were written in grown-up writing and I struggled to make them out, but something told me I should keep this note, that it was important. I tucked it back under the lining, never realising just how significant it would become.

AT SCHOOL, I was always on the outside looking in. Everyone gravitated towards their own little groups, never inviting me to join in. It hurt, but I tried not to care. Being weird and from the scheme didn't bring the privilege of friendship. People from the scheme didn't have time for anyone who was different.

The rest of the kids mostly ignored me when they weren't laughing at me behind my back. I would hear them calling me a weirdo and a freak. I knew they were right—I *was* different to them. I felt different, like there was more than one of me. I could hear the voices inside my head chattering amongst themselves, deciding what I should do, taking control of my life, making me do things I didn't want to do.

After a while it stopped bothering me, I kind of got used to them being around. They were company for me, I guess. They were my friends—my only friends. They could be kind and caring, taking away all the bad things; or they could be mean and nasty, whispering bad things in my head and making me do things I knew I shouldn't.

Like the time our dog, Lassie, went missing. She had been my only friend until my others arrived. She managed to get out the house one night and never came back. I wouldn't have done that, and neither would my mum. It had to have been one of them, hadn't it?

Out of all the voices, there was one who was the loudest—she even gave herself a name—Samantha. She made me laugh, she didn't let anyone calling us names bother her. Samantha looked out for me. But she had a cruel side. Nobody should mess with Samantha.

When Samantha was around, I didn't need to hide away, she made me feel ten feet tall. We'd huddle together for hours, her whispering away to me, making me giggle. I knew other people pointed and laughed, but I didn't care, at least I wasn't alone anymore. She wasn't scared of anything or anybody. She had the answers to all my questions. In a world of grey, she was my rainbow.

At home, I'd stare at myself in the mirror, reaching out and touching the face staring back at me. I didn't want that face, it felt like a mask that didn't quite fit. Only when Samantha's face stared back at me did I feel like I belonged somewhere.

One day I plucked up the courage to tell Mum about the voices—I wanted her to know it wasn't me doing bad things. I watched her body stiffen and her mouth drop open so wide I could see all her fillings.

'You know, hen, people are going to start talking about you if you tell them you hear voices in your head. They'll say you're not right in the head.'

I didn't mention them again. To anyone.

THURSDAY WAS MY favourite day. It was the day Mum got her money from the post office before she came to school to pick me up. At three o'clock on the dot, I'd be the first in the class ready for the school bell ringing. First in my class to rush out the doors, a huge grin spread across my face when I saw her at the school gate. Mum never forgot to come and get me, not like some of the other kid's mums, who would come racing up to the gates at the last minute, as though they'd forgotten they even had a kid. My mum wasn't like that, she was always there for me.

At the school gate, the other mothers would watch me—suspicion mixed with fear written across their faces. No doubt their kids had told them of my strange outbursts in class. In their small cliques I'd hear them laugh as I walked by hand-in-hand with my mum.

'Hold your head up high, hen,' she'd whisper through gritted teeth. 'Don't let any of those stuck-up bitches look down their noses at you.'

I'd grip her hand tighter and together we'd walk past them, me straining my neck to hold my head as high as I could. For some reason that would send Mum into a fit of giggles. Those were the days when everything was okay in my world and Mum was still a proper mum.

4

SITTING IN THE car, these were the thoughts squirming inside my head, trying to untangle themselves from the chaos they were in. Screwing up my eyes, I willed my brain to hold on to the good memories of Mum before everything went wrong. I tried to go back, but Alex's voice pulled me from my memories.

'We're here,' she said, and opened the door, bundling me out of the car into my new life.

Clutching onto my plastic carrier bag containing everything I owned—a carrier bag, I'd soon learn, would forever define me as a kid from care—I forced one foot in front of the other as I made my way reluctantly up the path. My mouth was dry as I chewed at my lips, tasting a spot of blood. Would they like me? Would they want me to stay? *Nobody is going to want you to stay Rebecca. You're a little bitch and everybody hates you.* 'Shut up!' I screamed inside my head.

The Reids were an average couple living an average life in an average house. Or so they must have thought. Then I arrived. A little bundle of chaos wrapped in layers of anger and mistrust, ready to wreak havoc on their lives. *Serves them right really for being interfering do-gooders.* The thought popped into my head from nowhere. I ignored it, painting on my best smile. I wanted them to like me. I wanted a new mum… And a dad. I wanted a dad more than anything. A dad who would love me the way dads were meant to love their little girls. I didn't want my others ruining my chances for me.

Once inside, Mrs Reid fussed over me, giving me a glass of milk and a biscuit while she, Alex, and Jim did some grown-up talking. I sat back and nibbled on my biscuits quietly, watching, waiting, and drinking it all in. Mr Reid was there too, reading his paper. He gave the impression that he wasn't interested in me, just looking over at me briefly and winking. My heart sank as I took an instant dislike to him. His gaze told me he wasn't going to be the kind of dad I was looking for. I could see the kind of attention he was paying me, his head slowly turning around on the stump of his fat podgy neck, his little beady eyes boring into my soul. I'd shivered as he watched, and I felt his eyes peeling back my skin, exposing the blackness that lay beneath.

I wrapped my arms tight round my small body, trying to protect myself, but it was impossible, his eyes never left me for a minute. I heard the voices whisper inside my head. *Keep an eye on that one. He knows what you are, Rebecca.* I gave myself a shake and started to listen to what the grown-ups were saying. They were talking about placements and meetings, the words meant little to me, other than I would be staying here for a while.

Jim began putting his papers back into his bag as he and Alex stood up. They were getting ready to leave. Jim must have noticed the look of panic on my face.

'It's alright hen, I'll be back at the end of the week to see how you're getting on. You'll be fine.'

'Come on Rebecca, I'll show you your bedroom.' Mrs Reid took my hand and gave it a small squeeze. I watched her face tighten as I felt Samantha squeeze her hand back harder.

Compared to my room at home, this one was warm and cosy. Mrs Reid told me it had been built specially for girls like me. I felt cold fingers running down my spine. There was a small single bed, neatly made, a straight-backed chair, and a small chest of drawers, but no mirror. I thought that was strange. I remembered my mum always looking in the mirrors at home, fussing at her hair, fixing her lipstick. Even towards the end, when it made no difference to how she looked, she would still do it. I wondered about a house that had no mirrors in the bedrooms. What secrets were they trying to hide?

The windows were framed with heavy, old fashioned, red velvet curtains, and firmly shut. Opening the curtains slightly, I watched as a fly buzzed angrily against the glass. I knew exactly how that fly felt—trapped.

Closing my eyes, I thought about my bedroom at home. The walls had been grubby, with dark, discoloured patches of damp decorating the cold plastered walls, the wallpaper peeling as though it was trying to tear itself free from the dirt. Mum had done her best with what little she had. She tried to brighten it up with posters from magazines, using them to cover the worst of the damp. My duvet didn't have a pretty pink cover like the one here at the Reid's; it had no cover and the only pattern had been the filth from the men who had come into my life. But it had been mine. This room wasn't. I didn't belong here.

I opened my eyes. The fly was squashed dead between my thumb and forefinger. I didn't remember doing that. *Murdering bitch. That's what you are, Rebecca.*

5

IN 1993, WHEN I was seven years old, things began to get worse. I believed it was all my fault—if I hadn't been such a freak, if only the others who lived inside me hadn't made me do bad things, then none of this would have happened. My dad wouldn't have left me, and things wouldn't have gone so horribly wrong. I wanted to be good, I really did, but sometimes they wouldn't let me. Maybe if they hadn't been here then everything would have been alright. But what I didn't realise then was that they probably saved my life.

Things had just been trundling on, we were all muddling along together in our own way, me, mum and my others. As long as I didn't talk to her about them, she just let me be.

'You'll grow out of it, hen, it's just a phase,' she'd laugh.

Then a bombshell hit our lives. A bombshell in the shape of Annie Reilly, the woman who moved into the house two doors down from us. Annie Reilly's presence changed everything.

Before Annie arrived, Mum hadn't gone out much. She preferred to stay at home curled up on the couch with me watching the telly.

'I'm a homebody, hen,' she'd laugh, when I asked why she never went out like the other women on the scheme who were always going out to the pub and to parties.

Then Annie happened. A tiny woman who had moved to Glasgow from Ireland. She had a mass of red curls and a fiery temper to match. The rumour was that she hadn't chosen to move to Glasgow, but she had been forced to leave her home. Everyone had something to say about Annie and none of it was good.

'Lock up your men when Annie's about, she's a good time girl, that one,' the neighbours would whisper knowingly over their garden fences. Annie didn't give two hoots about what the neighbours said—laughing in their faces, she'd stick up two fingers at them, and just carry on doing what she did. I soon discovered exactly what a good time girl was, when my mum began spending more and more time with Annie.

I would be left to my own devices as she would shroud herself in tight fitting dresses, wafting a cloud of cheap perfume around the house as they got ready for a night out. My face would darken and the two of them would laugh, 'Och, you'll be fine hen, I've left some crisps and fizzy juice in the kitchen for you. Just don't answer the door or make chips,' Mum would call over her shoulder, as the two of them flounced out the door. Before Annie, Mum would never have left me in the house on my own.

They would return in the early hours of the morning, sometimes bringing strangers back to carry on the party. I'd get up the next morning to find them passed out on the couch, surrounded by empty cans of lager and ashtrays full of cigarette butts. Tiptoeing around them, I'd make an attempt to clear up some of the mess before searching the cupboards for something to fill my belly for the day ahead at school. I didn't think I liked good time girls very much. I definitely didn't like my new mum and I hated Annie Reilly with a passion. So did Samantha.

When I asked Mum why she was spending so much time with Annie, she told me she felt sorry for her. 'She's not had the easiest life, hen, her mammy and daddy were murdered when she was wee and she grew up in a children's home.'

'But why doesn't she just go back home, Mum? Why is she here all the time?'

'She's not got a home or any family, hen. She moved over to Glasgow for a new start and got in with the wrong crowd, ended up being chucked out her last house.'

'But why is she always here?' Samantha had made me ask.

'She's here because she's got nobody else, I told you. Now stop being such a spoiled, selfish wee bitch, and quit with your constant questions,' Mum snapped in reply, raising her hand to slap me away.

It's ok, Samantha soothed. *I'm watching her. I've got your back, Rebecca.*

We might not have had much money or anything in the way of luxuries, but Annie's house was even worse—it was a dump. I hated it when Mum dragged me round there. Her front door had been battered by the weather, leaving it covered in a thick layer of dirt. Inside, the rooms were all dusty and covered in spiders' webs. I'd imagine giant spiders scuttling into the walls whenever they heard us coming. The windows were filthy, letting in just a tiny sliver of light, which highlighted her only armchair and a mound of mouldy newspapers. She didn't even use her kitchen, but a rusty microwave balanced precariously on the papers, surrounded by the remnants of takeaway dinners, half-eaten offerings to the rats, who, to be honest, were probably the only visitors brave enough to step into the dump that was Annie's home.

There was a smell clinging to the inside of her house. It came from the walls—a dirty, dangerous smell that stuck in my nostrils, giving me a hunch that something terrible was about to happen. Mum was shocked that anyone could live in such a state and so she invited Annie round to our house most days. She offered Annie an escape, and Annie grabbed that lifeline with both hands, not caring who she was kicking down in her attempt to claw herself back up.

Their afternoons together turned into Annie staying for dinner.

'We can make ours stretch a wee bit further, can't we, hen?' Mum said, ruffling my hair. I'd just nod in agreement while the voices were whispering. *Watch out for that Annie, she's bad news.*

Quickly, it seemed like Annie was always at our table for dinner and, before I knew it, she was there for breakfast every morning too. I think she had stopped going home. I'd get up in the morning and marvel at how her tiny frame filled our springy sofa, her red hair fanning out like a ring of fire around her small, pinched face. She was strangely fascinating.

One morning she woke up and caught me staring at her. She threw out her hand, narrowly missing me but grabbing me by the neck of my dressing gown.

'Get me fags, wee girl,' the words spitting from her mouth, her eyes narrowing as I shook my head defiantly. She hissed, 'You'll no be as cheeky when I get yer mammy to make ye earn yer keep.'

Coughing, she howked up a gob of green spit and I ran before she aimed it at me. I heard her cackle like a witch as I ran to the safety of the bathroom. I closed my eyes and allowed one of the others to breathe slowly for me, calming me down, relaxing me.

Before long, Annie's presence filled our tiny house. Her shadow seemed to eat me up; leaving me cowering in the dark as she gradually sucked the life and the love out of our house. The changes started slowly; the nights curled up with Mum in front of the telly faded away, until they eventually stopped altogether. Within a couple of months, I found myself spending more time in my room, the sounds of Mum and Annie's raucous laughter reminding me of how lonely I was.

That's when my others really took over. The chatter in my head grew louder, more insistent. Sometimes they talked to me but sometimes they talked about me. *Nobody loves Rebecca, do they? No wonder Rebecca is on her own. Rebecca is dirty. Rebecca is bad.*

They'd call my name as I was falling asleep, forcing me to wake up. They would tell me to do things, things I didn't want to do. Things I didn't remember doing. Waking up in the morning with the tell-tale cuts and scratches on my thighs, the razor blades hidden under my bed. None of that was me. Was it?

When Annie and Mum started bringing their 'friends' back from the pub, I'd bury my head under the covers, trying to shut out the noise. The sound of their voices and tuneless singing drifting through into my room. They would become louder, the laughter turning into screams and yelps, followed by the sound of slapping and grunts. Then silence. It was the silence that scared me the most.

Despite the changes at home, I was scared that one day that Mum would just get up, walk out, and leave me. I was scared my others would leave me too. I didn't want to be alone—the thought terrified me. Pulling the covers over my face, I'd lie in my bed, taking comfort from voices chattering in my head. It didn't matter that they were mean to me, at least they were with me. At least I wasn't alone.

Sometimes, the noises coming from my mum's room would rouse me out of my sleep, the deep gruff voices, muffled screams, and the sound of someone crying in pain while the deeper voices laughed. The smell of smoke would drift into my room, making me cough. It was a funny smell though; it didn't smell like the cigarettes Mum used to buy when she was feeling a bit flush. It smelt like the next-door neighbour's house. She had a cat that was old; it peed all over the house. Mum's new cigarettes smelled like that, like cat pee.

I'd try to hold my breath for as long as I could, so that it wouldn't go up my nose, but soon everything in the house smelled of it, giving the kids at school something else to laugh at me for.

I remember waking up early one morning, bursting for a pee. I'd crept along to the bathroom, scared to make a noise in case I woke anyone up. I never knew who might be staying over at our house. Pushing open the door I found my mum lying on the floor. She had a funny band tied round her arm and there was a black teaspoon and a needle lying on the floor. I screamed for help, but it was Annie who came running through.

Her eyes blazing, she slapped me hard, hissing, 'Shut the feck up, girl, and get yerself away back to your room. Your mammy was awful sick last night, and I had to go and get some medicine from the doctor. Now mind don't tell a soul, the social will come and get you if they think yer mammy's sick, ye know?'

'I don't want you here,' I screamed, my face screwed up in an impotent fury. At that, Annie slapped me hard across the face again.

'I said shut the feck up. Stop yer snivelling ye brat. There's nobody else here, ye silly wee bitch. Now get yerself away back to your room. Yer mammy's just sick. The doctor said she'll be fine once she's had a sleep.'

I stared at her, eyes wide. My cheek was burning from her slap. I didn't believe her. I'd have heard the doctor coming to the door and the men that had come into the house last night didn't sound like any doctor. I looked at my mum lying on the bathroom floor, her eyes dancing in her head and a small line of drool making a track down her chin. I screamed again and I ran.

Safe in my room, I let the others take over. They wiped away my tears, they promised me everything was going to be okay. *We'll take care of it for you, Rebecca.*

It wasn't me who took the little bags of brown powder from the secret stash in Annie's bag. It wasn't me who took the rat poison Mum had left under the sink and mixed the two powders together. It couldn't have been me. Could it?

I watched them as I floated above in the room where Annie was in a deep sleep. I watched them shake her and smile when she didn't wake up. I watched them tie a funny band round Annie's skinny arm, tap at the crook of her elbow until a red vein popped through her transparent skin. I watched them plunge the needle deep into her arm. I watched as they got her up on her feet, she was so off her face she had no clue what was happening. They told her they were taking her to a party. She giggled as they led her, stumbling, out the back door and into the bin yard. Laying her down among the rubbish, they sat and watched Annie's eyes roll back in her head, her mouth beginning to froth and her body twitch. I watched from above as the last breath left her body.

Dumped like the rubbish she was, the black bin bags ripped around her, spilling their putrid contents over her cooling body, the needle still sticking out of her arm. I floated back down to my bed and slept soundly that night.

Two days later, I heard a scream as the neighbour tripped over the bin bags and fell into the dead body of Annie Reilly. I didn't remember how it had happened. How could I?

Nobody mourned Annie's passing. 'Just another junkie,' they'd whispered on the streets.

I thought things might have returned to normal with Annie gone, but I couldn't have been more wrong. It might have been quieter without her presence, but it felt like something evil had been left behind. I watched, helpless, as Mum sank into a dark depression, often not leaving the house for days. She brushed off my attempts to comfort her and she certainly offered none to me. *Bitch,* my others would mutter at her. They would use me to dig my fingers into her arms, pull at her hair and call her names. I don't think she even noticed it wasn't me. She seemed to just exist—nothing more, nothing less.

Gradually she stopped washing or taking care of herself. She stank, but didn't seem to notice and, if she did, she didn't care. I didn't like this new mum, I hated her, we all hated her.

Then one morning, I'd come through to the living room to find she'd tidied up a little, and I felt a small flutter of hope that she'd come through the worst. Then I spotted the empty wine bottles on the floor. She must have seen my face drop.

What's up, hen? Mammy's been shopping,' she giggled as she slurred her words. 'Got you a some treats too, through in the kitchen, stuff for your dinner and some sweets.' She grinned, I cringed.

She looked at herself in the mirror, poking and pulling at her hair and her face as though she was trying to form it into something normal. She winked at me, 'Your auld Mammy's still got it, hen.' I wondered if she could see the monster staring back at her.

Then the men started coming around. They would bring her drink and cigarettes, she'd dress up for them in clothes that showed more of her body than they covered. The red lipstick like a slash across her pale gaunt face. 'Make yourself scarce, hen,' she would hiss at me when the knock at the front door came.

SCHOOL QUICKLY BECAME my only escape from what was going on at home. The months rolled into a year, and nobody seemed to notice that I turned up to school unwashed and unkempt. I'd be the kid waiting for my mum to turn up at the gate at the end of the day. The Thursday treat days had become a distant memory and the other parents would look on in horror when she turned up drunk and abusive. I'd just become like every other kid in the school, blending into the background, invisible and left to my own devices.

The only person who cared was my teacher, Miss Ovens. She was perfect, just like a princess, tall and slim with long, dark, shiny hair that bounced when she walked. Her brown eyes were like velvet and they smiled all the time. Real smiles, the kind of smile that reached her eyes and made them twinkle. I thought she was magical. She made everything fun and even the kids who normally mucked about at school sat up and listened to her. Even my others behaved when Miss Ovens was around.

It was Miss Ovens who first noticed I was becoming even quieter than normal. One day before break, she took me aside and asked me to help her set up the classroom. 'Is everything okay, Rebecca?' she'd asked.

The truth was sitting on my tongue ready to tumble out, but I remembered the lesson that was drummed into the head of every kid who lived in the scheme—don't tell anyone what really goes on at home because the social might come and take you away. We'd been taught that social workers were the bogey men, and if we told them anything, they would turn up and steal us away from home. How could I tell my teacher I was more afraid of the bogey men than I was of my mum and her so-called friends? I wished I could have told her the truth.

But I couldn't risk being taken away. Home might have been Hell but it was still my home, Mum was still my mum and I held on to my hope that things would return to normal. So, I lied and I told Miss Ovens that everything was fine.

'I've just fallen out with my pals,' I told her, keeping my fingers crossed behind my back. She wasn't to know I had no friends to fall out with and the few that I'd had before had stopped talking to me as things at home began to spiral out of control. I'd see their mums and dads looking at me in that way that grown-ups do when they feel sorry for you but don't want you anywhere near their kids.

Things reached a new low the day Mum didn't turn up at home time. She hadn't told me I was to make my way home; she hadn't called the school to say she wouldn't be there. It wasn't like her, and I felt the fear seep into my veins—she'd never forgotten me before.

I stood at the school gate, frozen at the dread twisting in the pit of my stomach. Something must have happened to her. She wouldn't just abandon me like this.

I could sense Miss Ovens watching me from the classroom window. I tried to blend into the background, to hide from her gaze. But she waved me towards her. My heart sank. If I told her my mum hadn't come for me, she might tell the social. But I was seven years old now and lots of kids my age, and younger, walked home alone. I tried to convince myself of this. *Mummy's gone and left you.* The voices giggled. Then Samantha's voice came through, taking charge. *Tell Miss Ovens that your mum said you've to walk home yourself today because you're old enough.*

She was right, I knew my own way home. I turned and dragged my feet across the playground with them whispering in my head. Miss Ovens was sitting at her desk, her head bent over the books marking our classwork.

'Miss,' I ventured quietly.

She looked up from her marking, her eyes smiling as she saw me standing in front of her desk. That minute, I wished with all my heart that Miss Ovens was my mum.

'Hi, Rebecca, is there something wrong, sweetheart? No mum to pick you up today?' She tilted her head as she looked at me.

I shook my head. 'No, miss, I just forgot that I was to walk home myself tonight. Mum hasn't forgotten about me.' It sounded like someone else's voice coming from my mouth, but she didn't seem to notice.

'Well why would I think that? Has your mum forgotten about you? Do you want me to call her? Or I could give you a lift home if you like?' Miss Ovens sounded worried now.

Inside I panicked, thinking that maybe I shouldn't have said that about my mum forgetting? What if Miss Ovens phoned the social now? I scrabbled about inside my head looking for the right words to make things okay again.

'N-n-no, it's okay. Mum says I'm a big girl now and it's time I got some more re-spons-ibi-lity.' I didn't know who had said that.

Miss Ovens had looked at me for a moment as though she could read my thoughts. She gave a soft sigh, then she smiled. 'Okay then, Rebecca, as long as you're alright about walking home. For what it's worth, I think you're a very responsible young lady and your mum is lucky to have you as her daughter. I'll see you tomorrow then, sweetheart. Now safe home.'

'Thank you, miss,' I whispered, turning away, the tears welling up in my eyes. I wished I had told her truth. I wished she could have seen inside of my head. It might have made a difference. It might not have ended the way it did.

6

JIM HAD TOLD me that my stay at the Reids was only to be for a short while. I'd only meant to be there for a couple of weeks, yet here I was, two years later, still there. At almost twelve years old, I was starting to get worried I was going to end up in the children's home. I'd heard Mrs Reid on the phone to Jim plenty of times, looking to see if he'd found somewhere else for me. *Nobody wants you, Rebecca*, my voices taunted.

I tried my best to be good for them. I'd follow Mrs Reid around the house, like a little puppy trying to help her, trying to please her. But my others always seemed to make it go wrong. They smashed her favourite cup when they made her a cup of tea, they burnt her most expensive pan, but the worst of it was when they wet the bed. I woke in the morning in a cold damp puddle. I was mortified when Mrs Reid caught me trying to stuff the sheets into the washing machine. She didn't need to yell at me, the look of disappointment that crossed her face told me exactly what she was thinking as she handed me over clean sheets without saying a word.

That night when I went to bed there was a protective sheet over the mattress, the kind they used in babies' cots. Inside my head, the voices laughed. Over and over, the chatter between them went on, driving me mad. Under the covers I'd bring out the blades, the sweet sensation of blood flowing silenced them.

After that, I stopped trying. I resigned myself to being a disappointment again.

Everyone thought the Reids were lovely. In public they would be all over me, buying me the best of everything, but behind closed doors things were different. Mrs Reid worried and fretted, pacing constantly while Mr Reid leered at me from behind his newspaper. There was no love in that house, no communication, only silence and hidden looks.

I'd learned to be quiet, to be invisible. Sometimes I'd feel like a little ghost, floating through the house unseen and unheard. Christmases and birthdays had come and gone in a whirlwind of glitter, wrapping paper, and expensive gifts. But it was all for show. Gifts were for display, not for playing with.

Jim would pop in regularly to see how I was getting on. He was taken in by the Reids too. I'd tried to tell him I wasn't happy. He'd nod, make some reassuring noises, but nothing was ever done about it. I didn't want to make a fuss; I didn't want him to leave too. If he left, I might have to stay with the Reids forever. He called me hen and ruffled my hair, which Mrs Reid tutted at. But I liked it. It felt like home when he called me that.

On one of his visits he asked to speak to me on my own. 'Are you okay, hen?'

I didn't see the point in telling him again how unhappy I was.

I shrugged my shoulders.

'Mrs Reid says you've been a bit difficult lately, breaking things, being clumsy.'

Furious at having to take the blame for things I didn't do, I'd decided to test him out about my others.

'Jim, do you ever think that other people are telling you what to do?'

He'd laughed. 'Aye, all the time hen, my boss is always telling me what to do.'

'No, not like that, I mean like other people inside your head, making you do things you don't want to do? Saying things to you?'

I watched his forehead and nose scrunch up as he looked at me.

'How do you mean?' he asked.

I got the feeling I maybe shouldn't have said anything.

'Nothing, it doesn't matter,' I stared down at the ground.

'It obviously does matter, hen. What sort of things are they telling you to do?'

I didn't know what to say, I wished I'd kept quiet. Mum had always said I shouldn't tell anyone about the voices, about the other parts of me. I should have listened to her.

'Nothing really, just like when I broke Mrs. Reid's cup and that... Like when I do naughty things— it's not really me.'

The words tumbled out of my mouth, even though I didn't want them to. They were answering for me again.

Jim just stared at me. A look flitted across his eyes, something that screamed out at me that he thought I was crazy. I wished I hadn't said anything. I had a strange feeling in my belly; something was telling me that I shouldn't have mentioned it. But he just gave me a small hug and told me everything would be alright.

THAT NIGHT I went to bed but the voices wouldn't let me sleep. I wanted to run away, to hide, but they wouldn't allow it. They were constantly there, fighting to be heard, telling me what to do, how to behave, how to act. I wanted to jump out of my skin to escape them. But there was no escape. I covered my ears with my hands and I sobbed, 'Please leave me alone, please...

Please… Please.' But they continued until finally I fell asleep, exhausted.

The next morning, I woke up on the kitchen floor, the Reids towering above me.

'What on earth are you doing here, Rebecca?' asked Mrs Reid.

I looked around me, confused and unsure. The memories of the previous night fuzzy inside my head. The kitchen knife was still clasped in my hand. I curled my hand around it, anxious they wouldn't see it.

'Answer us, girl,' barked Mr Reid.

'I-I don't know…I-I-I think I must have had a bad dream and sleepwalked.'

My face flushed as a knot of anxiety threatened to overwhelm me. Mr Reid pushed his fat, ugly face closer to mine, his saliva splattering over my cheek, his rank breath lingering in the air.

'You can't remember? What sort of idiot are you? Who gets up in the middle of the night, goes to sleep on the kitchen floor and doesn't remember a thing about it?'

I heard Samantha's voice slip from my tongue.

'I'm not a fucking idiot…'

He lifted his hand as though to strike me. Mrs Reid grabbed at him, I clambered up and ran into my room, slamming the door behind me.

I hid under my bed, examining the small cuts on the top of my thigh, I traced my fingers over the patterns the scars were forming, and began to pick… Outside I could hear the Reids arguing—those loud whispers that adults do when they try to hide what they're saying from kids. I picked harder, tears streaming down my face until I fell asleep curled in a ball where I was.

THINGS SETTLED DOWN again after the kitchen incident. My others had gone quiet—their voices just a dull rumble in my head—but that was okay, I could deal with that. Until, Mrs Reid started leaving me at home on my own with Mr Reid. I didn't like being left alone with him, it made me feel uncomfortable, but I was too scared to tell Jim. I didn't want to disappoint him again.

Besides I knew I had an important meeting coming up to talk about where I was going to live next, and I didn't want to ruin my chances by complaining. It was better just to keep quiet, I decided.

Mrs Reid didn't mean any harm leaving me with him. She probably just wanted to get away from him and I didn't blame her. She was kind in her own way, even though she did have lots of rules for me to follow. I had to make my own bed in the morning, and I had a list of chores to do around the house every day. I hated doing the chores, frightened the others would mess them up and I'd get into trouble again. But they let me be, most of the time, only coming at night now, when I was on my own. Anyway, chores gave me something to fill my time.

I had thought I might have made some new friends—they had moved me to a new school, but the kids there weren't very friendly. I guess they knew I was in care. I would see them all, heads gathered in small huddles, whispering, looking over their shoulders, pointing and laughing.

'That's the lassie from the Reid's,' they would giggle, pointing over. 'Remember the other one who stayed with them? She didn't last long.' Turning away from me they would snigger and continue to mutter under their breath. I wondered what had happened to the other girl who had stayed, and I vowed to ask

Jim the next time he came around. Only I never got the chance to ask him what happened to her.

Life at the Reid's was getting worse. Grown-ups were funny; they thought kids couldn't hear things. But it was hard for anyone to miss the muffled shouts, the slamming doors, and the unmistakeable awkward silences at the breakfast table. Mrs Reid became more and more distant, as Mr Reid became increasingly close. It didn't feel right at all.

Mr Reid would feign interest in me when Mrs Reid was around, he would bring me sweets home from work or sidle up beside me on the pretence of helping with my homework. He gave me the creeps; he made my skin crawl, and took me back to a time in my life I didn't want to remember. I didn't like the way his hand would linger on my leg just a little too long or the way he'd lick his fat, greasy lips when he looked at me over the table whenever Mrs Reid's back was turned.

Mrs Reid started to go out more often, slamming the door behind her and leaving me and Mr Reid on our own. I didn't like these nights. I stopped going for a bath when she went out, after finding him standing outside the bathroom door waiting for me. He'd looked almost disappointed when I came out dressed in my fluffy PJs and oversized dressing gown. He'd looked at me and muttered something about the lock on the door being broken and him having to take it off to replace it. I knew that there was nothing wrong with the lock on the door at all.

Next were his offers of lifts to school or turning up at the end of the day to pick me up. I hated being cooped up in the car with him, trapped. His eyes would roam over my small body as I struggled to push myself into the seat trying to make myself invisible. He'd talk about how I should be grateful for all the nice things I had now that I lived with them. I wasn't stupid, I knew exactly what he was doing. *He better be careful,* Samantha whispered in my ear at night. *We all know what happens to people who hurt Rebecca, don't we?*

When the letters addressed to Mrs Reid started arriving, Mr Reid began to back off a little. At first, she would throw them straight in the bin. But when they kept arriving, she would tear them open, scan them quickly, look at me, and burst into tears. I'd hear the two of them arguing into the small hours.

Her voice shrill as she cried, 'You told me you wouldn't do it again, how could you? You got away with it the last time, with that other wee girl because I lied for you. I can't do it again. I won't do it again. It's sick what you're doing. You're sick in the head, and I'm not going to be party to it anymore

She sobbed. I listened and wondered.

Having no friends at school had its plus points, nobody bothered about the wee girl who sat in class at every break and scribbled endlessly. If only someone had taken the time to look at what I was writing—someone other than poor Mrs Reid— maybe things would have turned out differently.

Things came to a head when Jim came to speak to me about my LACC review which was due soon. He explained that LACC meant 'looked after and accommodated' because I was staying with another family. I didn't have a clue what he was talking about, but I guessed it must be important because there would be lots of people at that meeting, teachers, doctors and his boss too.

That day, the Reids pulled him aside asking if they could have a 'wee word' before he left. His face dropped as if he knew what was coming, as if he had been there before. An expression of weary acceptance slid over him. I knew then that it would soon be time for me to move on.

'Listen, son,' said Mr Reid. 'We didnae want to do this to the wean, y'know. We know she's gone through hell and back, but me and the wife, well, we're no cut out for this. It's too much at our age.'

He lowered his voice and whispered something to Jim, something I couldn't hear. Something I obviously wasn't meant to hear. I just sat back in my chair and smiled sweetly. Well, at least I thought it was a sweet smile, I'm not so sure given the way they all looked at me.

Jim nodded and scribbled something in his book. His face sagged, he looked tired and drawn, and I knew I was the cause of it all. I didn't care, I didn't want to stay with the Reids anymore. My bag was packed and had been since I knew that Jim was coming around. I'm not sure if I'd packed it or if it had been Mrs Reid.

I saw the way she looked at me when she caught me coming out of their bedroom. She knew what I'd been doing or so she thought she did. What she didn't know was that it was her bastard of a husband who was the one that should be sitting here in my shoes, waiting to get passed to some other place to take care of him. That bastard that thought it was okay to watch wee lassies like me, he was just like all the rest of the monsters.

I did feel sorry for Mrs Reid. She didn't deserve all this. She was nothing like my mother. But she'd had to pay the price. That's what Samantha had told me. Samantha was right. Mrs Reid had been taken in with his fuckin' lies; his fuckin' lies telling her he had caught me climbing into his fuckin' bed.

In my head, I quickly slipped back into the vernacular of the housing scheme I'd come from. As if I would climb into his bed willingly. *He's a dirty auld bastard and I'll see him pay*, I thought. Only I knew that I wouldn't see him pay, I slowly realised, the only one paying any price was me, wasn't it? Stupid wee bitch that I am.

The adults carried on their conversation as I zoned out of it all. Apart from the drugs and the visitors, life at the Reid's had turned out just the same as at home really. My mind wandered back to my mum and my past.

7

1994

AFTER REASSURING MISS Ovens that I was okay, I made my way home from school, my heart heavy as I realised life was never going to go back to the way it had been before. All the way home, the voices taunted me: *Stupid Rebecca. You're worthless, Rebecca. Don't even know why you are here. Nobody loves you, Rebecca. You know what you need to do to take the pain away, Rebecca, don't you? Do it, Rebecca, do it… Do it… Do it.*

I ran home trying to escape them, straight into my room. I watched from above as they pulled out the razor blade from under my mattress and began scoring deep into my thighs. The warm trickle of blood soothed me and the voices gradually grew quieter: *Good girl, Rebecca. Make it all better… All better now.*

Mum had given up on all pretence of normality. I watched as the days merged into nights. The stench in the house was starting to take over, suffocating me. But even more worrying was the appearance of syringes lying around the house. I knew this was bad as we'd had the drugs talk at school. Needles were dangerous. *Look what had happened to Annie Reilly,* whispered Samantha. *I'll always protect you, Rebecca.*

Mum sank deeper into the pit she was burying herself in, and I'd come home from school most days to find her slumped on the threadbare couch, her jaw slack, her eyes seeing nothing. Our house was bare, even our TV had gone. Two men had turned up, battering at the front door one night. Their fists nearly made their way through the flimsy panels before Mum had sent me to answer it for her. As usual, she was too far gone to be of any use to anyone never mind being in any fit state to look after me.

The men at the door were huge, like big bears. Their presence filled the doorway. They smiled widely at me, but I knew their smiles weren't real because they didn't reach their eyes. Holding the door open just an inch, I told them Mum was at work, but they just laughed out loud. It was a joyless laugh, harsh, dangerous, not one that invited me to join in.

'Aye, hen, the only work yer ma does is on her back at night when it's too dark for the punters to see her face.'

They pushed by me, storming into the living room. Ignoring Mum, passed out on the couch, they calmly ripped our TV from the wall. A patch of crumbling plaster the only evidence it had ever existed.

'Tell yer maw she still owes us a grand. We'll be round to get it. If she's not got the cash, we'll get it from her one way or another. Or from you.'

I cowered down and slumped to the floor as they walked out the house, slamming the door behind them. Mum just lay there, oblivious to it all. Tears flowing down my face, I punched her hard. She didn't even flinch. I wanted to kill her. *We will*, they whispered.

Before the drugs had took hold, Mum had been really pretty, with long blonde curly hair and big blue eyes. Now she looked just like all the other addicts who prowled around the streets—her eyes sunken under the dark bags that had appeared and taken over her face. Her once golden curls were now like damp rats' tails clinging to her cheeks. Yet, she still insisted on putting on that bright red lipstick.

Standing in front of the mirror she would smear it across her mouth, preening and fixing her hair.

'Looking good Stella,' she grinned to herself in the mirror.

The woman who stared back from the mirror was invisible to my mum, but I saw this monster's face every single day. That's what she'd become. A monster.

I didn't care much about what she did until she started bringing the men back home almost every night. Everything was okay when she met with them away from the house. The few times she'd brought them back before, she had waited until I was tucked up in my bed. None of the men knew I was there. But she was getting weaker as her addiction took a stronger hold of her.

'Be a love, Rebecca,' she would whine. 'It's too cold out there for your auld ma, here's a quid. Away and get yourself some sweeties and keep out the way for a couple of hours.'

I did as I was told, glad to be away from her. But one night it was so cold outside, I thought it would be safe for me to just sneak back in while she was busy. I planned to slip upstairs to my room and hide under my covers. But when I walked in through the back door, I knew right away something was wrong.

My mum was slumped across the sofa, a needle sticking out her arm and a man was pushing his feet into his shoes and readjusting his trousers… My mum's skirt was bunched round her waist. He watched me coming in, a sly leer crossing his face.

'Well looky-looky, what have we here? A wee dolly to play with?'

I glared at him with all the venom a ten-year-old could muster. 'Fuck off, dick,' I snarled. Samantha was back.

He laughed. 'Feisty wee thing, aren't ye, hen, hmm? I'd beat that cheek out of you, so I would.'

I didn't like the way he was looking at me or the way he was getting closer to me, his smell almost knocking me sick.

'Well, the auld bitch might have her uses after all, with a wee sweetheart like you around, hen,' he sneered, pinching my chin in his rough grubby fingers. He put his stinking mouth right up to my face whispering, 'I'll be back round tomorrow night, tell yer ma Harry said he wants the wean at the party too.' And with that, he slunk out into the night, leaving his stench behind him.

Harry did come back round the next night and the night after. At first, he'd bring me sweets and comics, lulling me into a false sense of security, kidding me on, acting like a favourite uncle. But the act soon dropped. He started bringing other men too. After a few months the treats stopped. I was just expected to do as I was told with no rewards.

I cried to start with, clutching onto my mum, screaming at her as they tore me from her arms, begging her not to make me go with them. But she just stood there, stony faced with that red slash across her mouth, stuffing the money that my uncles handed over into her grubby grey bra. She wouldn't meet my eyes. She'd just shuffle out of the room leaving me behind. It wasn't her they came to visit anymore.

I started to retreat into myself. I'd let my others take over, watching from above as my body lay still and the men did what they came to do. When it was over, my others would sooth me, take away the pain. They'd bring me my blades and help me make the tiny cuts in my legs, wrapping me in their whispers until I fell asleep.

But I'd wake up to the harsher voices: *Dirty little bitch, it's all your own fault, you don't deserve anything else. Bitch, bitch, bitch.* This was the voice I would hear as I sunk into a dark and restless sleep. A sleep full of nightmares, of demons sitting on my chest trying to crush the life out of me.

Sometimes when the men came, Samantha would take control. She wouldn't let me lie down and take it, she'd fight back, clawing at their faces, their arms and their legs as they tried to pin me down. This sent my mum into a rage. The spittle would spray from her mouth as she screamed at me, blaming me for us having no money or food, blaming me for scaring the men away. I didn't care though; I'd happily go without food for the day if it meant the men didn't come and visit.

Without money for drugs, my mum would just lie on the couch and I'd watch her thrash about, sweating and shouting in pain. She would swear at me, screaming in terror at the monsters coming out the walls. I knew the monsters weren't in the walls; they were lying on our couch and waiting behind the door to come and get me. Sometimes her terrors were so fierce that she would cling onto me, holding me so tight I couldn't even breathe. I'd cling back, crying, trying to reassure her that we'd be okay. Even among the terror, my need for affection, any form of affection, took over.

It never lasted. She'd push me away, convinced that I was one of the monsters. She'd cower into the couch trying to escape from me, while I crawled into the corner and cried. It frightened me when she was like that. I'd pray somebody—another grown up—would come and help her. But they didn't. Around our way, nobody ever heard anything. Nobody wanted to get involved in what happened behind closed doors.

AS LIFE BEGAN to spiral out of control, my behaviour got worse. I was driven by the voices in my head. I'd refuse to do what I was told. The men started turning away, and Mum began to beat me.

'*Bitch*,' they would scream at her, their voices spewing anger from my mouth.

'Shut up,' she'd screech back. 'You owe me. I gave up my life for you, you brat.'

Curling up into a ball to protect myself from the blows, I retreated further and further into a black hole from which it was becoming harder to escape. Mum was clever though, she knew not to hit me where other people might see it—the bruises and welts from her brush were hidden beneath my clothes, but every one of them left a memory imprinted that would follow me for the rest of my life. Memories I was too young to understand yet, but which would shape my future. Memories that would shape who I'd become.

Hiding in my bed, I would try to make myself small and invisible. I'd been trying to do this for years, but it had become more difficult as time went on. Night after night I'd huddle under the covers and sometimes under my bed, praying that the monsters wouldn't come creeping in the dark.

The monsters under my bed and through my door were real, there were no warm cuddles from a mummy or daddy reassuring me that they weren't true. No night light or torch to offer me protection. No. I was on my own and no match for the monsters, especially the one with the bright red lips and sharp nails that dug into my arms as I struggled to escape. The fag breath breathing a hissed warning of what would happen if I didn't behave, and a lascivious laugh as the monster turned and left the room and left me to my fate.

The monsters were very real for me.

8

1998

I STOLE A last glance back at the Reid's house and buckled my seat belt. Mrs Reid stood at the window watching me, I think she might have looked a bit ashamed. I hope she felt shame, I hoped that the shame would follow her to her grave and beyond. *So here you go again, Rebecca*, they said, as I followed Jim Aitken into the car. *Same shit, just a different day. Where are you going to end up now?* They giggled. I didn't.

I looked at the rear-view mirror and realised that Jim was talking to me. I watched him for a minute. He was all right for a social worker, he wasn't the bogey man I'd been threatened with. Although he hadn't done anything about the Reids until my others had stepped in, he *had* listened to me when I'd told him about my others. He hadn't laughed or accused me of lying.

I started as I was snapped out of my daydream by the sound of his voice.

'Did you hear what I said to you?'

I shrugged.

'You're a wee daydreamer, hen, aren't you?' He chuckled.

'So, do you want to tell me what happened at the Reid's then? I thought you liked it there?'

'Dunno,' I muttered, not really wanting to tell him anything. They were telling me not to tell him too much.

Ssshhh. The words came from inside my head. *Tell him nothing.*

'Maybe they were too old to look after me?' I hesitated as I offered this up as an explanation.

Jim just laughed. 'The Reids have been fostering weans for years, hen. They've still got a good few years left in them. Were you giving them a hard time? Being cheeky?'

I shook my head. A voice from within me snapped, 'Why, what did they say I done?'

Jim looked at me in the rear-view mirror; his eyes narrowed as he recognised the change of tone in my voice. 'Mrs Reid said that you were maybe a wee bit too forward for your age. Your behaviour made Mr Reid feel a bit uncomfortable.' His eyes seemed to bore into me, demanding that I gave something back.

My face flushed but inside a rage was burning.

'I fuckin didn't!' I spat the words at him.

A look of shock crossed his face. 'Rebecca, don't speak to me like that! What the hell has got into you, girl?'

But I was beyond listening. By now I was tearing at my hair, screaming and kicking the back of his seat. My mouth was spewing out curses as I began to break down.

Jim pulled the car over. He came round to my door and opened it up, taking a step back as he did, as though he was terrified I would lash out at him.

Something inside me snapped and I slumped back in my seat. The tears were streaming down my face. I didn't know what was happening to me.

He pushed in beside me, putting an arm around me. 'Rebecca, hen. Are you okay?'

I shook my head and cried. 'N-n-no,' I cried. 'I don't know w-w-what's w-wrong with me. Can you help me please?'

'It's okay, hen. I know, you've had a rough couple of years, what with your mum, not knowing what's happening with you.

Do you remember I spoke to you about seeing someone about the voices you said you were hearing?'

I nodded.

'Well, I wasn't going to tell you until after you had settled a bit, but I've managed to get you an appointment to see someone, a doctor.'

I looked up at him, my eyes wide. 'Will they send me to the nut house?'

He smiled kindly, 'We don't call them that, Rebecca, and no, nobody is going to send you to hospital. We just want you to get better. We don't want you feeling this way.'

'Okay,' I whispered, wiping my nose with my sleeve.

'Here, hen, don't use your sleeve.' He pushed a hanky into my hand. I used it gratefully and gave him a watery smile.

'I'm sorry, Jim.'

'Och, it's okay, don't worry about it. Tell you what, why don't we stop and get a Maccy D's as a wee treat?'

I smiled. 'Yes please'. But inside I was still worried—I'd seen a doctor before, after my mum died. They'd made me see two doctors, one who looked at my body and another who talked to me a lot. They had asked me lots of questions about what things were like living with my mum. They asked about visitors and people touching me. They took lots of pictures of old bruises and scars. I heard them saying that I'd been abused. I didn't know what that meant, but by the look on their faces when I told them about my uncles and the parties, I guessed that it was something to do with them. I didn't want to have to talk about all that again. But I couldn't find the words to tell Jim that. He was trying his best. I didn't want to let him down.

Jim got out from the back seat, stopping to make a call on his phone. He had his back turned to me, but I could still hear what he was saying. 'It's me Marie, Jim. Listen, I think we are going to have to have a chat about the Reids, I'm not happy about sending any more kids there until we've investigated further.'

I smiled. He believed me.

As he chatted on the way to McDonalds, I realised this treat was to soften the blow he was just about to give me.

'I wouldn't normally spring something like this on you hen, but the placement we had lined up for you has fallen through.'

I didn't need to hear the words that came next, I already knew what he was going to say. I was going to the Children's Home. *Nobody's child Rebecca, that's you. Little orphan Rebecca. Nobody wants her because she's dirty. She's bad.* I put my hand to my mouth, not sure if it was to stop the voices escaping or to stop myself being sick.

Everyone knew what the children's home meant. It was only the kids nobody else wanted who ended up there. I'd only ever been in one for a meeting, before I went to the Reids. The noise had been horrendous, kids screaming and shouting, everyone staring at me, the walls closing in on me, trapping me.

'It won't be that bad Rebecca, I promise you, we are looking for somewhere else for you, I promise.' Jim tried to reassure me. I nodded, blinking back the tears.

'I'm not hungry anymore,' I whispered. 'I don't really want a McDonalds now, thank you.'

I ignored the look of dejection on his face as we drove out of the car park and back onto the main road. It was his own fault. He deserved it.

9

BY MY TENTH birthday, the visits from men to our house had grown more frequent. The others inside me would chatter amongst themselves angrily.

Dirty bitch. It's okay, we'll look after you… No we won't. Dirty bitch deserves it…Kill them, Rebecca, stab them in the heart. Sshh, Rebecca, sleep now. Kill the bitch. She should pay, Rebecca, she should pay… Dirty bitch. Rebecca, you are going to die. You deserve to die.

The day it happened, I knew as soon as I woke up that it was going to be a bad day. My nightmares the previous night had been so real, I was still terrified. The others had gone silent. I was on my own. That morning, Mum had seemed different—there had been a nervous excitement about her. She was buzzing about all over the place, humming to herself. She told me that I had to be a good girl because Uncle Duncan was coming round after school to take me to a special party.

'Good girls get pretty new dresses for parties.' She laughed. Sometimes I think she forgot what age I was. A party dress for fuck's sake, I was ten years old. I felt confused though; I never got new clothes and I'd never ever been to a party before. Maybe this time things would be different, I thought. Maybe it would be like a real party, with music and a DJ like the rest of the kids at school talked about? Part of me bubbled with excitement, but deep down I knew it wouldn't be that sort of party. I could imagine the kind of clothes he would bring me.

He was disgusting, always wanting me to act way younger than I was. He would bring me sweets, but the sweets that Uncle Duncan brought me were not the sort that the other kids got as treats. These sweets made me feel all fuzzy inside, as though the world around me wasn't real. It didn't really matter what I wanted though, did it? I did know that Duncan was the least favourite of all my 'uncles'.

He'd been coming around for about a year by then. Sometimes he would bring a boy with him. He was a lot older than me. He didn't say very much. He just did whatever he was told to do. He'd always have a smile on his face though. Sometimes he would go downstairs with Mum, leaving me with Uncle Duncan and other times he'd come and watch us. Sometimes he'd touch.

He creeped me out more than Uncle Duncan, with that sly smile on his face, saying nothing. The last few times they had come around, he'd brought the wee girl who lived next door in with him. I'd seen her before, out playing in her garden... I hated her. *Everyone loves her, Rebecca. Look at her—she's so pretty. Not like you, Rebecca—dirty and bad.*

I didn't want her hurt, though. I wouldn't have let her get hurt. But Samantha did. *I'm only looking out for you, Rebecca,* she'd whisper, as she pulled me into the corner and kept me safe. *I'd do anything for you, Rebecca. Anything.* She made me close my eyes when they hurt the little girl. But I heard her scream.

I'd tried to tell Mum about Uncle Duncan. I told her he frightened me and that he made me do things I didn't want to do. My bottom lip trembled and my voice shook as the words came tumbling out my mouth. Her lips grew tight, her eyes narrowed. I felt a surge of relief, she was angry, she was going to stop it. And then her hand cracked off the side of my head so hard I saw stars.

'Shut up, you little bitch. Don't you ever let me hear that filth come out your mouth again.' I knew then if I went to any party with Duncan Campbell and that boy, I'd never escape from that life.

I came home from school at half past three the day it happened. I'd hurried home, something inside me telling me not to go for my usual wander in the woods. All day at school I'd had a strange fluttering inside my tummy, not the nice fluttering you get when something good is going to happen. It was a bad fluttering, it was a warning.

I reached the front door and as I ran indoors, I found my mum slumped on the couch with her needles and tin foil, off her face. There were so many shapes and shadows all merging into one inside my head, the voices were loud but I couldn't hear what they were saying. I vaguely remember going upstairs and hiding under my bed, hoping and praying that Uncle Duncan had maybe forgotten to visit. There was an old fork lying under the bed and I'd used it to stab at my legs, the dull pain of the prongs drowning out the fear in my head.

I heard the front door bang open. The rush of heavy feet and the mutterings of my mother, so far gone she didn't know where or even who she was, never mind that I was slowly dying inside upstairs. I heard the feet make their way up the stairs, two sets, one lighter than the other. I remember the door being pushed open and the monster with the red slash for a mouth barging in.

'Get yersel out and ready, Uncle Duncan's here to take you to a party,' the monster's high-pitched voice shrilled in a silly, sing-song tone. Laughing, the monster retreated from the room clutching at the small brown wrap that Duncan had pressed into her hand, and then Duncan's feet were there at the foot of my bed. He lowered himself to the floor, his stubby fingers were cajoling and poking and prodding under my bed, drool slobbering down his crusty chin, his eyes sinking further into his face as the gravity pulled at them. He was waving a plastic bag towards me.

'Come on, hen. Got you some pretty clothes in here for our party.'

I sensed that this was going to be bad, as bad as it would ever get.

'Come on out, hen, don't be making me look fur ye; it will only be worse if you don't do what I tell ye. Did yer ma no tell ye tae be nice tae yer Uncle Duncan? Ah've got sweeties fur yer.'

I tried to flatten myself into the floorboards, willing them to crack and splinter underneath me and send me out of his reach. My tiny body shuddered as I smelled him getting closer. That greasy fat smell that oozed out of his skin. His breath was stinking too; it smelled like dog breath and his fat pudgy fingers dug into my skin, into places I didn't want him to dig.

I shut my eyes tightly; I didn't want to think about it anymore. I screwed them shut tighter, willing him to leave and not come back, trying to imagine a life that wasn't this one. The only problem was my imagination wasn't that good. This was the only life I knew, the only life I could expect to live until I died. I suddenly realised that I couldn't live the rest of my life like this. I couldn't and I wouldn't. I screamed to myself. Nobody heard me, apart from me. I heard him puffing as he waddled his way towards my hiding space.

'Come on out, hen,' he wheezed, 'Ah've got a wee surprise for ye.'

He gave a guttural laugh and I knew exactly what his surprise was. He brought it to me every Thursday, every week, and had done so for the last year.

My mum said Uncle Duncan was a good uncle to have, he always made sure that he left us plenty of money after his visits.

She told me I was just to shut up and be a good girl and do what he told me to do.

'After all,' she said, 'you're just going to have to get used to it, it's what you're going to be doing for the foreseeable, hen, it's the way of the world for folks like us.'

I hadn't known what she meant, but I did know I didn't want Uncle Duncan's surprises anymore. I didn't want any of my uncles to visit me anymore. I didn't want sweeties, special parties, or dresses. I just wanted it to be me and my mum. She might not have been the best mum, but if my uncles weren't there, then maybe things would be all right. We could manage without them. If only my mum didn't let my uncles visit. If only I'd been enough for her.

I heard him get closer as his breath grew heavier and the smell more pungent; the tears squeezed through my screwed-up eyes, burning a grimy track on my dirty face. I took a deep breath and began to inch my way out on my belly from under my bed. His black shiny shoes were the first thing I saw, and I remember thinking how strange it was that such a disgusting man would have such clean shiny shoes. Raising my eyes, I took in his short stubby legs encased in crusty brown trousers, the stains of his vile life ingrained into them. My eyes looked up further and saw his pudgy hand reach down to his button and pop it effortlessly, before slipping down to the zipper, lower and lower...

From nowhere came an explosion, it was so loud I thought it would bring the house down. The colours exploded as the sounds crashed around my head and into my ears. I gasped, perhaps this was my escape, I looked up, but Uncle Duncan clearly couldn't hear the noise, his fat dirty fingers were going lower and then I knew, it was me—it was my head that exploded, nothing inside the house. Inside my room, nothing had changed. Only me, only I had changed.

I didn't want Uncle Duncan's surprise, I wasn't going to take his surprise, I drew my hand back under the bed and retrieved the fork. I pulled it out and looked up at Uncle Duncan, his face a twisted mess of evil pleasure, and I plunged the fork straight into his leg just above his knee, just above the dirty stain that told a thousand stories. Then he heard the explosion; then it was real to him. He had heard me, this time.

'Ya fuckin bitch!' he screamed, grabbing at his leg with one hand, while he tried to swipe and kick me at the same time. I was too quick though. I jumped away and watched him crash down on my floor. When I stabbed him, he got really angry, almost like he was going to kill me angry. I was scared. He *was* going to kill me. I knew he was. I'd almost prepared myself to die, thinking at least it would be all over.

He started, and roared a curse, but it died on his lips as he watched me advance towards him. Something must have clicked inside his head, a realisation that I was not a walkover. Perhaps this time he was afraid the neighbours would hear and this time they would care. He turned and he ran as though the hounds of hell were after him. Perhaps they were.

Collapsing onto the floor, the tears were ripped from my eyes. I heaved, spewing the contents of my stomach across the carpet. I felt a sense of calm wash over me as the others put their arms around me, clutching me close.

Something stirred inside me and I rose quietly. I slipped into the kitchen. Only it wasn't me anymore.

I could see Mum lying slumped over the kitchen table, that vacant look in her dull eyes, the drool running down the side of her mouth. Her breathing was shallow and the tell-tale signs of her medicine; the tin foil, the spoon, and the needle, lay close by. I heard the voices whisper to me, telling me to pick up the knife that was lying on the side of the sink. I wasn't allowed to touch knives, but they whispered that it was okay. I was in a trance as I slowly made my way past my mum's slumped outline and picked up the knife by the handle. I felt a hand close over mine. We became one as we united against all that was evil in this house.

Everything turned black, then a roaring sound like a waterfall hitting the rocks filled my head. The atmosphere turned heavy, the room coal black before turning red, warm, and sticky. All over the place. All over me, like the blood red paint we had used at school to paint Santa Claus for the Christmas Fayre.

I looked round the room. I was alone. I looked down at my hands, they were sticky, warm, and very red. I looked at my mum, her eyes were staring, and her mouth was open, screaming with no sound coming out.

Did I cause all of this? I wish I could remember but I can't. I only remember wee snippets. I do remember looking in a mirror back at my own house. Well, it looked like a mirror, my reflection in it, watching me but, in the reflection, my eyes were somehow different. It made me smile. The voices had gone, my others had left; left me on my own. In the kitchen. With the blood. With the knife. With her.

It all went grey then, before it exploded into a bright shower of red again. Everywhere was red, and I was on my knees on the kitchen floor, holding my mum's head in my hands. She was like a fountain of fire and the bright red blood sprayed all over her, over me, and over the grease that covered the kitchen. My hands held a knife and I woke up screaming.

Four of them came to get me. The clatter of their feet and their muffled shouts a welcome distraction from what lay before me. The neighbours must have heard something and reported it. Finally, I thought, how long had they closed their ears to what was going on? How long had they pretended that they couldn't hear, couldn't see?

If only they'd done something sooner.

If only...

10

AFTER SIX MONTHS on the unit and a few failed foster placements, I'd been over the moon when I'd been told of a couple looking to adopt an older child. The Nikolics had no children of their own, although they did have a young girl staying with them on an emergency placement at the moment. I was excited but scared too. After everything, it was hard to believe that anyone would want me. My tummy was full of butterflies, I wasn't far off my thirteenth birthday, and I knew this could be my final chance.

The preparation visits I'd had with the Nikolics had gone well, I'd been on my best behaviour and even my other selves hadn't messed it up. I'd had a few appointments with the doctor Jim had referred me to—Dr Sullivan. I liked her, she listened to me, and she listened to us. She understood.

I did feel a bit anxious about the other kid staying with them, though. What if they only picked one of us to live with them? What if they liked her best? *Who's going to want you to stay with them Rebecca? Nobody wants you… Nobody loves you.*

I tried to do what Dr Sullivan suggested to manage my other selves. She had been teaching me how to think about places where I might feel safe, to write things down. She even suggested I make up a place in my mind for all my other parts to meet and talk to each other. That had made me laugh a little, the thought of them all meeting up inside my head. But it had helped. I was learning to find ways of keeping a grip on reality when they were all getting too much for me; breathing and making small fists in time to my breath. But the nightmares didn't leave, they still paralysed me when the demons took over at night.

When moving day arrived, Jim came to pick me up at the unit. He smiled at the sight of me standing at the door, my bags packed and all ready to go.

One of the support workers had laughed.

'She's been ready and waiting since seven this morning, Jim.'

Jumping into the back seat, I quickly drifted off into a daydream about my new life, wondering what it would be like to live as part of a proper family.

Jim was talking to me again. I could see his lips moving in the rear-view mirror. I had no idea what he'd been saying.

He gave a little smile. 'Still away in a world of your own, hen?'

I nodded, not knowing how he wanted me to answer. Although I liked him, I still didn't know if I trusted him. It was hard to let go of everything I'd been told about social workers.

'I was telling you about the Nikolics and Melissa. I know she's a bit younger than you, she's just six, but she'll be a wee bit company for you, eh? Just like having a sister?'

I processed that bit of information with a mixture of excitement and fear in my belly. A sister sounded good, I'd always wanted a sister or a brother.

'Aye, sounds okay. Melissa sounds posh.' I giggled, and Jim looked at me sharply.

'Don't go making assumptions about folks, hen, not based on a name. How'd you like it if folk judged you because of your background?'

My face grew hot with shame. I knew he was right. I could remember all too clearly the judgements others had made about me when my life had started turning upside down. How the kids at school had withdrawn from me as my mum's life spiralled out of control. And after 'that day' it got worse. When I'd gone back to school, they all wanted to be my friend, didn't they? Childish curiosity made them want to befriend the freak whose mum had only went and got herself murdered. The playground had been full of gossip, despite the teachers' efforts to stop it. I'd heard them whispering in corners when they thought I wasn't listening. I was always listening and watching. I could hear the playground chatter in my head now.

'D'ye think she done it? Ma maw says she did, that they found her gouging out her maw's eyes and stuffin' them in her mooth.'

'Naw, ma da says that it wiz her da, he came back and found her daein it wae a punter and stabbed her through the heart.'

'Naw, she's no got a da, he's in the Big Hoose.'

'It wiz wan o' her punters, that's what ah heard the polis sayin'.'

It had only stopped when it was decided that I'd move to a new school nearer the Reid's. At first, they thought that the familiarity of my old school would provide me with some stability amid the trauma of what had happened. But when I was found in the girls' toilet trying to cut my wrists against a crack in the cistern, they quickly realised that this familiarity was making the situation much worse. I never went back.

While Jim chattered on, I thought about what had happened to my mum. I knew, we knew, my other selves and I. We'd all been there. The nice policewoman and another social worker had asked me lots of questions. They'd taken me to a room with lots of soft chairs and funny dolls that had girl and boy bits added. I didn't like those dolls. I'd sat on the couches, my hands tucked under my legs and my head tucked into my chest. I answered all their questions, but it wasn't my words that came out of my mouth.

One of my others told them about my mum and all the needles and tin foil. They told them about the men who came to the house and how they sometimes got mad at me. But they didn't tell them about them visiting me though or the games they made me play. But they had known. The doctor who had examined me had told them. The nice policewoman had come back to see me when I was at the Reids. She'd met me with Jim and explained that they'd been unable to find the person who had killed my mum. She talked about lots of fingerprints and footprints being found. Mostly mine and Mum's. My prints were all over my mum's body, but they said it was because of how they'd found me. I heard her whispering to Jim about 'key suspects' and 'rings'. I'm sure she mentioned my uncle Duncan, but I'd just sat quietly, like a good little girl.

Pulling myself out of my daydreams, I nodded at Jim who just shook his head and smiled.

'We'll stop off at McDonald's on the way.'

I smiled. 'Yes please.' Jim knew how much I loved McDonalds.

He finally pulled his car up at the familiar golden arches.

'Where are we again?'

I'd completely forgotten the name of the place that the Nikolics lived.

'Kirkie, hen, or Kirkintilloch, if we give it its Sunday name.'

I tried the name out on my tongue, rolling it back and forward. It tasted good; it gave me a good feeling. 'And this is where I'm going to be living forever?' I looked at him hopefully.

'Aye, hen, well, no here in McDonald's, mind, but just five minutes up the road.' He laughed at his own joke, pleased at the obvious look of delight that was plastered over my face.

McDonald's was busy with the usual chatter of tired and harassed parents accompanied by their hyper kids. I sat soaking in the atmosphere as I shovelled a chicken burger and chips into my mouth. An adult sized one, not a kid's meal. Jim had raised his eyebrows at my order, clearly, forgetting the survival instinct of kids who didn't know where the next meal was coming from.

I don't think I even tasted the food. I was so engrossed in my surroundings. I smiled as I watched the toddler on the table opposite, intent on her finger painting all over the windows with tomato ketchup while her mum was lost in a conversation on her phone. I laughed inwardly as the toddler, now bored with the window, proceeded to run her fingers all down the back of the expensive cream jumper her mum wore. *That'll teach you*, I thought, happy at the child's small act of rebellion against her neglectful mother.

Back in the car, I quizzed Jim about Melissa, trying to work out how much competition she would be. *Of course, they'll like her more than you, Rebecca. Who wouldn't?*

I closed them off while he told me that she was staying with Mark and Teresa as her mum had been in a car accident and was in hospital. I felt sorry for her, but my others whispered in my head. *She's got a mum Rebecca... You've got nobody... Dirty, bad Rebecca... Why should she have a mum and you don't? Nobody wants you, Rebecca... They won't want you, Rebecca.*

Remembering what Dr Sullivan had told me, I breathed deeply and made small fists, in and out, in and out, until they faded.

Jim motioned for me to look out the window at the canal, where a boat was coming into view.

I watched the brightly painted barge move leisurely along the water, the passengers on board waving at the dog walkers at the side of the canal. I was mesmerised, I'd never seen anything like it. Jim explained that the road over the bridge was built specially to allow it to open up to let the barges pass through. I watched; my eyes wide with amazement. I wasn't going to let anything spoil this for me. This was my chance for a new start.

Once the barge had passed, we carried on up the hill. The road lined with shabby, tired grey houses, and I let out a sigh of relief as we drove past them and came to a school and a small shopping centre. The smell of chips from the chip shop on the corner wafted through the car's air vents; and despite just having wolfed down my McDonald's, it was making my mouth water. I hoped I was going to live near here and we could maybe get chips on a Friday night.

Passing by the shops, we followed the road down, the houses becoming bigger and brighter, their gardens filled with a rainbow of colours. There was a small putting green, a bowling green, and a huge park taking up most of one side of the road. My head was spinning with all this space. I'd never seen anything like it before. Back at home the parks had been no-go zones, either full of dog shit, broken glass, or used needles. Everything here looked so clean in comparison. I shoogled up and down in my seat with excitement, eager to reach our destination.

Finally, Jim pulled up in front of the Nikolic's house. Although I'd visited before, I couldn't remember any detail. At the time I hadn't been taking much in, scared to let myself believe that I was finally going to have a real home. A real family. Now, I felt like I was seeing it all for the first time.

The house was painted white, the windows neatly framed with blue curtains and a vase of fresh flowers in them. I don't ever remember flowers in our house, not even plastic ones. I could see toys scattered in the garden. This house looked loved. I leaned back in my seat, suddenly anxious, not knowing what I should do next, or even how I should behave. What if they were just like the Reids? What if they were worse? Thoughts bounced around in my head as I waited for Jim to tell me what to do next. As though he had heard those thoughts, he turned around and smiled, the corner of his eyes crinkled up, matching the smile on his face.

'Right we are, hen. Home, well at least for the next wee while.'

Nodding, I clutched onto my bag and waited for him to open the car door. I hid behind him as he walked up the path, me shuffling behind him.

The door opened and a woman with dark curly hair stood smiling at us both. It was Teresa. I could vaguely remember her face from before. She was wiping her hands on a towel and I could see they were covered in flour.

A small girl—that must be Melissa—stood beside her watching us intently as we walked towards them. My hands were sweaty and my mouth felt as though it was full of cloth. I clutched onto Jim's arm with one hand. My bag in the other.

'Hello, Rebecca.' She smiled. 'This is Melissa.'

She pushed the small girl gently forward. She looked as anxious as me. We stared at each other for a minute before she offered a shy smile. I tried hard to mimic it; hers reached her eyes. I don't think mine did. I hoped nobody noticed.

'Come away in both of you. Melissa and I have been baking cakes and they're just out of the oven. Jim, you'll be wanting one with your cuppa, I'm guessing.' She laughed. It was a warm, tinkly laugh. I looked at her eyes, and they matched her smile. I breathed out, a sense of relief washing over me.

'Mark's out in the garden. You know what he's like, Jim, always pottering about in the greenhouse. Melissa's been helping him, haven't you love?' Melissa nodded shyly. Jim reached over and ruffled her hair. Something inside me snapped. *See, even your social worker likes her better, Rebecca. No wonder—look how cute she is. You've no chance here...* I gripped onto his hand tighter. He seemed to sense my change in mood. He ruffled my hair too and smiled.

'Melissa, why don't you take Rebecca upstairs and show her your bedroom. You'd like that, Rebecca, wouldn't you? Me and Mrs Nikolic can do the boring paperwork while you have a look around, eh?'

I looked down at my feet. *Go show her, Rebecca. Show her who's boss. You want to stay here, don't you?*

I looked up at Jim and nodded.

'Right, Mrs Nikolic, let's get that paperwork sorted.'

'Oh, Jim,' she laughed. 'Mrs Nikolic, indeed. It's Teresa. Now, away through to the kitchen and I'll shout Mark in from the garden.'

Their voices faded into the background as they left us standing looking at each other. Melissa looked nothing like me. Her skin looked fresh and healthy compared to my dull, lifeless complexion and lank greasy hair. *What a pretty little girl. Wonder who is going to be favourite around here, then?* I pulled myself up to my full height and followed her.

She took me into a large double bedroom with two single beds perfectly made with matching white duvets, covered in tiny pink rosebuds. Between the beds were two small bedside cabinets with little heart shaped lamps on them and under the window a huge desk, big enough for two. It was the perfect room for a child, but not for a thirteen-year-old.

The carpet was a dusky pink and so deep I could feel my toes sink into it. I drank in my surroundings. Photographs of a woman who looked like an older version of Melissa were lined up carefully on the window ledge. A large, expensive looking teddy was tucked up under the duvet, its glassy eyes staring at me as if laying claim to the room on Melissa's behalf. I looked over to the other bed, an assortment of soft toys waiting for me to claim them. *They think you're just a stupid little kid, just like her. They don't know, do they? You're bad. Dirty and bad.* My hands clenched into two tight fists. I felt myself start to float away. I was watching it all play out. It wasn't me anymore.

I could see Melissa watching me, as though trying to gauge my reaction. I could hear the voices of the grown-ups float up through the open window. I watched as I turned slowly to Melissa and said, 'I want that bed,' pointing at the one that was clearly hers.

I wanted to shout, 'I don't want that bed. I don't care what bed I sleep in!' But I couldn't say a word. I wasn't in control.

She shook her head. 'N-n-no, you can't. Teresa said that one was mine. We went to the shop and bought you some teddies of your own for your bed. I chose them especially for you,' she offered hopefully.

I watched as I inched closer. My face pushed right into hers, and hissed, 'I'm not a fucking kid. I don't want the fucking teddies and I want that fucking bed. If you want to stay here and not get sent to the children's home, you'll do as I say.'

Melissa's mouth opened with a yell threatening to escape. My hand found its way over her mouth.

'Be quiet. Don't you dare scream. If you do, I'll scream even louder and tell them you did this.' My T-shirt was lifted and my nails drew across my skin leaving tiny welts, little drops of blood forming at the sharpness.

Melissa's mouth dropped open, her eyes wide. She nodded, screwing up her eyes as though she were forcing the tears back in.

'The bed's yours,' she whispered, as she edged away from me, fear etched across her pretty little face. My head began to spin as I found myself standing in front of Melissa, I had no idea where that had come from.

'Girls!' A voice shouted, along with the sound of footsteps running up the stairs. Pulling my T-shirt down, I stepped back over to the bed I'd chosen as the door slid opened. Teresa put her head round the door, stopping in her tracks as she watched Melissa transfer her belongings to the other bed.

'Is everything okay, girls?' she asked.

Melissa nodded. 'Yes, Teresa. I decided that I liked the other bed best, I hope you don't mind. Rebecca said it was okay.'

'If you're sure, Melissa,' she said, looking directly at me.

I smiled. I couldn't speak. Out of the corner of my eye I saw Melissa nod her head. I said nothing.

'Come down and get some juice and biscuits, girls,' said Teresa as she left the room, apparently satisfied at Melissa's explanation.

Leaving the bedroom, I pulled Melissa close to me and whispered into her ear, 'It's all going to be okay.'

I smiled and, taking her hand, we made our way down the stairs.

11

JIM WAS PUTTING some papers into his rucksack as we came downstairs. Teresa sat on the sofa next to Mark, who had his arm thrown casually around her shoulders. He smiled over at me. I stared at him, not quite trusting myself to smile back just yet.

Standing back at the door, I peered out shyly and hid my hands, which were balled into tight fists, my nails digging into my skin. I watched Melissa run over to them, throwing herself onto their laps. They looked like the perfect family. A wave of resentment surged inside me as I took in the picture in front of me. Perfection. Would I ever fit in? I wondered.

Melissa turned and looked at me, I tensed... Would she say anything? Her mouth opened and the words began to form on her lips...

'Rebecca has... I mean, I've given Rebecca my bed. I-I-I think she'll like it better.'

The words tumbled out, causing her to stutter and I caught my breath, waiting for the adults to work out what had gone on. They said nothing.

Breathing out, I clenched my fists and forced my mouth into the widest smile. Out of the corner of my eye, I watched the adults look at one another and smile indulgently. Relieved, I breathed out quietly. Inside my head, the others giggled.

Jim talked about the process of adoption. He explained that there would be lots of meetings and assessments to make sure things were working out. He talked about supports and reviews, but I was taking nothing in. *Nobody will want you, Rebecca. You're damaged goods. A bad girl.*

I knew they were right, why would any family want someone like me when there was a cute six-year-old girl crying out to be loved? I tried to block their voices, I tried sending them away to their special place, but they chattered on.

They quietened as Teresa and Mark talked about the new school I'd be going to, swimming lessons I'd join Melissa in, and family holidays they had planned for next summer. My head was spinning, I'd never been swimming before and as for a holiday, well, that was just a dream. I listened to Jim talking about regular contact and monitoring. He finally came to the end of his lists and stood up to leave. Suddenly I felt nervous again, I clutched onto his leg, tears forming in my eyes. I didn't want him to leave. He looked down at me. He was smiling, but I was sure I could see his eyes mist over too.

'Come on, hen,' he chided. 'It's going to be okay. You've got a cracking family here. Teresa and Mark are great foster parents, and Melissa is a lovely kid. You'll love it, and I'll be back at the end of the week to see how you're getting on.'

Reluctantly, I let him go, watching every step he took away from me. All at once, I felt alone again.

'I'm feeling tired,' I told Mark and Teresa when they came back into the living room. I rubbed my eyes and feigned a yawn for effect. 'Is it okay if I go to my room for a while?'

They nodded, a look of concern on their faces.

'Oh, alright then, love,' said Teresa. 'Just half an hour though, eh? We don't want you shutting yourself away from everyone, you're part of this family and we're looking forward to getting to know you.'

She asked Melissa to go and help Mark in the garden for a while. I stood at the door watching them, before slipping out quietly, making my way upstairs to our room. I threw myself onto the bed Melissa had reluctantly handed over.

I grabbed my case. A hand-me-down fished out of social work supplies, it was battered and torn, just like me—my whole life bundled up into an overnight case and a carrier bag. How sad was that? *Just like you, sad, bad, sad and bad, bad and sad.*

'SHUT UP!' I shouted at them.

In my case was my memory box. All care kids had one. It was probably the most valuable possession I owned; it was something that proved I was somebody, proved that I'd belonged somewhere at some point in my life, no matter how many times I'd been shunted around the system.

Mine contained very little: my jewellery box, with a dog-eared photo of my mum and the silver chain, that had turned green, with a little half of a heart hanging from the end of it.

Holding it close to my chest, I thought about my dad. I wondered if he ever thought about me. If he knew what had happened, he would have turned up and got me, wouldn't he? The voices inside my head argued over it, I tried to shout over them, to tell them my dad was real, that he cared, he just didn't know where to find me, that was all. They didn't listen. They didn't hear. They drowned me out.

I remembered about the letter tucked up at the bottom of the box. Over the years I'd taken it in and out the box so often it was almost disintegrating. I smoothed it over and began to read it from memory.

Dear Rebecca,

If you're reading this letter, then it means your mum gave you the necklace. I have the other half; I keep it close every day. I should never have gone. I should have stayed and been your dad. Your mum wouldn't let me. I should have fought harder for you. I'm sorry. Just forget about me. I'm not worth knowing. A real dad would never have left you.

Sorry

Love Dad xx

Over the years I'd read this letter repeatedly, wondering about the man who was my dad. Samantha would whisper: *See, your mum got everything she deserved, Rebecca. All this is her fault. She stopped your dad from loving you.*

I tucked the letter up and placed it carefully underneath all my memories in hope that the truth would make itself known in the end.

I thought about Mark, Teresa and Melissa downstairs, a mum, dad and kid. A proper family. I wondered if Mark would be like a dad to me. Would he care for me? He didn't seem to be anything like Mr Reid, but I knew I had to be careful. I couldn't let myself get too close just to lose everything all over again. And Melissa? She was cute—too cute really. How would anybody love me with her around?

It's okay Rebecca, I won't let anyone hurt you ever again. I'm here. Anyone who tries to hurt you needs to get through me first. Samantha's voice was loud and clear, drowning out the others. Everything would be okay. Wouldn't it?

12

I'D BEEN LIVING with the Nikolics for about six months and things had started to settle. Even my other selves had quietened down and mostly left me alone. Apart from Samantha. She would always be there for me.

Jim still came out once or twice a week. It seemed to me like the adoption process was taking forever. I overheard Teresa tell Mark that she thought it was strange.

'It's not normal, Mark, none of the social workers we've ever had come out this often. I wonder if there's something about Rebecca they're not telling us?'

I couldn't hear Mark's reply as the washing machine chose that moment to go onto the spin cycle. But the comment was enough to send my mind into overdrive. Did they suspect something about me? Did they think there was something wrong with me? I fretted endlessly. What if they decided to get rid of me? I couldn't let that happen. I wouldn't let it happen.

Before long, the night terrors and the restless nights chasing the demons started up again. I was exhausted, but I had to keep up the pretence. It was more important now than ever.

More and more I'd feel myself disconnecting from the world around me. Moments and hours would pass where I couldn't remember a thing. I felt like a big black empty hole. I was frightened. Every look, every whisper I heard from Mark or Teresa convinced me they were going to send me away. They were watching my every move. Everyone was. I knew it. I could feel it.

I heard Teresa on the phone, speaking to Jim, asking him to come out and see them. They were worried about me. My world started to spin and Samantha's voice hissed in my ear. *Nobody fucking cares about you, Rebecca. You'd be better off dead.*

Jim came the next day. He looked kind of resigned, as if he had been expecting their call. He shut himself away in the living room with Mark and Teresa while I went upstairs and gouged a hole in my leg. Nobody knew, only us.

I was taken back to see Dr. Sullivan. She asked me lots of questions about living with Mark and Teresa—were they treating me well? Had anything happened? I told her the truth. I told her how much I liked staying with them and I was scared my others were going to ruin it for me. I'd tried doing everything she had taught me, but it wasn't working.

She gave me some tablets to take. They made me feel funny, it was quieter in my head when I took them, but the voices didn't like that. They didn't like the tablets closing them down. I was drowning and I didn't know what to do.

WEEKS TURNED INTO months, and life was slowly returning to normal. I was doing everything I could to prove I was good, to make Mark and Teresa want me. I wanted to stay here forever. I didn't want to be sent back to the unit. The Nikolics were my last chance, and I wouldn't let anyone or anything ruin it.

I still didn't like the side effects of the medication I was on, they made my brain like cotton wool, but I knew Dr Sullivan wouldn't let me stop taking them, and I didn't want to risk Mark or Teresa becoming even more concerned about my mental health. So I made up my mind to stop taking them. The only thing was Mark and Teresa kept them under lock and key and administered them to me. But I knew a few tricks from my time in the children's unit. I knew how to tuck the tablet under my tongue and spit it down the toilet later. And if that didn't work, I'd make myself throw up after taking it.

Slowly the nightmares began to creep in again, my other selves wheedled their way back into my head. I stopped recognising myself in the mirror. Teresa and Mark became the monsters I wanted to avoid, and my others made Melissa the focus of their attention.

At night we would sit on Melissa's bed, our sharp fingers poking and prodding at her, forcing her out from under the covers. We whispered threats, her face would turn chalk white and the fear would slip like a mask over her plump little cheeks. A part of me felt sorry for her—she hadn't done anything wrong—but my others kept going.

Drawings depicting our family were found under my bed, drawings where I was always scribbled over in a fury of black and red crayon, lying as though I was dead, just outside of the safety of the family home.

'Disturbing,' I heard Teresa whisper to Mark, as she crumpled up yet another terrifying drawing. 'This girl seriously needs help. If I'm honest, I'm starting to feel a little frightened of her.'

Mark would shrug his shoulders. I got the feeling that he was reluctant for Teresa to raise her concerns officially. At night I'd hear the two of them talk in their bedroom when they thought I was fast asleep. I discovered they couldn't have children of their own and Mark was desperate to be a father. He clearly didn't want to be seen as a failure by admitting to the professionals they were struggling to cope with me. This was his only chance of being a dad and he wasn't going to take any chances of ruining it. Mark believed it was just a phase I was going through. Teresa wasn't quite as sure as he was. The drawings were getting darker, the injuries to my body, drawn in a crude childish scribble, becoming increasingly disturbing. When I started wetting the bed, Teresa became more and more upset. I'd catch her watching me carefully as though trying to catch me out.

'This can't go on. She needs help, professional help,' I heard her whisper to Mark one morning after having to strip my bed once more.

I sat in the toilet, rocking back and forth, the pain in my head becoming intense. *Bad, bad Rebecca. They're going to send you away.* The razor blade against my skin soothed me, it made the voices disappear.

13

LIVING WITH ME was starting to have an effect on Melissa. She slowly began to unravel in front of us all. Gone were the breathless giggles and smiles, replaced by a sullen and tearful child. She was terrified to tell anyone what was really going on.

At first, it was little things that would go missing, a pair of Teresa's earrings or a few coins from her purse. A few days later they would turn up squirrelled away among Melissa's belongings. She didn't even deny it. She knew there was no point. I could see Teresa struggling to understand what was going on; she had no idea how to deal with the situation.

I'd watch her in the kitchen, staring absently out into the garden, a small tear tracing its way down her face. I tried to play on her confusion.

'Poor little Melissa. She's just missing her mum.' I'd offer in her defence. But when I started to show up with unexplained injuries, the tension really ramped up. I'd brush it off blaming my clumsiness, but Teresa was having none of it.

'Why are you doing this, Rebecca? We know it's not Melissa stealing and drawing these vile pictures, we know it's you.'

I swallowed my rage, but my knuckles were white and my nails dug into the palms of my hands. I could feel the warmth of the blood and I imagined raking my nails down Teresa's face. *Do it*, whispered Samantha. But I didn't. I wanted to bide my time.

I heard Mark and Teresa talking in bed not long after this conversation. Teresa was crying, she was worried about both of us. She begged Mark to confide in Jim. 'Before it's too late,' I heard her say.

'I'm not giving up on that kid, Teresa', Mark had replied. 'We can help her, I know we can.'

The next day Jim came over. Sitting quietly outside the living room door, I listened to them telling him about what had been going on. I heard them cry as they told him. They didn't know how much longer they could keep us both with them. *Rebecca's getting sent away... Dirty little girl... Nobody wants you... Everybody hates you.* The voices in my head were getting louder, it was harder to ignore them and harder to keep them away from everyone else.

I heard Jim get up and make his way to the door. I ran back upstairs, anxious for him not to catch me. I was lying on my bed when he came into my room.

'Hey Rebecca. How are you doing, hen?' He asked as he sat down beside me.

I shrugged in reply. I was scared to open my mouth. I didn't know who was going to answer.

'Are you taking your medication like Dr Sullivan told you?'
I nodded.

'Are things becoming difficult again, hen?'

I knew what he meant—he meant was I going crazy? Were my others telling me what to do? I pulled the pillow over my face so he wouldn't see them.

He kept on talking, reassuring me everything was going to be okay. He told me he wanted me to go back and see Dr Sullivan. He'd managed to get an emergency appointment with her the next day.

I didn't reply.

'Rebecca, hen, you've not really got any choice, you know? We are worried about you. I need you to go to see the doctor. I don't want you to end up in hospital.'

Hospital. The word jerked me back into reality. I didn't want to go to any hospital. I wanted to stay here with Mark and Teresa. I wanted them to be my new family. I pulled the pillow away from my face. Jim's face fell when he saw my tear stained cheeks.

'Och, hen, you're a wee soul, you know that, don't you? Listen, I need to speak to Mark and Teresa again, I'll be right back up to see you.'

He was only away a couple of minutes, before he was back trying to reassure me, telling me things would all work out. He said he'd take me to my appointment with Dr Sullivan. I wondered why he would be doing it and not Mark or Teresa, as they usually did. Jim didn't say, he just gave me a small hug and said he would see me at two the next day.

I liked Dr Sullivan, but she was not as easy to manipulate as most adults. She seemed to be able to see deep inside me, and I'd quickly learned that staying quiet was not an option during our appointments. She expected me to open up and talk. She didn't mind which one of me spoke during our meetings. That's what I liked about her—I trusted her, but now I was worried Jim was going to take me there and I'd be sent to hospital.

The rest of the day passed in a bit of a blur, there was a dark fog inside my head and it wouldn't clear. I floated in and out of myself. Teresa was trying her best, popping in and out of the room, trying to tempt me with my favourite foods. I refused to eat. She wouldn't leave me alone though, reappearing every so often, offering me treats.

'Come on, Rebecca love,' she said. 'It's just you and me in the house, Mark's taken Melissa out for the day.'

So that's why I hadn't seen her since Jim had left. I wondered if perhaps Mark had taken her to the children's home. But I knew he hadn't, all her stuff was still here.

Rebecca's going to the doctor tomorrow… Rebecca's getting sent to the funny farm… She's a bad girl… That's where the bad girls go. They were all talking inside my head, talking about me. I couldn't stand it anymore.

Teresa, bless her, kept on trying. She refused to give up on me. She even tried to reason with my others when they answered her, often in angry and aggressive outbursts. I watched her from above, I felt sorry for her. She didn't deserve this. She deserved better than me.

I begged them to leave me, to let me be myself. I wanted to stay here with Mark and Teresa. But they just laughed at me. *We're not leaving you, Rebecca, you need us. Without us, you are nobody… You're nobody… Who is ever going to love you apart from us?*

I watched from above again as Teresa sat down on the bed beside my body and hugged me hard. I wished I could float back down there and be me and pause that moment forever.

Mark returned with Melissa. I heard him whisper to Teresa: 'How's Rebecca? Is she any better?'

Teresa gave a bitter laugh, 'Mark, she's not going to get any better. I think we need to accept she needs more help than we can give her.'

See, told you so. You're going to be carted off tomorrow. Never coming back here. They don't want you.

'Shut up… shut up… just shut the fuck up,' I muttered over and over, my hands over my ears trying to stop their voices.

I sat on the couch in the living room. Mark and Teresa were in the kitchen and Melissa had gone upstairs to our room. I listened to their conversation.

'Dr Sullivan will know what's best for her,' said Teresa.

'I just don't want to give up on her, my heart breaks for that little girl and everything she has gone through,' replied Mark.

'I know, love. Mine too, but she really does need some professional help and I think she needs to be somewhere else to get it. It's not fair on Melissa, is it? I know you want to help them both, but seriously, Rebecca needs way more than we can give her. For her own sake... and for ours.'

I couldn't listen anymore. I knew what was going to happen. I was going to be taken away tomorrow and there was nothing I could do to stop it.

Pushing open the kitchen door, I watched as Mark and Teresa hugged each other. He had tears in his eyes. Teresa turned and saw me standing there. 'Oh, Rebecca love, I didn't know you were there.'

I could see the guilt in her eyes. Turning, I slowly walked out the door and the others slammed it hard behind me.

Back upstairs in the bedroom, I stood at the door watching Melissa play with her teddies. She must have sensed my presence, as she turned to look at me. The fear shone from her eyes.

'H-h-hi Rebecca...d-d-o you w-want to p-p-play?' She stuttered.

Ignoring her, I threw myself on my bed and buried my head in my pillows. I heard her tiny feet pad out the door and run downstairs.

You need to sort her Rebecca... It's all her fault... She needs to learn a lesson.

14

I LOST ALL sense of time when Melissa left the room. A mist descended and the room became a strange mix of shapes and figures all blurring into one. I no longer knew where I was or who was in control. Their voices became one inside my head as I tried to pull myself out of the darkness.

Outside the room, I could hear the ordinary sounds of Teresa, Mark and Melissa. I tried to shout out to them, to come and save me, to take me away, but my mouth would make no sound. I sunk back onto the bed and gave in to my voices. I let them take over.

When I opened my eyes, I had no idea how long I'd been gone. The house was quiet and I could see the darkness had slipped through the gap in the curtains. It must be night time. I looked across the room, I could see the small shape in the other bed. Melissa curled up in a world full of her own dreams. I could see her blonde curls peeking out the duvet and a small fist clutched tightly on to a teddy.

My heart was breaking. She looked so innocent. *Not like you Rebecca. Dirty Rebecca. You aren't innocent, are you?* I placed a finger over my lips in an attempt to quiet them.

Slipping out of the bed, I tiptoed over to the mirror, I gazed at the face peering back at me. It wasn't me. Her dark eyes stared lifelessly back at me, dark hair like snakes swirling around her head. Her mouth opened, I lifted my hand to my face and felt my own mouth mirroring hers. *You know what to do, Rebecca. It's time now.*

I watched as my body glided across the room, I held my breath as she grabbed the child by the hair. Holding one hand over her mouth, she pulled her into a sitting position. She thrust a knife into her hand, forcing her to grasp her fingers around it. Melissa was terrified, I could see her face scream. Dragging her out of bed, I watched as my hand raised with the knife poised to strike.

'Noooooooooooooooooooooo!' I screamed. I forced myself down, back into my body. Roughly I pushed Melissa back onto her bed. I smiled at her, my eyes glittering. I felt no fear at all. Only a sudden clarity in my brain. This was the right thing to do.

I hoisted up my top, exposing my pale belly, I lifted the knife high and, watching Melissa, I plunged it down hard into my stomach.

I felt a sweet release as the blood began to pump out, stark against the white sheets on the bed. My breath came hard and fast. A rush of blood filled my head and I closed my eyes, melting into the sensation. *'Scream,'* growled my others.

I opened my eyes wide and emitted a piercing scream that shattered the dark silence. I looked up, Melissa was standing over me, her face chalk white. I lay down and laughed.

The house burst into life, a riot of noise and sound as Mark and Teresa came charging into our room. By this point, Melissa was hysterical and I was catatonic. I felt as though I was drowning. I could feel myself being sucked from my body. I watched, my eyelids flickering, my body still, Teresa's mouth gaping in a soundless scream while Mark shouted garbled words into the phone.

'Police, ambulance, now… stabbed… child… foster… social work.' The words made no sense to me, but I knew exactly what had happened. They had won.

Teresa stood silently in the corner; her hands clutched tightly as though in prayer. Mark held the bedsheets against my wound, stemming the blood. I watched everything happen around me in slow motion. I looked at myself lying on the bed, my hair fanned out around me, the blood saturating the bedsheets. My eyes were closed. Mark and Teresa were watching over me, a look of anguish on their faces. A terror that would never leave them. Melissa stood in the middle of the room, rocking back and forth, screams spewing out of her mouth. Her eyes were dead. It was over for her now.

The next thing I knew, I was back on the bed, jolted into my own body. The room was full of people, the static of police radios and a sea of green as the paramedics rushed to my aid. By this time, Melissa was crumpled in a heap on the floor, sobbing wretchedly with a policewoman standing over her looking unsure as what to do next. Memories reared inside my head, screaming at me, tearing at my eyes, and sending me back to that day. To Samantha. To Mum. To death.

A blur of faces surrounded me until one came into focus. It was Jim. He was staring at me with a strange look on his face. Pity, fear, love, terror? I didn't know, the emotions seemed to play out like a film across his face. The room went black.

I WOKE UP to the hiss and beep of machines around me. Slowly opening my eyes, I watched the green flashes across the black screen play out a stable line, a sheet of paper slipping out into the metal tray underneath. I could see the back of a woman dressed in a pale blue nurse's tunic and Teresa lying across the bundle of my bedsheets where she'd fallen asleep watching over me.

Stealing a glance around the room, I noted that Mark wasn't there. The door to my room whispered open and in slipped Jim. Worry was etched across his face. He clearly hadn't slept, the wrinkles across his brow were more pronounced than ever. I wanted to giggle. They looked as though they'd been ironed into his face like creases in a shirt. He sensed my stare and looked across the room at me, his eyes misty as he walked towards me. Teresa stirred and came around quickly, realising I was waking.

I listened to them, my eyes closed so that nobody could see the smile lighting them up. I heard Jim's voice whisper 'Goodbye' in my ear, and the door click over as he left the room.

The next few days passed quietly. I wasn't in any immediate danger but was being kept in hospital for observation. I wasn't fooled, I knew that there was another reason I was being kept there, the adults wanted some time to talk about what would happen next.

I wasn't stupid, I knew I wouldn't be allowed to go back to Mark and Teresa. Not now. Not after that.

There were lots of whispered conversations taking place in the rooms around me. The adults would come in and look at me. Sometimes they would smile, other times a mixture of fear and pity would mask their faces. There were lots of questions thrown at me every day. Questions about my other selves. Questions about me.

Dr Sullivan came back to see me. She asked me about the night it had happened.

'Who did this to you?' she asked. I shrugged my shoulders. I didn't know. All I knew was that it wasn't me.

'Were the others there, Rebecca? It's okay, you can tell me, nobody is in any trouble, we just want to help you.'

I looked at her, wanting to trust her. She had no idea how much I wanted to trust her. I wanted to trust someone, anyone, who would help me escape from this madness I was trapped in. Her face was expressionless, she didn't look angry or as though she didn't believe me. She looked like she was happy to stay there all day just waiting for me to talk.

I listened inside my head. Silence. I looked around me, the room was clear, there was no mist, I could make out the shapes of the bed, sink, drip and all the other hospital equipment. I looked back at Dr Sullivan. She was still there, just waiting.

Opening my mouth, I tested the words coming out to make sure they were mine.

'How's Melissa?' I whispered.

She lay her hand across mine gently. 'Melissa will be fine. She's going to be okay. It's you we are worried about, Rebecca.'

Her smile was reassuring, my voice had been my own. There was no sign of the others. It was now or never. And so I spilled my guts to the doctor, nobody stopped my words, nobody stole them to turn them into something else. I told her everything. Everything I could remember from before. Everything that had happened to me and everything I had done. I told her about the others living inside me. I told her about the good parts of them and about the bad.

As the last words left my mouth, I flopped back on the bed. Spent. Done.

I didn't hear much of what Dr Sullivan said after that, only her thanks for my honesty and the words I'd been dreading for such a long time. 'Rebecca, I think we are going to have to have you come into hospital for a period of assessment and treatment.'

After that the room went black and I disappeared.

15

I CRIED MY heart out the day they transferred me to Kintyre House, the adolescent inpatient unit in Glasgow. They could call it whatever they wanted to, but to me, it was still the nut house. I'd asked if Teresa and Mark would be coming to see me before I was moved. The nurse looking after me just shook her head. They had left me too. Along with my others. Abandoned again. Only Samantha was left. She would never leave me. She promised.

I was heartbroken. All I'd wanted was to be a part of a family. I hadn't meant to hurt Melissa or the Nikolics. I had only wanted them to love me. But my others had put a stop to that. It was their fault I was alone again. I felt bad for the Nikolics and for Melissa, they hadn't deserved me, or Samantha. They were decent, genuine people who had only tried to care for me. *Bad little Rebecca, she ruins everything...* hissed Samantha as I waited to be taken to the hospital.

Even Samantha couldn't be trusted properly, I thought bitterly. There were two sides to her too, and heaven help anyone who got caught on her bad side. Her sly side. Her evil side. Just look at what happened to Mum, and Annie Reilly. That had been down to Samantha... Hadn't it?

The nurse from my ward accompanied me to Kintyre House. We had to go through a secure door to enter and then another two after that.

'Am I going to be locked up?' I whispered to her.

'The doors are all locked but it's just for security, love,' she replied, shrugging her shoulders.

She didn't understand, she didn't even care. I couldn't be locked up, the very thought of it terrified me. I had visions of being locked in a room and the men coming back and nobody being there to stop them. I pulled away from her and started running in the opposite direction. But she came right after me, catching me in seconds. In a rage, I began kicking and biting at her, desperate to break free. I was screaming and cursing, the voice coming out my mouth didn't belong to me.

The disturbance must have caught the attention of ward staff. As if by magic, doors hissed open and four nurses came towards us. Their words were quiet—an attempt to diffuse the situation—but the sight of them in their nursing tunics sent the fear of God into me and my attempts to escape became even more violent.

I'm sure I broke skin and caused a few bruises, but it didn't matter. I ended up face down on the floor, with one nurse at my feet and the other at my back, my hands and feet restrained. It took four of them to lift me and escort me to the admissions room. My feet dragged and I cursed and spat at anyone who looked at me.

The room they put me in was empty, apart from the seat I sat on and a small table with another seat beside it. They were all securely attached to the floor. Looking around, I noticed the scuffs and gouges on the walls. Clearly, I wasn't the first person to be unhappy at being placed here. One of the nurses who had restrained me sat on the seat opposite me. She had given up trying to explain what was going to happen.

Inside my head, the others were clamouring for my attention. I screamed at them to shut the fuck up. I watched the nurse as the curses spilled out my mouth. Her face never changed expression the whole time. I wondered who she could see, me or them? I wondered whose voice she could hear, mine or theirs?

One of my others stood back and tried to calm me, she helped me breathe by taking slow deep breaths and gently clenching my fists. She urged me to lie down in the corner with my knees tucked up to my chest and she soothed me to a state of calmness. Best of all, she managed to stop all the others shouting.

The door opened and a tall, skinny man entered. I shrunk back, trying to disappear into the wall. I knew it, they were coming to get me. My heart rate increased, and a scream worked its way into my mouth. I watched him say something quietly to the nurse and she left the room. My scream spewed out my mouth and my body prepared to fight.

The man didn't come near me. He didn't begin to undress and no evil words left his mouth. Instead he took a seat at the table and set out a notebook and pen in front of him.

I watched him, through my fingers, unsure of his reaction. My screams had died away.

He looked up from the table. 'Rebecca,' his voice was soft. 'I'm Doctor Sanderson, the consultant psychiatrist for the ward. Would you like to take a seat?'

Don't trust him Rebecca… He's going to lock you up… He's going to hurt you… Bad Rebecca… Dirty Rebecca.

'Shut the fuck up,' I snapped.

The man looked at me. 'Is there someone else with you just now, Rebecca?'

Don't fucking tell him Rebecca… Tell him nothing… He can't help you… Only we can help you.

'Fucking leave me alone,' I screamed, clutching my head in my hands, desperate to claw them out.

'Rebecca, it's okay, I understand. I'm here to help you and I'm quite happy to talk to anyone else who is with you just now if that's what they want? If that's what you want?'

I shook my head, taking my hand away from my face. I had to ignore them, I had to remember what Dr Sullivan had told me. I stared at the table and chairs, focusing on them, taking my thoughts away from my others. I felt myself starting to reconnect with the room, my thoughts becoming clearer. I sat up with my knees still clutched to my chest.

He smiled at me, 'The seat's more comfortable, but if you are happy there, then I'm happy to chat to you from here.'

His words were soft and reassuring, even if I didn't understand what he was talking about. He would scribble short notes down on the paper. Curious, I eventually shuffled over to the chair and sat down across from him.

He lifted his hand and laid it gently across mine. Something snapped. I grabbed his pen and stabbed it into my hand.

I WOKE UP to find myself in bed in a small, sparsely decorated room. The walls were painted an institutional pale blue and there was a small rectangular window at the top of the wall. I tried to focus, to think about where I was… who I was. I looked down at my body, covered in a quilt which matched the colour of the walls. I still had my clothes on and I appeared to be unharmed.

A noise from the far end of the room made me look up, and panic rose in my chest as I noticed a shadowy figure sitting on a chair in the open doorway. The figure was staring at me. I clutched the blanket to my chest and began to scream.

'Shh,' it said.

I screamed louder.

The figure stood up and moved towards me. By now, my screams would have woken the dead.

The lights snapped on, the cold fluorescent strip hurting my eyes as it fizzed to life. The figure was at the foot of my bed and was trying to reassure me. The pale blue tunic she wore made me realise it was a nurse. Another head popped through the door.

'Everything alright in here?'

'Yeah, it's fine, Linda,' said the nurse. 'She's just woken up and I think the poor soul was a bit frightened. Can you go fetch her something to drink and a wee slice of toast?' She turned to me as she said this, nodding her head.

I nodded back at her, not sure of what I should say or what I should be doing.

'You alright now, love?' she asked.

I shrugged. *If I was alright, I wouldn't be lying in this bed in this bloody nut house, would I?* I said nothing.

'You gave us all a bit of a fright, thankfully there was no harm done to your hand though, just some bruising.'

I looked down and saw a small bruise spreading out from the black-red spot on the back of my hand. The memories came back in slow motion… A room… A doctor… A notebook…

I checked to see if the nurse was angry at me, but she was smiling.

'Linda's just away to get you a drink and some toast. My name's Tricia and I'll be staying with you just until the doctor comes back to assess you.'

I let her words sink in. Samantha chattered inside me, I zoned out of her voice.

'Why am I here?'

'I think the doctor is best to answer that question, Rebecca, love. Let's just say you've not been very well recently and hospital's the best place to be to get you back on your feet.'

The door opened and the nurse called Linda came back in. She had a drink and some toast on a tray. The smell made me realise how hungry I was. I also realised I was bursting for a pee. I made to get out of my bed.

'Where are you going?' Asked Tricia.

'I need a pee.'

'Okie dokes, just a minute until I unlock your toilet door.'

She took a bunch of keys from her pocket and unlocked the door. I slipped inside and went to close the door behind me. But Tricia had come in with me. I stood looking at her, the confusion must have been clear on my face.

'It's procedure, love, you're on special obs. I need to be with you. It's just to keep you safe.'

My face burned with shame as I tried to wiggle down my trousers and underwear. To give her her due, she did turn her back a little to afford me some privacy.

Back in the room, I wolfed down my toast and drink. Sitting on my bed, I asked Tricia what was to happen next. Just as she was about to explain, there was a knock on the door and the doctor from earlier on came in. And so my journey to recovery began.

ALMOST TWO YEARS later, and after what had seemed like endless rounds of care planning, review meetings and sessions with psychiatrists, occupational therapists and nursing staff, the big day came. It was my discharge planning meeting, time for me to go out into the big, bad world again.

Although I'd never have believed things could get better, I had to admit that twelve months in Kintyre House had left me feeling like a new person. Intensive support and therapy had taught me to come to terms with my diagnosis of Dissociative Identity Disorder. It had felt good to give it a name, not to have to hide it anymore and not to be afraid of being labelled "crazy" by others. In here, it was perfectly acceptable to be myself, or indeed ourselves.

My others had learned to take a back seat, and staff had taught me plenty of coping mechanisms and ways in which I could relegate them to that back seat when they began to play up. I had finally learned to live with my condition as opposed to it controlling me.

My consultant had explained my condition was likely to have been caused by the trauma I'd experienced as a child. I cried my heart out at this. It was the first time I had ever openly acknowledged what had happened to me back then and they helped me understand the abuse had not been my fault. And best of all, for once, my others hadn't butted in to tell me any different.

I looked around the table, thinking how different things were compared to the first day I came onto the ward. I no longer viewed staff as the enemy and felt I was at the table as an equal now. It was a good feeling and one I was determined to hold on to. The meeting was coming to an end and it had been decided I'd move into supported housing to begin with. I'd have regular contact with the community mental health team with a view to me moving on to independent living by my eighteenth birthday. They even had a college place lined up for me.

My new social worker was coming the next day to help me move. I hadn't seen Jim Aitken since the day of the incident with Melissa. Like everyone else, he had abandoned me. But I didn't care anymore—I'd learned to let him go. I didn't need him. I didn't need anybody anymore. This was my new beginning. I'd finally learned to live with who I was, but I'd never forget my past.

Inside, I was buzzing. Life had just started to get better. If only I'd had a crystal ball and a magic wand, I may just have pressed pause at that moment and left it there.

PART TWO

2018

16

HER HEART POUNDING following yet another nightmare, Rebecca Findlay slumped back down in bed, the darkness her cover as the moon peeked through the small gap in the curtains. Her ears pricked up at the sound of the car crunching its way slowly up the drive.

He's back. You know what's going to happen now. 'Shut up,' she muttered. She was too tired to listen to Samantha tonight.

A gentle thud as the door closed over, as though the driver was trying to deny their presence. Soft footsteps approached the front door and she heard the key slip easily into the lock. He was trying to be quiet.

The door gave the game away with its undeniable whine as it closed. A soft shuffle as shoes were slipped off, before he made his way up the stairs. He was home. Lucas was back and her stomach clenched, as his footsteps drew closer followed by the soft noise of the bedroom door being pushed open. She closed her eyes and sighed, she knew exactly what was coming next...

Who could have known that such violence could be so silent? It was almost as though they'd perfected the art of keeping it all behind closed doors. Stifled sobs as the blows came reigning down; silent screams as the feet made contact with the soft underside of the belly. Each punch and kick silent in their brutality. The level of control was measured for maximum impact as each blow was delivered. And then it was over. Just like that. Spent.

Lying back on her pillows, she tried to fight the sleep she knew she so desperately needed. Her body was exhausted from the onslaught and her mind alive with the battle that had gone before. But Rebecca knew sleep wouldn't come alone tonight; she knew what demons awaited her, and she wasn't sure she could take it anymore. She was drained. She was empty.

She slowly became aware of the morning sunlight creeping through the curtains; the evidence of the night sharp in the first light of day. Like her life gone before her, the vase gifted to them on their wedding day lay shattered in pieces across the floor with a smear of blood as though the hands that had caused the hurt were still scraping their way down the walls. On the rug lay several shiny beads, an assortment of sizes, the pale, watery sun reflecting the shattered mess that was their lives.

Stepping gingerly out of the bed, fearful of waking Lucas, Rebecca slowly picked her way across the debris, across the landing, and into the bathroom. She started as she caught sight of her reflection in the mirror. Staring back at her was a woman she recognised from times gone by. Dark shadows framed her eyes, hair lank and lifeless, and skin as grey as the dead.

Surveying the effects of the night before, she clenched her fists ten times matching each clench with a deep breath. The repetition soothed her, it brought a sense of calm to her inner turmoil and she knew that, with careful attention, she could bring order to her day. Carefully laying out her tools—primer, foundation, blusher, eyeshadow, mascara, and lipstick, in that order—she stared into the mirror, seeing only the demons from the night before. The sharp light behind her accentuated the horrors. Ten deep breaths, ten clenches of her fists. She stepped into the shower and prepared to begin the application of her mask for the day.

Returning to the bedroom, she stood and watched Lucas breathing softly, his face buried in the pillow and his arms covering his head. He looked so peaceful, so rested, so calm. Memories flashed before her eyes as he gave a soft sigh and stirred. Turning over in the bed, stretching in anticipation of another day, Lucas began to stir. Tears filling her eyes, Rebecca slipped out the room again quietly before he came to. She didn't think she could face him after what had happened.

'It's getting worse every time—it can't go on much longer,' she thought, as she hastily dressed for the day in the spare room. Transformation complete, she reviewed her appearance in the mirror. She was ready to present herself to the world again.

The phone rang as she reached the bottom of the stairs. She considered ignoring it, but it could be work. Sighing, she answered.

'Hi, Rebecca speaking.'

Silence. She slammed the phone down, she was sick of these silent calls, this was the fifth one this week.

Lucas was already in the kitchen when she walked in. He looked straight at her as though she were a stranger; like he didn't recognise her. His eyes were blank, giving nothing away. His breathing steady, he stood perfectly still as though trying to predict her next move.

'Can he not see that this is all his own doing?' Rebecca asked herself. 'Has he no insight at all? Does he forget it all as soon as it's over? Is it only me that's left with the aftermath of his destruction, day after day, while he just gets up and gets on with things as though nothing has ever happened?'

No words were spoken, yet their unspoken communication sparked with electricity, creating a dark tension in the room. The underlying message given was clear. This was not over. Not by a long chalk.

Rebecca watched as Lucas ate his toast, cleaning up the kitchen methodically as he went; opening the cupboards to check the tins were facing the right way, stopping to rearrange the mugs so the handles faced outwards, and wiping down the surfaces until every possible germ was obliterated.

She counted off the rituals in her head; tins, mugs, surfaces, cutlery drawer, and fridge. She knew it off by heart and knew that he would have had already been through the living room with a fine-tooth comb making sure that each cushion was plumped and sitting at the perfect angle, each magazine arranged neatly across the coffee table, and each book spine pushed in to align perfectly with the others. She knew exactly what would happen if things didn't look exactly the same when they returned from work.

She tilted her head and looked at him as he prepared to leave for the day.

'For Christ Sake's, Lucas, I don't know why you're so obsessed with things in the house. I think you might have OCD you know,' she sneered. 'You really are so screwed-up, folk must wonder why I put up with you.'

She watched him, daring him to speak, daring him to contradict her. As she predicted, he said nothing. He just stared back at her, and she could almost see the counter accusations poised, but remaining firmly on his lips. Rebecca knew that he wouldn't argue back, she would never let him win.

She smiled as he shook his head and left the house, watching his shoulders slump and the air hang heavy around him. She could almost hear the self-doubt nagging away inside his head already.

She waited until he had left and almost gleefully dropped some breadcrumbs on the counter and pushed the mugs out of line. It gave her a small sense of satisfaction to break her own rules, no matter the consequences for Lucas.

Satisfied that she'd ensured his day had got off to a bad start, she picked up her keys and slipped out the front door to begin her own day, but not before she checked and re-checked the door to ensure it was locked.

17

FOLLOWING HER NORMAL daily routine, Rebecca began to plan for her day ahead. It was crucial for her wellbeing; she couldn't afford for the old fears to slip back into her mind—she couldn't go back to the days of not knowing who she was. To stay well she had to stay focused. Fear gripped her stomach as thoughts of her past and her loss of control drifted through her mind. She pushed them away, those memories couldn't be allowed to slip their shackles and attack the new Rebecca.

Her others had all but retreated now, back into the shadows. Apart from one—Samantha—and Rebecca had gradually become used to her being around. In a bizarre way, she found it kind of reassuring, having Samantha in there. They mostly existed side by side. Sometimes she would let Samantha take control of the parts of life she struggled to cope with. But she remained wary of giving her full control, because she was well aware of the dark side to Samantha and she knew exactly what she was capable of when pushed.

Only Rebecca's therapist knew about Samantha. Not Lucas, and most certainly not any of her work colleagues. Despite the open-minded environment she worked in, she was all too aware there was still an underlying stigma about mental health. Too many peoples' views were fashioned by the tabloid headlines, and she wasn't entirely convinced her colleagues would be any different. She couldn't imagine them being as accepting of her if she were to tell them she was host to another person inside her. Besides, Samantha had her uses, she allowed Rebecca to shake off the shackles of her past and have some fun at the expense of others.

Reaching the bus stop, she noticed the queue was busier than normal. The previous bus couldn't have arrived yet. She sighed. She hated her routine being broken. Clenching her fists inside her coat pocket, she took ten deep breaths while she thought about heading back to catch the train instead. But that would mean upsetting her usual plans, and she didn't think she could face the upheaval today, she was still worn out from the night before.

She could easily have taken a lift into work with Lucas, he had offered her often enough. Rebecca didn't drive, she'd never felt the urge to learn, preferring to spend her time before work planning rather than fuming in endless traffic jams. Besides, it gave the others in the office something else to gossip about.

'He must be a right bastard to live with,' she could almost hear them whisper. 'Making her get the bus, while he drives himself into work in comfort.'

She smiled to herself. She loved it when a plan worked out, and this one was working perfectly. Well, almost perfectly. She shook her head to rid herself of any doubts that might be lingering.

Standing at the bus stop, Rebecca shivered. Something made her check over her shoulder. She felt the hairs on the back of her neck stand to attention; someone was watching her. She could feel it. This wasn't the first time either, it had been going on for a couple of weeks now.

With a sense of foreboding, she discreetly checked her surroundings, but her fellow passengers were all engrossed in their phones, oblivious to the panic washing over her. Glancing around the busy street, she was convinced she saw someone move in the bushes behind the bus shelter. She started, but then it was gone. Cold fingers ran down her spine. She pulled her coat tighter as though to protect herself. She willed the bus to hurry. Had she locked the door? Checked the windows before she left? The panic was rising, fuelled by the voices in her head clamouring to be heard. *It's watching you Rebecca…Behind you…You can't escape.* 'Shut up' she muttered, startled by the stares of the other passengers. 'Shit, I must have said that out loud.' She fixed the glare on her face, pulled her shoulders back, and stared straight ahead.

When the number 88 finally arrived—seven minutes late— she pushed her way on ahead of the others, who stood back to let her go, perhaps a little perturbed by her behaviour.

She felt sick as she realised all the single seats were taken. She didn't want to sit next to anyone, but she knew it would look strange if she stood when there were still seats available. Scanning the chairs, she looked for the safest place to perch herself until she reached her stop: a young man plugged into his music, the tinny rattle escaping from the white buds pressed into his ears. At least he wouldn't attempt to strike up a conversation.

Hands clammy and heart racing, Rebecca sat down gingerly at the very edge of the seat and held herself rigidly, eyes fixed on the floor, while taking silent breaths to calm her for the rest of the journey. Today was not a good day. Today it could all go terribly wrong.

She was already in the office when her assistant Emma Mitchell breezed in. Emma greeted her with a cheery wave and a smile, dumping her oversized bag on her desk. Rebecca grimaced in irritation. Emma grated on her nerves. Samantha didn't like her much either. Emma always managed to look perfect, but would glibly insist it only took her ten minutes to get ready. Rebecca didn't trust anyone who felt the need to hide themselves behind a mask of thick makeup.

Rebecca glanced at Emma's bag thrown on the desk, scattering a shower of paperwork in its wake. It wasn't even half-past nine in the morning and already she'd used her calming-down routine five times. Today was most definitely not going to be a good day.

The moment passed and she opened her desk drawer to reassure herself that her own papers were still neatly stacked, just as she'd left them the night before. Sighing in relief at the expected order, she sat back and eyed Emma carefully. *Bet you wish you were more like her,* whispered Samantha. *She's just so chilled out. Relaxed and effortless. Not like you, Rebecca.*

Rebecca frowned, irritated at Samantha's interruption. Things had been going off kilter recently and she didn't like it. Afraid Emma would notice her acting oddly, she moulded her face into an acceptable expression and glanced over at her. She knew she'd nailed it when Emma shot her a worried look.

'Another tough night, love? Honestly, I don't know how you put up with it.'

Rebecca pretended to wipe away a tear. 'It's not that bad, he's just stressed with the changes at work, you know? The funding is under review. It's hard for him too, he doesn't mean it.'

Rebecca watched for Emma's reaction, pleased when she saw the look of pity cross her colleague's face. Her plan to have others question her husband's behaviour was working and she knew they gossiped about it behind her back, struggling to work out why such a self-assured woman as herself would put up with a man like him. They don't know the half of it, she thought grimly.

She accepted Emma's offer of a cup of tea—the panacea to every catastrophe in this place. If only tea could solve everything else.

Rebecca found herself thinking back to when she had first met Lucas. It was hard to believe it had only been two years ago. They'd gelled quickly and after a whirlwind romance, tied the knot in Gretna last year. It had been a perfect day, married in the Old Mill Forge, over the anvil, just the two of them with witnesses they'd pulled from behind the hotel bar. They had been full of hopes and dreams for the future.

Well, Rebecca had hopes and dreams, whether they'd matched Lucas's was a different story. He had been no match for her determination. When she wanted something, she was determined to make it happen. Nothing, or nobody stood in Rebecca's way, not anymore.

They both worked in the third sector in the East End of Glasgow. Funding was always tenuous and the challenges and frustrations of working with their client groups meant their working life could be difficult and extremely busy. Theirs was not a normal nine-to-five life, their working hours most definitely anti-social. Still, at least it meant she wasn't forced to spend too much time with her husband.

Lucas was senior support worker at Space to Grow, mostly working with men who had been referred by the courts for behavioural change programmes. Many of his clients had been charged with violent and sexual offences and often had underlying mental health and addiction issues that had never been addressed. It wasn't the easiest client group to work with and Lucas often found himself at the end of their threats and sometimes their fists.

She thought he must have the patience of a saint. She knew what she'd do with them. Her project, Phoenix, worked with the women who had suffered at the hands of the men Lucas worked with, and as such she didn't have any patience for his client group.

She was shaken out of her thoughts by Emma plonking her tea down on her desk. Hiding her irritation as some of the liquid slopped over the side of the cup, splashing onto her notebook, she smiled her thanks and switched on her computer. The ping of the incoming mail reminded her of how busy the service was. The constant influx of referrals meant they were always on the go.

She enjoyed her work, she knew what some of these women had been through at the hands of violent partners, and she took great pleasure in the role she saw herself playing in helping them turning their lives around.

As the manager, Rebecca didn't do a lot of one-to-one client work, but she'd sat through enough of the conversations to know about the women who used the project. It's my pleasure to get involved in their lives, she thought wryly as she considered the very real benefits her position had brought her. She also enjoyed reminding herself of just how far she had come in her life.

While Phoenix was open to both men and women, the majority of the clients who came along to the project were women. There was still a huge stigma for men, especially men in the west of Scotland, to admit to having been a victim of abuse. This angered Rebecca, but not for the reasons her colleagues might have thought—Rebecca loathed weakness, and especially weak men. She viewed any man who was unable to stand up and talk about their experiences as weak, and if she were brutally honest, she thought that men who let themselves be abused were even weaker. Of course, she could never say that out loud in front of her colleagues. Besides, they weren't really her views, they were Samantha's… Weren't they?

Turning her attention back to the present, she decided to let Samantha out to play, and brighten up her morning a little.

'Emma, did you not complete the monthly returns I left you yesterday?' Rebecca called.

She smiled as Emma looked up, panic written across her face.

'What returns?'

'The ones I left on your desk,' she sighed.

She watched the confusion on Emma's face as she shook her head.

'No, no there were no forms when I left last night, I'm sure of it.'

'Oh, Emma, really? You're getting worse, you know? I think you pay more attention to those crime novels you constantly have your nose stuck in than the work we have going on here. You know those returns are due with the funders today.'

Rebecca stood and walked over to Emma's desk; she indicated the mess of papers lying there and looked at Emma. 'How the hell can you find anything here?' Picking up a pile of committee papers she pointed to the returns below. 'These ones,' she snapped. The ones she had slipped onto Emma's desk that morning before her poor colleague had arrived.

Emma's face fell.

'Rebecca, no way. They weren't on my desk. I know they weren't, I'd just this minute put those committee papers down before I made your tea. The returns weren't there, I promise.'

Rebecca saw the cloud of self-doubt cross Emma's face like a shadow. She smiled inside, careful not to let it show on her face.

'Whatever, Emma, just get your act together. Remember you're due your appraisal next month.'

Rebecca turned and walked back to her desk, a smirk plastered across her face, imagining she could hear Emma questioning herself uncertainly.

BEHIND REBECCA'S BACK, Emma bit her lip, barely holding the tears back. It was always the same. She knew those returns hadn't been on her desk. She'd tidied everything yesterday before leaving, and they'd not been there. Emma also knew Rebecca hadn't mentioned any deadline for completion. She might be scatty at times, but she always took note of important tasks like these. She knew how important the returns were, and she would never take unnecessary risks with funding. Her job relied on it too.

She couldn't prove anything, but Emma was sure that Rebecca was behind the sudden appearance of the returns. It wasn't the first time something like this had happened. Not just to Emma. Other colleagues had mentioned important paperwork, client assessments, funding applications going missing; or turning up for meetings only to be told they'd already taken place. Rebecca always seemed to be in the background when things went wrong.

But Emma couldn't prove any of it and, even if she could, nobody would believe her—everyone loved Rebecca. They would put her claims down to jealousy. Emma vowed to take more care of her work and to start keeping things in a locked drawer. She sat down at her desk, glancing over at Rebecca. She couldn't help but notice a look of worry cross her usually serene face.

That wasn't like Rebecca at all. She wondered what had got into her. She was normally in complete control. The bitch deserves to be rattled though, she thought, turning back to her own paperwork, determined not to let Rebecca spoil her day.

MEANWHILE, REBECCA SCROLLED through her emails, trying to focus on work to rid her mind of her paranoia. She couldn't take her mind off the silent calls and the feeling she'd had of being watched recently. It was really rattling her. She tried to tell herself she was being ridiculous, but she couldn't shake off this unease.

She was busy sorting emails into order of priority when a name she recognised popped up. James Aitken? She scrolled through her memory bank trying to shake the name free. James... Jim... Surely not. Not him, not here. Her heart skipped a beat and the colour drained from her face as the memories came flooding back.

If this was the same Jim Aitken, then things were not going to be alright. Things could go very wrong. He could put a real spanner in the works if he recognised her and started blabbing about her past. Rebecca wasn't prepared to let things go wrong. Not now, just as her plan to destroy Lucas was coming to a head.

Using her breathing techniques to remain calm, she opened the email and read it closely. He wanted to meet her. Her heart dropped like a stone. The fears came rushing back, threatening to expose her weakness, she couldn't let this happen. She couldn't let anybody see her like this.

They're coming to get you Rebecca. They are going to find you out. Let me sort it for you. LET ME!

'Please just leave me alone,' she muttered.

'Deep breaths,' she told herself. 'You've got this, you can do it.'

Her fists clenched underneath her desk and she sucked in at the air greedily, all the time glancing around the office to make sure nobody seen her mask slip.

18

OH REBECCA, DID you really think I'd leave you alone? I shouldn't really say this, but I've had so much fun playing with you.

Do you feel my eyes on you? Can you feel my breath whisper across your skin? Can you feel me brush by you?

Every day you crumble just a little bit more, and here I am standing in the shadows, watching you.

I'm the only one who knows who you really are, who can see beneath the lies you try so hard to hide behind. But there is no hiding from me, Rebecca. You're wasting your time trying.

That noise behind you, the hairs on your neck standing up, only there's nobody there when you turn around... Is there?

Is this real, Rebecca? Is it all in your mind? Are you going mad again? You will be by the time I'm finished with you, you little bitch. Just you wait and see.

19

ANOTHER DAY, ANOTHER crisis. Jim Aitken made his way to his office in Glasgow's East End. He wondered what fresh hell awaited him today. He'd only recently moved back to work in Glasgow and was finding things were a bit more stressful than his last post in Killearn, a small village in Stirlingshire, where the most controversial cases he had worked on were older people being forced to sell their homes to pay for a move into care.

Due to staff shortages and sickness levels, he was also working most weekends, covering duty, and it was beginning to take its toll. His hands shook as he swiped his pass to gain entry into the building. Once inside, he cupped his hands over his mouth and nose and breathed deeply. He grimaced; he could still smell the stale booze on his breath. He reached into his pocket for a mint. He was going to have to knock the drink on the head, but he needed something to get through each day and recently things had started to get worse.

He had been in social work most of his life and had made his way through almost every department from Children and Families to Older People. He'd now found himself in the world of Criminal Justice. He was getting tired of it all, tired of the misery of other people's lives, tired of all the red tape and paperwork he and his colleagues found themselves mired in these days. Jim just craved a quiet life—a normal life.

More often than not, he'd find his mind wandering back to his past, but those memories came with a cost. Not one he was sure he could afford to pay.

'I'm weary,' he thought, slumping down at his desk. It was covered in a mountain of case files he could never hope to control.

He hadn't had an easy life. Growing up on a tough housing scheme in the North of Glasgow, he'd witnessed many of his old pals fall victim to drugs and crime, or end up married with four kids before the age of twenty-five. Jim had been determined that this life wasn't for him and he'd worked hard to get his qualifications and get a job with the council. But he'd also played hard too.

He'd been a good-looking lad and hadn't been short of female admirers. He was the first to admit that he'd sometimes taken advantage of the attention and hadn't always been the perfect gentleman when it came to love. There had been one girl, well, woman really, he got embroiled with. The woman who had changed his life.

Ten years older than Jim, she had turned his head until she had started getting a bit too heavy with him. She had been looking for something Jim wasn't ready to give: commitment. And so he had run for the hills. He'd heard through the grapevine he had broken her heart, but the old Jim hadn't cared. More recently, as he grew older, his regrets had grown heavier.

Life had paid him back though; karma was most certainly a bitch. In his mid-thirties, he'd met and fell in love with a woman who changed his ways forever. He had thought his life was complete. When he came home from work one day and found her in bed with the guy who lived next door, his world had been destroyed. Devastated at his loss and his pride in tatters, he'd turned to drink.

His life had spiralled out of control and if it hadn't been for his manager at the time, he'd probably have ended up dead. Getting him the support he had so badly needed, his manager had also arranged for him to be transferred out to the tranquillity of Killearn. The move had probably saved his life. That and his dog Cooper, a golden Labrador, who had given Jim a new purpose in life.

As he grew older, he'd hankered to return to his roots. Using the money he had saved over the years, he'd bought himself a smallholding on the outskirts of Bishopbriggs, where he now lived with his dog. Just the two of them. He was lonely, but he had resigned himself to this way of life.

Things had been going well for him, he'd started to make plans for retirement and had been looking forward to escaping the rat race. Until she had turned up. She had turned his world on its head and that was when he had started to turn to the drink again.

His quiet was shattered when his colleague, Nicole Holten, bounced into the room. The waft of her patchouli oil mixed with a faint whiff of tobacco snapped him back into reality.

'Hey Jim. Morning! How are ya doing?'

That soft Canadian twang always sounded out of sorts here in the heart of the East End, he thought, but she never failed to make him smile, even if her timekeeping and reliability stressed him out.

She had joined the team just six months before him and the two of them had gravitated towards each other as they struggled to find any common ground with the rest of their colleagues.

'A bunch of fucking tree huggers,' Nicole had laughed when they had gone out for lunch on his first day on the job. Jim had smiled, glad to find a kindred spirit.

'Hi Nicole. Yeah, am okay, just don't know where to start with this lot.' He waved his hand at the manila folders scattered across his desk.

'Yeah, I hear ya! And I say let's start with a coffee, and it's your shout, buddy.'

Jim laughed. 'Instant or am I buying?' He already knew the answer.

'Buying for sure. Don't you dare be giving me that instant muck they keep in here.'

NICOLE WATCHED AS Jim left the office. She suspected he needed the coffee more than she did, given the tremor in his hands and the smell of stale booze coming from him this morning.

She waited a few minutes to make sure he hadn't forgotten anything. Satisfied he had left the building, she walked over to his desk and flicked through the paperwork. She sighed, his desk was a disaster—the paperwork was in such a mess, she didn't know how he could function in this chaos. Still, at least he would never know she had been snooping.

She grinned when she spotted the file she had been looking for. Snatching it up, she noted the liberation date of the prisoner. Perfect. He had been let out last week, which would make things so much easier for her.

Back at her own desk, she pulled out her personal mobile and tapped in a message, pressed send and shoved it back in her bag. She looked round the office she shared with Jim, it was grim. The paint was peeling off the walls and it was always too hot or too cold. No budget to replace the windows or the heating, they had been told. Not her problem, she thought. She wasn't going to be here forever; she'd be gone soon and for good. She was counting down the days.

Life hadn't turned out quite how she had planned—she had ended up living in London where she had studied psychology, and then gone on to complete her social work training before finally taking up a post as a Probation Officer in Carlisle.

When Probation had been privatised, she'd had thrown in the towel and taken the decision to move up to Scotland. She'd told Jim she always had a soft spot in her heart for Scotland— her dad had originally been from Scotland and its landscape reminded her of Canada where she had grown up. She had clammed up when he probed a little more into her background, making it quite clear she didn't want to talk about her past.

She quickly realised Jim was one of those men who loved to pry into other people's live. He was clearly lonely, living on his own with just his dog for company and was forever asking questions which she batted away with ease.

Life in Criminal Justice had been good for her, she had taken to it like a duck to water, relishing the freedom she had in terms of her daily work with clients, compared to the system back in Carlisle, where everything had become target driven.

Fairly outgoing in nature, Nicole had quickly established a rapport with her clients. She knew some of them had initially thought they would be in for an easy ride with the blonde, blue-eyed Canadian, but she had quickly disabused them of that notion. She was firm but she was fair. Those who played by her rules got on just fine, those who didn't... Well she made sure they ended back up inside, one way or another.

Drumming her fingers on her desk, she looked at the clock. Jim was taking ages with those coffees. Had it been after eleven, she would have not been surprised if he had stopped by the pub on the way to get them, but it was only ten and too early for the pubs to be open. He was probably gabbing to someone.

For all his faults, she liked the man. He could talk a bit much and he loved to stick his nose into everyone's business, but she had worked with worse folk than him. Besides he had a Labrador. He'd invited her round for dinner one night and she had fallen in love with Cooper. He'd reminded her of her own dog, Buster, a chocolate lab, who had passed away just before she moved back to Scotland.

The aroma of the freshly brewed coffee brought a smile to her face as Jim returned, but not as big a smile as the text she received just as he walked through the door.

20

CLOSING THE OFFICE door behind him, Lucas leaned against it, grateful for the support. His body was shaking and his head was in a spin. Rebecca's attack on him the night before had left him tired and bruised, and not just physically. He was emotionally drained. It was a relief to get out of the house.

He was thankful that, for today at least, he would be on his own. The rest of his team were out on a staff development day. He'd managed to wangle his way out of it. He hated team days with a passion, all that oversharing and false bonding made him cringe. The idea of sharing his deepest thoughts and experiences with his colleagues made him sick to the stomach.

In his line of work, reflective practice was actively encouraged, with an unwritten rule that staff would be open about their own life and willing to share their experiences in order to reflect, grow, and develop. He gave a short laugh. He had absolutely no desire to share his experiences or his thoughts with anyone else, let alone his colleagues. What happened in his own life and his own mind was his and his alone to keep. If he were to share what really went on, he could just imagine the revulsion his colleagues would show. Or would it be pity? Or both? He wasn't sure, but he certainly wasn't willing to take the chance.

Being married to Rebecca was killing him. Rubbing his hand across the stubble on his chin—he'd not been able to face looking at his reflection in the mirror to shave this morning—

he thought about his wife. He couldn't fathom her out at all. Most of the time it was like being married to two different women, one loving and one lethal. His whole life was spent walking on eggshells, fearful of triggering her temper.

He took a deep breath, determined to make the most of his time in the office on his own. There was nobody here to watch him, to spy on him. Here, he at least had some semblance of control, unlike at home where he had none at all.

He put a lot of effort in at work to stay on top of things, always striving to maintain the image he wanted others to have of him. He didn't want anyone to see the real Lucas, to know what went on in his private life and who he was. The thought of losing everything he had achieved filled him with terror and now it seemed like his nightmare was about to come true.

With a cursory glance around the office—double checking that he really was alone—he decided to leave the phone on answerphone mode. He didn't want to be disturbed. He slid open his desk drawer and pulled out the letter. It had arrived at the house the day before. Thankfully, it had been delivered when Rebecca was out or she would have demanded he open it in front of her—she didn't believe in privacy. Well, not for him.

Hands shaking, he shook the letter out of the envelope. It fell to the table, the words staring accusingly at him. He could feel Rebecca peer over his shoulder, imagining her face if she knew the secret he was hiding. He would never be free of his past and he would never be free of his wife. She had made that perfectly clear. Lucas was trapped, every which way he looked, there was no escape.

When he had first met Rebecca, he was only looking for a quick fling, nothing serious and certainly not marriage. Although deep down he craved the normality of a family, his past experiences had shaped the man he had become. He didn't know if he could trust himself. At forty-two, he was ten years her senior, but Rebecca had cast a spell on him. She wasn't like other girls he had been with. She was confident and didn't seek approval from anyone. She made him feel alive, she made him believe he was in control, that he was calling the shots. She would go out of her way to please him. She sucked him in and before he knew it he was standing at the alter saying: 'I Do.'

He knew their domestic situation was toxic. She had quickly turned from the kind and considerate woman he had married, to a bitch who had him by the balls and was not prepared to let go. But Lucas was torn between the two versions of his wife— the calculating manipulator, and the Rebecca he'd catch staring into space, pain etched across her face as her body shook; the Rebecca who would wake in the middle of the night, terrified, whispering of demons and shadows.

Everyone who knew Rebecca sang her praises. God, even the neighbours thought she was a bloody saint. She was always in and out of Mary Pickens' house next door, taking her home baking and soup; having cosy little chats with her. He suspected Rebecca was painting Mary a very different picture of their home life to the one he experienced. He knew exactly how twisted and vicious his wife could be.

Some nights, for fun, she'd turn the television off and start throwing things around, screaming at Lucas to stop; begging him to leave her alone, while he sat open mouthed at the performance she was able to put on. She was clever, though; she wouldn't keep it up for too long, knowing just when to stop before someone called the police. It was after those nights she'd nip next door to see Mary.

He'd leave the house and catch Mary peeking from behind her net curtains, eyebrows raised and lips pursed. He'd see the other neighbours cast disapproving looks his way, their pointed whispers after another one of Rebecca's shows.

He wished he could tell them all, but how could he? He didn't have the guts to say it aloud. He didn't have the courage to deal with the consequences of speaking out; Rebecca's wrath and the disdain of others who would think him weak to be abused by a woman. Just like before, with his father. He never had the guts to say no then, or maybe he didn't want to say no... Maybe he deserved this?

He knew he should leave her, but something stopped him. Pride? Stubbornness? Fear? That sense of self-doubt she managed to instil in him that left him feeling as though he were going mad at times. He wasn't quite sure. But one thing he knew was that, the way things were going, it could only end in destruction. The only question was: who would be destroyed first?

He opened the drawer, pushing the letter to the back and pulling out his mobile. The mobile that Rebecca didn't know about. Quickly, he tapped out a message.

'I need to see you soon. Text me pls.'

While waiting for a reply to his text, Lucas thoughts were drawn back to the letter in the drawer. His hands trembled as he pulled it out. He stared at that one simple sentence typed out in the middle of the page. A sentence that could rip his life apart at the seams.

I know who you are and what you are. Your time is coming.

It had been hand delivered, just like the others—no postmark to give him a clue where it might have come from.

How the hell could anyone know his secret? He had buried those memories deep inside and reinvented himself a long time ago. Nobody knew his background, and nobody knew the man he was now. The fear rested in his chest, waiting to explode and swallow him whole. His fist slammed down hard on the desk. This wasn't how things were meant to be.

Until his father had ruined everything, Lucas had been a quiet and unremarkable child. At school, he had been the class swot, never speaking up and no trouble at all. The kind of boy teachers struggled to remember at parents' evening.

He could remember clearly his mother's anger when she had been called to see the headmaster. Lucas had got into a fight with one of the school troublemakers. Lucas had instigated the fight, busting the older boy's nose and knocking him almost unconscious. That incident had earned him a week's suspension from school. But that hadn't been as painful as his mother's reaction. As soon as they had returned home, she had grabbed him by the throat and pinned him to the wall, warning him to keep his mouth shut about what went on at home.

It was at that exact moment Lucas knew his mother had always known what was happening. Had always known what his father was. But all she cared about was Lucas drawing attention to himself and thereby risking attention being drawn to what really went on behind closed doors. He'd returned to school and retreated back into his shell. But Lucas had changed that day, and the damage was done.

A bead of sweat ran down the side of his face; he wiped it away, blinking back real tears at the same time. If Rebecca discovered his past, then it would all be over. It would be the end of them, of him. But perhaps that would be for best, he thought—they couldn't keep on like this. It felt like one of them had pushed a self-destruct button and the explosion was going to happen no matter what.

He was ashamed; ashamed of what they'd become, ashamed of what she'd reduced him to. Ashamed of the man he was. Ashamed of the past he couldn't escape from. He couldn't help himself and there was nobody he could confide in. How could he tell anyone who he had been, or who he was now?

His mates all saw him as a man's man, the kind of guy who loved football and a boy's night out. None of that had changed since he'd met Rebecca. She had made sure of that. At first, he'd been delighted to have met a woman who didn't try to pin him down, one who encouraged him to keep up his outside interests and friends.

'We're not joined at the hip,' she used to tell him, laughing. It was only when it was too late that he'd realised this was just part of her game, part of her manipulation. Who would believe him if he had told them what really went on when he returned home from a night out?

So, to everyone else, Lucas was just the same as he always was. One of the lads, a good laugh and a decent guy who did the best he could for those he worked with. But nobody saw the price he paid at the end of the day; how his wife made him pay.

Maybe if his lifestyle had changed then others would have recognised the signs. They might have noticed a change in his personality, his reluctance to join in like he used to, his excuses to leave and go home early. But she wasn't stupid, she knew exactly what she was doing.

She was like his mother in so many ways, always careful to ensure that appearances were kept up with those who already knew him. To make sure that they didn't suspect. To make sure that she was seen as the 'understanding wife'. She knew exactly what she was doing. And so he'd returned to the only solace he had ever known. Lucas Findlay really was his father's son and now he felt like time was running out.

Slumping forward, he buried himself away in the dark empty office, trying to escape his memories… A thousand needles were drumming inside his head, not sure of where, or who, he could turn to. It felt impossible, and the arrival of this letter might just be the needle with the potential to deliver the final blow.

His phone pinged, signalling an incoming text.

'Free today at 3. Usual place?' He smiled.

The text was quickly followed by another, a different number this time. 'You better have those files ready. Your shipment is due soon. Don't be late.'

21

OH LUCAS. SO you got my little note, did you? Just as well wifey didn't see it, eh? We all know what would have happened then.

Wifey doesn't like Lucas having secrets, does she?

Well guess what, Lucas? I know all your secrets. Yes, that's right, all of them, every last dirty little one of them. You can try all you want to convince yourself your daddy made you do it. Poor, poor Lucas, the bad man made you do it. Only you know that's not quite true.

You know the truth, Lucas.

I know the whole truth, and maybe it's time everyone else did too.

Tick tock, Lucas. Your time is running out. I'm watching you.

22

REBECCA FELT HER pulse quicken as goosebumps prickled her skin. The email from Jim Aitken had reawakened old memories. She felt the scars at the top of her thighs tingle, and she tried to ignore the urge to take herself away somewhere quiet and open them up again.

Although she couldn't be sure it was the same Jim Aitken, her gut was telling her it was him. She'd half expected their paths to cross at some point. She didn't think he'd have left the Glasgow area and, professionally, they had so much in common it had almost been inevitable. Rebecca wondered if perhaps, deep inside, she had always hoped this day would come.

After the incident at the Nikolics, after he' whispered goodbye in the hospital, she hadn't seen Jim again. He'd been replaced by a new social worker, and nobody had told her where or why he had gone. She'd spent years feeling angry at him for abandoning her, just like everyone else had. *Nobody loves you, Rebecca. They all abandoned you. But not us. We never left you.*

She clenched her fists under her desk willing the chatter to clear. She had spent so long creating this new life for herself, planning her revenge, she couldn't risk Jim Aitken waltzing in and exposing her. Not now.

She noticed he had sent the email two days ago. Well another day waiting for her reply wasn't going to kill him, was it?

She closed down her emails, not in the right frame of mind to deal with them right now. She found her thoughts drifting back to when she'd met up with Lucas. He'd be shocked if he were to realise she had manipulated their meeting. She smirked as she revelled in her unerring ability to get exactly what she wanted.

As soon as she'd seen his profile picture on the online dating site, she'd known he was the one. She wasn't going to let him go. What Rebecca wanted, Rebecca took. And she wanted him. But not for the reasons he'd thought.

She was too clever for him. Rebecca had never put her real profile on the dating site. For her, it was simply a means to an end. When Lucas had responded to her, she made use of the 'connect with me' tool to delve further into his background. To her delight, she found they had lots in common. They both worked in the voluntary sector in the same area. In fact, it was a miracle that she hadn't bumped into him before—the sector was so small, it could be almost incestuous at times. Once she'd sourced all the information she needed, she had closed down her account and set about using the information he had so freely provided to find him in real life.

She had learned he was due to attend a local awards ceremony and, while she usually avoided these events like the plague, she went out her way to attend this one. Luckily, Phoenix was also up for an award for their National Lottery funded Creative Writing Project and Rebecca had found it easy enough to wangle a ticket for her and Emma. It was almost all too easy, really.

On the night of the ceremony, she'd pulled out all the stops, hair and nails done, an emerald green, figure-hugging dress that meant she stood out from the Little Black Dress brigade. Even Emma had been impressed, her jaw dropping in disbelief as she opened the door to her.

'Bloody hell, Rebecca,' she'd gasped. 'You look stunning.'

Rebecca had blushed a little, wondering if she'd gone a bit over the top. Emma had reassured her, 'Absolutely not,' she'd said. 'You look amazing, see what a little effort can bring! Now let's go nail this.'

Emma's words had grated on her. The constant need to be valued only for your appearance was not something Rebecca bought into. She hated how people lived their lives for all to see on social media, pretending everything was perfect. But Rebecca knew the truth and she knew exactly what lay behind the filters they applied—she knew they would be horrified if they could see the reality of her life. But she had pushed those thoughts aside and sat back and let herself join Emma's world for the night.

As they'd walked through the doors of the ballroom, Rebecca had felt all eyes upon her. She knew she'd been right to choose that dress; the green had stood out in among a sea of glittery black. She'd known Lucas was bound to notice her. But first, she had to get through the deadly, dull networking element of the night, which she detested. That was much more Emma's comfort zone, really.

Still, what had to be done and all that, she'd thought as she'd plastered a smile across her face, ignoring the voices in her head telling her she was ugly and dirty, and had made her way across the floor to mingle with the other guests.

An hour later, heaving a sigh of relief, she'd made her way out of the crowds and moved to the side of the hall to find her target. She'd spotted him at the bar trying to catch the server's eye. She had made her way over and managed to squeeze into the empty space beside him. It had all been too easy. Lucas had turned his head and looked at her while she stared straight ahead being careful not to look at him.

The server must have taken pity on him because the next thing she'd known he had a pint in his hand and his mouth was forming some words clearly meant for her. Rebecca indicated that she hadn't heard him, forcing him to move his mouth a little closer to her ear.

'Can I get you a drink?' he'd shouted. Rebecca had smiled and shook her head, lifting her half full glass to him.

'I'm fine,' she'd replied. 'I'm only looking for some water, I've got a banging sore head.'

Lucas had smiled sympathetically and nodded his understanding. 'Yep, not my cup of tea either.' He said, waving his arm at the crowds in front of them.

She had readily agreed with him and moved a little closer. He indicated towards the foyer where there were a couple of comfy seats, the unspoken question obvious. She'd moved over to the seats, and Lucas had followed her, like she'd known he would. He hadn't even noticed she hadn't waited for her water. If he'd been a little more observant, he might have looked into her eyes and seen the dark depths of hell reflected there.

The noise of clients coming into the centre pulled her out her daydreams. She stretched her arms and yawned. She was dog-tired, sleep had evaded her recently and, when she did sleep, she'd wake up to her bed sheets tied in knots, evidence of the nightmares haunting her. *They are going to find you out, Rebecca*, the voice breathed into her ear. Clasping her hands over her ears Rebecca willed it to leave.

She opened up her emails again, clicking on the one from Jim Aitken. He wanted to meet up with her to discuss a new project for male perpetrators of abuse he was setting up. He didn't mention knowing her. Perhaps it wasn't him, she thought. But she wouldn't be agreeing to any meeting until she had done some digging of her own.

She marked the email as unread and left it in her inbox to deal with later, when she'd had time to formulate a plan. She gave herself a shake and pulled down the mask she needed to face the public.

She didn't notice Emma staring at her from the doorway, a strange smile on her face.

It was almost lunchtime and the centre was beginning to busy up. The corridors were buzzing with the sound of voices as a wave of clients made their way in out of the cold biting wind. Today, the timetable had self-defence and mindfulness classes, always popular sessions with the clients.

Rebecca watched as Emma went out to speak to some of the women. She liked to watch Emma—her easy nature intrigued her, and she envied the way others seemed to gravitate towards her. She wished she had the same self-assured nature, she wished she wasn't plagued by self-doubt and the constant chatter of Samantha's voice inside her head.

It took Rebecca every ounce of her energy to engage with people. She was suspicious of their motivations and constantly expected the worst from them. Samantha didn't help matters— she fed her paranoia, leaving her confused and afraid. The urge to cut herself was becoming stronger. Taking ten deep breaths and clenching her fists, she tried to focus on the women in the centre. Rebecca breathed in one more time before making her way out into the corridor.

As the manager, Rebecca didn't have to spend much one-to-one time with the clients who used the project, but she always made sure she went out of her way to touch base with them. Despite everything, her work was important to her—she really did care about these women. She wanted them to feel the project was somewhere safe, somewhere they belonged. *But you also want to keep an ear to the ground, Rebecca, don't you? You never know which one of them might know the truth about you… About us.*

'Shut up,' she snapped. 'I'm not a bad person. I really do care about these women and what goes on in this centre.' She repeated this to herself, trying to drown out Samantha's voice telling her otherwise.

Her eyes darted around, terrified someone might have caught her talking to herself, but everyone was too busy to notice her. Regaining her composure, she walked out into the busy foyer and was immediately greeted by Sarah Hardy and Kate Noble. The two women were as thick as thieves; they'd been coming along to Phoenix for as long as she could remember. She'd watched them turn their lives around from hopeless drug addicts who would do anything for their next fix to two strong women who had fought their own demons to become an integral part of their community.

She'd heard from the support staff that Sarah and Kate had been doing some great work with kids in the local schools to try to prevent them making the same mistakes they had. There had been glowing reports from teaching staff. The kids were both fascinated and inspired by the women. They had very few positive role models in their lives and seeing two young women coming from similar backgrounds as theirs make something of their life made much more impact than someone in a suit preaching about 'Just saying no to drugs'.

She looked at Sarah and Kate, thinking how different their lives would have been if it wasn't for her. They'd been over the moon when their creative writing project had won an award and it had continued to grow from strength to strength. If it hadn't been for me, those two would still have been in the bloody gutter trying to claw their way out, she thought bitterly. They should be grateful to me for the chances I've given them. She made sure that her true thoughts didn't show. *Not such a goody two shoes, are you, Rebecca? You use these women to make yourself feel better, to make yourself look good. I know what you really are though... Don't I, Rebecca?*

Rebecca dug her nails into her palms to rid her head of Samantha's mocking tone.

'Awrite, Rebecca?' said Sarah in that familiar nasal twang distinct to the schemes of Glasgow. It grated on Rebecca's ears, she'd taken years to cultivate a new accent, shedding the remnants of her own past with ease.

'Did ye hear about Kate here?'

Kate stood at her side with a huge grin plastered across her face. It was obvious she'd received some good news for a change.

'She's only got unsupervised access to the weans now.'

Kate had had a tough time of things—as well as dealing with her own addiction, she'd also been in a relationship with a man, Martin McCrae, who had used her as a human punch bag and wasn't shy of showing his fists in front of Kate's two children. She'd been addicted to him as much as she had been to the drugs and had found it impossible to leave him. Social workers had been left with no choice but to remove her kids from her care. Thankfully, her mum had been around, and the kids had gone to her rather than to the children's unit. A lucky escape for them, Rebecca had thought.

'Kate, that's brilliant news! You must be over the moon! See, all that hard work has paid off. You should be proud of yourself.' She forced her mouth into a smile as she said it.

Kate blushed and looked down at her feet. 'Aw, Rebecca, ah know. Ahm fair chuffed, so I am. I want to prove to ma weans that I mean it this time. No going back to that shit, I've got my head clear of that stuff now, and of him.'

Kate had done well getting rid of Martin, in Rebecca's opinion. He had been a right piece of work. With the support of Phoenix and her friends, she'd finally plucked up the courage to report his abuse to the police. Not an easy thing for a woman from the East End of Glasgow to do. In Kate and Sarah's world, the police were often viewed as the enemy, you didn't 'grass' no matter what was going on. But Kate had stood up to Martin and now the bastard was serving three years in prison, or the 'Bar L' as it was fondly referred to in Glasgow.

Rebecca smiled at the memory of him being sent down and his impotent rage at the part she had played in convincing Kate to report him. She was well aware that three years meant he'd more than likely be out soon, if not already. She also knew Kate would be vulnerable to his advances when he got out. Like most abusers, Martin would be likely to try every trick in the book to wheedle his way back into her life when he was released. Not because he loved her or had changed his ways, but because he recognised her as vulnerable, as someone he could coerce and control.

Men like Martin rarely changed, not even a spell in prison changed their behaviour. They usually just found new ways to abuse and to beat the law. They would all need to keep an extra eye out for Kate over the next while. She might be buzzing with confidence now, but Rebecca knew all too well what might happen if Martin came back on the scene.

Shaking her head, she smiled at Kate. 'You've done great, Kate, I'm so proud of you and your kids will be too.'

'Aye, ma maw is over the moon, Rebecca, and you know that if it wasn't for you and the rest of the staff here—' she swept out her arms '—I'd likely have been six feet under by now, dead from an overdose or a kickin' from that bastard.'

Rebecca looked at Kate and said seriously, 'Kate, you know you're the biggest factor in changing your life. Not me, not here, not your friends. Sure, we all chipped in a bit, but it was you who made the decision to change things and you should be proud of what you've achieved.'

She watched as the other woman's face flushed and she grinned widely. *Silly bitch believes you actually care, Rebecca.*

'Aye, okay, ah suppose. Anyway, all this bletherin' isn't going to get the room set up, is it?'

Rebecca smiled; Kate hated any form of praise. Like most of the women who came to the centre, she didn't know how to deal with it all. Despite how far she'd come, her confidence had taken such a battering she couldn't quite believe she was capable of doing anything positive for herself. She watched as Kate turned to Sarah, linking her arm through hers. *You'll never have a friendship like that in your life,* whispered the bitter voice in her ear.

'Right, come on, you. Our classroom awaits.' The two women made their way into the room to set up for the next group session, their heads close together laughing and chiding each other as they went. Rebecca watched them, a sour look masking her face.

You're pathetic, Rebecca. You know that, don't you? Getting all sentimental about your work. You need to focus. Maybe it's time for me to step back in. But look how that ended up the last time. Remember Mummy, Rebecca. Do you? A small voice hissed inside her head. She shook her head to get rid of it and painted her smile back on.

She made her way into the staff toilet and locked herself in one of the cubicles. Reaching into her bra, she pulled out a safety pin before slowly pulling her trousers down.

23

LUCAS RUBBED THE grit from his eyes, yawning widely. He needed to sleep. He couldn't sleep. His head was constantly racing. He rubbed the bristle on his chin, feeling his fingers tremble. He was a mess, physically and mentally.

He had managed to slip out and meet her yesterday. 'Her', he laughed. Christ, he was terrified even to think her name—afraid Rebecca was able to read his thoughts. If she knew what he was doing, she would probably kill him. And if she were to find out about his past, his life would be over. But somebody knew. Someone had sent him that letter—the letter that sat accusingly in his drawer, along with all the others, serving as a grim reminder of what he had done, of who he really was. It wasn't just the letter though. It was those files. He had to get them sent.

He felt sick.

He stumbled into the bathroom, the vomit rising in his throat. He just made it to the toilet as a stream of bile spewed up and hit the pan. Shaking, he sat until the tremors subsided a little. He stood up and, holding onto the basin, he stared at his reflection, not recognising the man staring back.

Splashing his face with cold water, he shivered as the panic drove deeper within him. He had to calm the fuck down—he couldn't let anyone see him like this. Thankful that nobody was around, he staggered back to his desk.

He unlocked the bottom drawer and pulled out a laptop. Firing it up, he swallowed down the bile in his throat. The desktop was bare apart from one folder. Unnamed. It didn't need a name. He knew exactly what it contained. His collection, and if he didn't send it over, there was someone else waiting in the wings to destroy him.

A knot of anxiety tightened inside his stomach as he thought about the man he was; he had tried his best, but he was weak. His fist punched the desk, knocking over his paperwork as he raged inside. Who the hell was he to offer support to the men who came to the service when he couldn't even support himself? He was as much of a victim as they were. No wonder Rebecca used him as an emotional and physical punch bag—it was all he deserved.

'I am a victim!' he yelled into the empty space.

The phone rang, startling him out of his self-pity. Picking it up, he tried to keep the tremor from his voice as he answered. 'Good morning, Space to Grow. Lucas speaking, how can I help?'

Answering the phone in here could be like a minefield, you never knew what was coming. It could be a referral, or it could be someone calling you to tell you they were thinking of ending it all. Sometimes there was nobody there at all, just that heavy silence of someone too afraid to speak. This morning though, it was a voice he didn't recognise.

'Morning, it's Jim Aitken here, the new Team Leader over at Criminal Justice. I'm looking to speak to someone about making a referral?'

'Morning, Jim, I can take that for you. I don't think we've spoken before, have we?' He struggled to keep the tremor from his voice.

'No, I'm pretty new to this department, and I'm just finding my feet, getting to know what's out there. Actually, it would probably be good if we could meet up at some point? You could give me a heads up on what you guys do over there and what's going on locally? Social Work isn't what it used to be, y'know. You move into a new area and just get thrown in at the deep end. Not like the old days where you felt part of the community, you knew what was going on and what was out there for people. Nowadays it's just paperwork and controlling budgets…Ha, listen to me prattling on here. So, that referral…'

Glad of the man's chatter as an escape from his thoughts, Lucas's breathing slowly returned to normal.

'That would be great, Jim, it's usually my manager, Anne Cater, who does all the networking stuff, but she's away sunning herself on a Greek island at the moment. So, if you're happy to chat with me about what we do, we could catch-up sometime?'

'Anne Cater, now there's a blast from the past! I remember her when she worked over in the Southside. A feisty wee thing she was then. She was one of the good ones, that project she worked in was a hellhole and she done good to get herself out. Anyway, enough of my wandering down memory lane, son! Aye, this week works for me. So, my referral, is it okay to do over the phone, or do I have another bloody form to fill in?' He laughed.

'No, no form filling, well, not for you, anyway. If you just give me the details, then I can get the referral on the system. We prioritise them in terms of court referrals and the usual stuff. So, what have you got for me?'

'OK, so this one's not long released from prison and I'm his supervising social worker. It was meant to be my colleague, Nicole Holten, but she's a bit snowed under at the moment.'

Lucas gave a sharp intake of breath, hoping the man on the other end hadn't noticed. But he had no need to worry, Jim was still prattling on.

'He's been in and out of the system since he was about eleven, the usual stuff—low level theft, progressed to housebreaking, assault, domestics, add in a few addictions and twelve years later, here's where we're at. I feel sorry for him, truth be told. His mother had a hell of a time with his waster of a father who was in and out of the Bar L for beating her up. She took him back every time, though. It's no wonder this one's ended up where he has.'

Lucas listened without really hearing what the man on the other end of the phone was saying. His heart was pounding. He stopped himself pressing Jim for more information on Nicole's whereabouts and tried to concentrate on the details he required.

'So, I'll just need to take some basic details, Jim,' he said.

'Aye, his name is Martin McCrae, he lives with his ma at 22 Westmark Street, you know, at the bookies just next to Parkhead Cross, son?'

Lucas quickly cut Jim's ramblings short, 'I'm just about to head out, if you want to just give me the basic details?' He hoped the man couldn't hear the irritation in his voice, but he wanted to end this call now.

'Aye, sorry, son, I can be a bit of a bletherer at times.' Jim laughed. 'Anyway, his date of birth is the first of September 1994. He'd been staying with a lassie called Kate and her weans, but things got a bit pressured with his addictions and things just kind of boiled over, ending up in a couple of domestics. But he's a decent lad, it's a shame really, he...'

'Aye,' said Lucas, cutting him off again. He knew all too well what Jim was referring to. He'd heard Rebecca talking about this case. This Martin had broken Kate down until she was hooked on heroin and had lost her kids. This guy was a bad bastard, a really bad bastard, not the type you'd want to mess with.

'OK.' Sighed Lucas. 'So, what is it you're looking for us to do with him?'

'I heard you ran the Re-Integrate programme?'

'Aye, we do, there's a new intake starting next week. I'll book him in with one of the teams if you want to bring him down?'

The Re-Integrate programme was designed for repeat offenders, offering them support to address the issues which led to their offending, allowing them to be reintegrated back into the community. Lucas knew it was most successful with participants who wanted to make a positive change to their lives, and he didn't think Martin McCrae was that type of guy.

'Aye, that's grand, I'll email you over a time once I've spoken to him. I'm meant to be going out to see him this week with Nicole, if she ever turns up. She's disappeared again…'

Lucas sensed Jim was about to launch into another rant and cut the call short.

Turning his attention back to the laptop, he transferred the files into a zipped folder and emailed them. He snatched up his phone and punched out a message.

'I need to see you, soon.'

BACK IN HIS office, Jim sighed. He was desperate for a drink. He considered nipping over to the Prince Charlie. A quick pint couldn't do any harm, could it? Glancing at his watch, he noticed lunchtime had passed. He could combine it with something to eat.

At first, Jim had used drink to relax, to chill out after a hard day at work. There was nothing wrong with it, he had told himself. Nearly all his colleagues used alcohol to take away the edge of some of the things they dealt with through the course of the day.

But that habit had slowly turned into a crutch and he'd soon found himself dependent on that crutch to get him through each day. A quick drink at night to help him sleep became a couple of pints after work to switch off, to a quick half at lunchtime to get him through the afternoon to the alcohol replacing his morning cuppa to kick start his day.

He bit down the urge for a drink and tried to focus on his work, he had tons of paperwork to get through and he knew he was going to have to make a start on it. Savouring the silence, it suddenly dawned on him that Nicole hadn't come back from wherever the hell she had been. This was becoming something of a habit with her.

He tried to suppress his irritation at Nicole, the need for alcohol becoming greater. Putting his hands out in front of him, he was disgusted at the tremors. He was still struggling after his excesses the night before.

He'd left work early the day before and gone home. After walking Cooper, he'd come back and poured himself a large whisky. One had led to another, and then another. He'd become maudlin after the fourth or fifth one, or it could have been the sixth or seventh, he couldn't remember. He'd passed out on the sofa, waking up at four in the morning with Cooper lying at his feet and saliva stuck to his face. He was pathetic.

He pulled out the faded photograph tucked away out of sight at the back of his wallet, and reached into his pocket for the small black velvet pouch that contained a part of his life that he could never tell anyone about. Holding them tight in his hand, the memories came flooding back.

The older he got, the guiltier he felt. He'd tried his best, or at least that's what he had tried to tell himself all these years. But events from the past were weighing heavily on his mind these days. He wasn't convinced he was being entirely truthful with himself. Had he really done his best? He'd let everyone down, including himself and that feeling of guilt was eating him up. And now he had been given a sign. He had to do something, he had to make amends. His hands shook, he really did need that drink.

24

REBECCA WAS BACK at her desk, the sharp sting of the fresh cuts on her thighs bringing her a release from the pressure she had felt building up. The centre had grown quiet; lunchtime was over and the afternoon sessions were well underway. This was the time that she would usually catch-up on her admin, but she was all over the place today.

Despite the cutting, she still wasn't thinking straight and there was a real danger that if she hung around, people in the office would realise there was something wrong with her. She couldn't risk anyone seeing her mask slip. She had to stay strong. She had to retain control.

Her mind felt as though it were packed tight with cotton wool. The thoughts were bouncing around inside her head as they tried to untangle themselves into some form of sense. It was impossible. She was drowning, her vision growing foggy.

She looked around. Her colleague's mouths were opening and closing but no words were coming out. She felt herself disconnecting. She had to get out of here.

Leaving Emma a hastily scribbled note, she grabbed her bag and quickly left the building to try to bring some focus to her mind.

Working in the middle of the busy East End of Glasgow meant quiet space wasn't always easy to find. In fact, finding any type of space could be impossible. Heading over to the Forge Shopping Centre was out of the question—it was always full of screaming kids with their mothers usually screaming even louder back at them. Walking round the streets wasn't an option either, there was always someone who knew her from work who would stop to catch-up, unburden themselves, or ask her questions. Rebecca couldn't face anyone just now. She couldn't risk them seeing Samantha. She needed to be alone.

She decided to make her way over to Tollcross Park—a haven of peace and tranquillity in this busy but downtrodden community. She left the offices on Helenvale Street and turned right onto Tollcross Road. She kept her eyes to the ground as she passed The Tavern Bar, not wanting any of the regulars there to recognise her. She passed the pharmacy and grimaced as she caught sight of a couple of the women who used to attend the centre, queue up for their methadone prescription.

Shaking her head, the thought that she couldn't save them all came to her. *I saved you, Rebecca. Don't you forget that. It was me. That could be you there, queuing for your fix, if I hadn't saved you.*

Rebecca clenched her fists tight and kept on walking. The smell from the takeaway at the corner across from the entrance to the park made her mouth water. She was starving, but she couldn't go in—she couldn't risk it. She needed to be somewhere quiet until Samantha was gone.

Reaching the park gates, she made her way through the park and over to the bench next to the now derelict Winter Gardens. Closed since the storms years ago, the place was usually deserted. Like most things, the City Council didn't have the funds to restore it to its former glory. At night, it was a haven for drug users and the homeless, but during the day it was an oasis of calm, the perfect place to seek solace. It was quiet, office workers and school kids looking for a sneaky lunchtime fag had long gone. Other than the odd dog walker or mum with her toddlers in tow, Rebecca had the place to herself for a while.

Sitting on the bench, she wrestled with Samantha for space in her head. She knew Samantha was right, she could have been one of those women queuing up for her methadone, or worse. She should be grateful. She could be selling herself down on Glasgow Green for the price of a fix. *See, I did save you, Rebecca. You should be more grateful.*

'But I'm tired of this. Tired of this life. Maybe I should just forget all those stupid ideas of revenge?' Rebecca often conversed with Samantha when she felt safe there was no one around to hear her. It helped her focus. Sometimes.

So, you're just going to let that bastard get away scot free, Rebecca? After everything they did to you? Maybe you did deserve it after all. Maybe you are just the dirty wee girl we all thought you were. Maybe we should have left you, Rebecca.

Rebecca shook her head. 'No, I'm not bad, I'm not dirty.' She sobbed, her voice childish now, her arms wrapped around her body as though to protect herself. 'Please, just leave me alone.'

Samantha's voice faded into the background as Rebecca allowed her mind to drift back in time. Her childhood memories were buried in a fog inside her head. She knew bad things had happened to her, she knew she had been in care and her mother had died, but events leading up to this were hazy.

Her other selves had saved her, they had taken over most of her life, protecting her from what was happening in reality. That's what her therapist had told her, what the psychiatrist and community mental health team had told her. Her disorder had occurred to protect her from the trauma she had lived through.

Rebecca sat up on the bench, tears were forming in her eyes and she didn't know if she had the strength to stop them. It was crazy how one email had the power to send her hurtling over the edge like this.

'Get a grip of yourself,' she whispered. 'You need to stop this. You are going to ruin it all.'

You always ruin everything, Rebecca... Spoil it all for everyone... You're a bad girl. It's all your fault. It's always been your fault.

'Shut up!' She shouted, not caring if there was anyone around to hear her. She placed her hands over her ears to shut out the voice that was threatening to take over.

She forced herself to focus on everything she had achieved since she had left hospital, using the distraction to quieten Samantha's voice inside her head.

Determined to make a new life for herself, Rebecca had taken up the college place that had been found for her when she was discharged from hospital. In the beginning, she had been overwhelmed by the freedom offered to her and had gone out partying every night. But hiding her diagnosis from her peers was difficult, especially when the alcohol left her pretty unstable. So she had buckled down and got stuck into her studies.

She had been surprised at her natural flair for learning, soaking up information like a sponge. For once, her own life experiences had a currency, studying social care meant the theory she read about—social depravation, adverse childhood experiences and trauma—were something she could relate to. The rest of the students were from a different background to her and she had found herself irritated by their ghoulish fascination of the life she had led, not that she ever told them just how real it was to her. Her peers were more interested in becoming the next TV criminologist than actually making a difference to anyone's life.

Rebecca had sailed through her assignments and exams and was awarded a distinction and a place at university to study social work. That had been tough, the placements had triggered memories of her own childhood and she spent much of her student life cutting herself to release the pressure she felt herself under. All through this, Samantha had been very much in the background, never quite leaving her, always reminding her of her goal in life: to exact revenge for what had been done to her.

Her degree taught her one thing: she didn't want to be a social worker. Too much red tape and not enough time with people. She'd watched, on placement, as social work staff bucked under the pressure of their role. And so she had left university and moved into the third sector, where there were more opportunities to spend time with people. To make her feel good about herself.

Although years of therapy had enabled her to learn to live with her past and her condition, she could never quite fully let it go. She had been obsessive about digging into the lives of those who had destroyed her, picking away at it like a scab.

Duncan Campbell's case had been well known, and she had been able to access a mine of information online about the man and his family. But even better was the gossip amongst the clients in the centre. Men like Duncan Campbell always left a long legacy behind.

She had discovered Duncan, despite his fondness for little girls, had been married to a woman and they'd had a child. A front for his activities, so the gossip went. Rebecca had dug around on the Internet, and using her contacts in work, it had been easy to uncover the full story.

Not long after starting work with Phoenix, she had discovered that Duncan had finally received proper justice. An article in the Glasgow gangland version of Hello Magazine, The Dagger, reported that he had been grassed up and jailed.

Duncan Campbell hadn't even lasted two weeks in prison before he had been found face down in the shower with a home-made shank having divested him of the one thing he used to wield his own perverted brand of power.

Rebecca had smiled when she'd read that. But what had really caught her interest was the rest of the report, where it told the woeful tale of the 'loving' partner left behind with Duncan's child. It was Lucas. Lucas had been the child born out of that unholy union. At eighteen, he had been old enough to be pictured and featured in the papers, and it was when she saw him that her plan began to fully form.

While studying, she'd shied away from developing any close relationships with her peers, preferring to remain in the background, observing, learning, plotting. At that time, the memories were still rattling around in her head and were a constant reminder of all that had happened. She had decided very quickly that one way or another she would get revenge.

Although Duncan was dead now, she knew his son was still out there. Free to live his life. It made her sick to think of him going unpunished. So, she had vowed to make him pay, for his own sins and for the sins of his father.

All her spare time was spent planning his downfall. He had grown into a man with a career and the kind of freedom his actions had denied her. It made her sick to the stomach to know he was out there pretending he was something he most definitely wasn't. It would have been too easy for her to blow his cover at work, to lay bare his sordid background. An anonymous tip off or a quiet word in the ear of some of the meatheads he supported.

She knew exactly what they would do if they found out that he was a child molester. But Rebecca didn't want to take the easy way and she didn't want to take the chance of him being let off by some lenient judge if she was to report him to the police, or some liberal social worker defending him for what he had done. No, she was determined to destroy his life the way that he and his father had destroyed hers.

She had vowed to hunt down her prey, trap him in her web and slowly drive him insane before taking him and his career down. He wasn't going to know what hit him.

He really believed he had got away with it all. But she knew where he lived, where he drank, and where he worked. She knew exactly what he was doing and when he was doing it. Rebecca was the hunter and he the target. She made it her mission to find out everything she could about him, which was easy when she had access to as much gossip as she did at the centre.

Her client's partners were often clients of his and these women loved nothing more than a good gossip. Rebecca wasn't afraid to take advantage of her position to dig as deep as she could. The spineless little pervert didn't even have a girlfriend and according to the women who came to the project, he was always out with different women and was known to use online dating sites. And that was how she knew she was going to trap him. Although the very thought of being with Lucas intimately made her want to throw up, she would do whatever was needed to get her revenge.

Rebecca sat up straight. She felt better now, her head was clearer. She stood up and looked around her. The park was still deserted but she could feel someone watching her. A rustle from the bushes behind her made her spin round but it was only a bird flying away. Samantha giggled inside her head. *Crazy little Rebecca. You're always going to be crazy little Rebecca.*

Rebecca shivered, there was something strange going on— the phone calls, the feeling of being watched. It was getting to her. But it wasn't just when she was out and about. She was sure someone had been in her house. It was just little things, so slight that they made her question herself. An ever-so-slightly opened kitchen drawer; a cup turned just off centre in the cupboard, a cushion out of place on the sofa. The silent phone calls when she was in the house alone. All these things served to feed her paranoia, the feeling that someone was watching her. She could feel eyes following her when she left the house. At night as she closed her curtains, she felt someone, or something, out there watching, waiting. She tried to convince herself that it was stress or exhaustion from a lack of restful sleep, but the knot of anxiety had settled in her stomach and it wasn't ready to let go anytime soon.

She hadn't seen anyone else in the park with her but the hairs on the back of her neck stood up. She hurried out of the park, almost tripping in her rush to be back amongst people. She ran most of the way back to the office where she was greeted by Emma holding out a huge bouquet of flowers. She thrust them into her face as soon as she walked through the door.

'Looks like your man is grovelling, love,' she smiled.

Rebecca had taken the flowers, fixing a smile onto her face. This wasn't Lucas's style at all. He knew she would detest any public displays. Sitting down at her desk, she grabbed the envelope attached and ripped it open.

TICK TOCK, DARLING XXX

'Everything okay, love?' Emma asked, as Rebecca's face drained of colour.

She shook her head as the card dropped through her fingers. Emma went to snatch it up and Rebecca stamped hard on her fingers.

'Ouch…W-what the fuck?' Emma gasped.

Rebecca grabbed the card and stuffed the flowers in the bin, then, ignoring Emma, she turned and fled.

25

DID YOU LIKE your flowers, Rebecca? All women love flowers, don't they? Especially flowers from a secret admirer?

But these didn't come from anyone who admires you. These were a gift from someone who wants to destroy you. From me. Your worst nightmare.

All those things moving about in the house. Is he messing with your mind? Is he disobeying your rules? Or maybe it's you? Maybe they have come back again, maybe they are making you do things you can't remember? Or maybe not…

When you pick up the phone, I love to hear your voice. Strong and confident at first as you ask who's calling, growing more hesitant as you listen to the silence. You want to slam the phone down, don't you? You want to close me out, forget about me, pretend I don't exist. But that's not going to happen, Rebecca. You're never going to forget who I am or what you've done.

I wish I could see your face on the other end of the line. I'll bet those pretty little brows of yours are furled all up, the shutters coming down as the others start to whisper in your ear. I wonder what they are telling you. Ignore me? Report me? Doesn't really matter what they say to you, they are not in control anymore, I am… I decide what happens to you now.

26

LUCAS LEFT THE office with plenty of time to make his meeting at three o'clock. With nobody around to see him slip away early, he felt fairly confident he'd get away with it without Rebecca finding out. Without a car, most of her work took place in or near the project, and he had ensured that this meeting place was far enough away that they wouldn't be spotted.

He felt the tension lift from his body as he drove by Alexandra Park and out of the grim surroundings of the East End to merge onto the M8. Traffic was light and, within ten minutes, he was taking the Charing Cross cut off bringing him to the Mitchell Library. He found himself gazing enviously at the students spilling out the doors without a care in the world.

He wished he could turn back the clock and start all over again, to be one of them, with his whole life in front of him. He found a parking space at the Granville Street entrance. He fed the parking meter and checked his watch.

In his eagerness to meet her he was half an hour early. He decided to walk round to the North Street entrance. Walking through the ornate doors and along the Victorian styled tiled corridor, he admired the sight before him. No matter how many times he came to the Mitchell Library, its grandeur and presence always managed to take his breath away. Despite the hum of those still in the building, it felt quiet, and a calm stillness settled over him as he sat down in a quiet spot in the main library to wait for her.

As was his way, his mind began to wander back in time and he found himself thinking back to when he first hooked up with Rebecca. He'd been delighted to meet someone he thought was on the same wavelength as him. Working in a similar setting she understood the challenges and frustrations.

After his rough start in life, he had grown up believing falling in love wasn't for men like him. His mother hadn't loved him, not really, she had just been in love with the idea of the perfect family. His father had been a bastard and that was him being kind. There was no other way of describing him.

Even as a child, Lucas could find no redeeming features about the man who had lived in his home. He had repulsed him yet fascinated him at the same time. Everyone in the scheme had known who his father was but not because he was popular. Uncle Duncan they'd called him, but not in a warm and affectionate way. No, Uncle Duncan was a pervert. A paedophile was how the professionals would have described him these days. Lucas knew his father hadn't loved his mum; she was much too old for him, not his type. And he most certainly didn't love Lucas. Everyone knew it was little girls his dad liked. But he chose to stay with Lucas and his mum because it suited him to have the disguise of a family to hide behind. His family were his respectable front for the community. His mum hadn't cared what he got up to behind her back. Duncan Campbell had made her an offer she couldn't refuse—he'd give her a child if she provided him with bed, lodgings, and an alibi whenever the police came around asking awkward questions.

She'd jumped at the chance. She wasn't the prettiest of women and she must have known the chances of her pulling a husband were slim from the outset. Realising that her time was running out, she'd bit his hand off when he made the offer. She'd told Lucas often enough, just how much she had sacrificed to have him. Lucas wished she hadn't bothered, he wished he had never been born.

Duncan was around as Lucas grew up but theirs was not a close relationship. At most he tolerated Lucas, and Lucas struggled to conceal his disgust at the man who called himself his father. The stench that wafted off him was rank; he never bothered to wash and rarely changed his clothes. He'd just sit in the spare room all day vegetating in front of the television before making a few furtive phone calls and slipping out the door like a big fat slug into the night.

Lucas could still remember some of his dad's friends who visited the house. It had been quite clear that they liked Lucas more than his father did, but their attention made him feel uncomfortable and he remembered it as the only time his mother stood up to his father. She told his father if any of the men laid a finger on Lucas, she would see them all locked up, including him. Duncan had laughed, but Lucas knew that inside he was afraid. His mother knew too much.

Lucas's dark fascination with his father grew as he became older. He found himself obsessed about knowing what he was up to. When he was thirteen years old, he had followed him to the houses on Blackview Road, right in the middle of the scheme.

Creeping behind him up the close, he watched as he went into the first house on the ground floor. He had crawled over to the door and peered through the letter box. He would never forget what he saw that day. He ran as fast as he could out the back and slumped against the wall of the yard where the bins were kept.

He had wept as the reality of just what his father was hit him. That was when the meaning of the word 'pervert' suddenly became all too real for him. Despite his disgust, Lucas couldn't stop himself from continuing to follow and to watch. He hated himself for it, but he didn't know how to stop. Watching his father awoke a darkness within him. He was ashamed, but what could he do?

Over the next few years, Lucas had thought he'd perfected the art of stalking his father. He wasn't to know that his father had been aware of his presence all along and had intended using his son as bait. Lucas had walked straight into the trap and there was no way out. He had found himself unwittingly caught up in a world he knew it was wrong to be a part of, a world he didn't want to be a part of. Or so he had tried hard to convince himself.

'So, you want to be a part of yer auld da's gang,' Duncan had leered, the drool pooling at the corner of his mouth the first time he caught Lucas following him.

Lucas had shaken his head.

'Too late,' spat his father. 'You've been watching me for too long. Ye think I'm daft? You think I didnae see ye? Of course, I seen ye, ya wee prick.'

Grabbing Lucas by the throat, he rammed him up against the wall. His breath was fetid, and the spit stuck to his face as each word was thrown at him.

'Too late for ye now, wee man. Ye seen too much. So, the only way I've got of protecting myself is by making sure you get yer hands dirty.'

Lucas began to snivel, shaking his head, squirming as he tried to escape from the man before him.

'I d-d-don't want to,' he cried. 'I w-won't t-tell anyone, I p-promise.'

Duncan Campbell threw his head back and roared with laughter.

'Yer nothing but a wee poof. A mammy's nancy boy. I cannae believe you're any son of mine.' Slapping him around the

SHARON BAIRDEN

head, Duncan pulled Lucas to his feet and shoved him in front of him.

'Y'know exactly where we going, don't ya boy?' He hissed into his ear, the spittle hitting Lucas's cheek and sticking there. 'So, go on, lead the way Macduff, you've been there often enough, watching. I reckon it's time you joined in.'

'N-n-o,' he stammered.

'Oh, ah think ye will, son. If ye don't, ah've got a few mates that widnae say naw to a wee shot of you, ye know whit ah mean?'

The meaning of his father's words was all too clear. Lucas knew exactly what his father's friends would do to him given the chance. He'd seen the videos they watched. The tears streamed down Lucas's face. He knew then he had no choice but to do what he was told. If he didn't then his father would beat him and pass him on to his friends. He knew, despite her threats, his mother wouldn't stop it, she wouldn't say a word so long as it wasn't happening under her roof.

Ashamed, he'd made his way to the house, dragging his feet through the close and into the dump that served as a home. He wept inside as the sights before him hit with a bitter reality. Lucas was about to become his father's son.

He tried to blank out most of what went on after, but over the years it became burnt into his brain. Duncan started taking him with him every time he went visiting. Lucas was powerless to stop it. Lucas had seen the grainy VHS tapes running in his father's room. He didn't want a starring role.

Sometimes he would be made to join in while Duncan took photographs. 'Souvenirs,' he called them. He had laughed when he said this, not a friendly laugh but rather one that chilled Lucas to the bone. On the way home, his father would tell him exactly what he would do with these souvenirs if Lucas didn't do what he was told.

And so Lucas had become his father's son.

Visits all blurred into one, as Lucas quickly got swallowed into his father's world. They visited lots of houses, houses with kids who had parents who didn't care and neighbours who were happy to turn a blind eye.

But they always returned to that one house. The one where it had all began for him. It wasn't just the girl who lived in the house his father was interested in, he'd managed to get the kid next door involved too. This kid was different, she had family—people who cared about her. Lucas had felt scared then. He knew it was risky when the parents cared, not like the other wee girl. Her mum was only interested in the small bags of brown powder his father gave her in return for time with her daughter.

Frightened of the other girl's parents finding out, Lucas had refused to take part until his father had pulled out some photographs. They were grainy but it was clear that Lucas was in these pictures and he hadn't looked entirely innocent.

Their last visit to the house was etched on his mind forever. His father had told him to wait outside, he would go and collect the kid and then they were going to a party. Lucas knew exactly what type of party his father meant; he had seen the clothes he'd packed for the child to take. It wasn't any type of party normal folk went to.

Twenty minutes later, he had watched, terrified, as his father had come blundering out of the house, his trousers covered in blood and his face contorted in rage. He grabbed Lucas by the throat, leaning right into his face, his breath foul as he rasped, 'Say a word, you little bastard, and those photos are going everywhere.'

'I w-w-won't say anything, I p-p-promise.'

Duncan let him go, throwing him to the ground and leaving him in a snivelling heap. Lucas lay there for an hour, unable to move, guilt flooding him at the relief he felt—not for the girl, but for himself.

When his father had been caught for the possession of child pornography six months later and sentenced to five years in prison, Lucas had been relived. He thought it would be an escape for him. But it had been the beginning of a whole new nightmare for him and his mum. With the news splashed all across The Dagger and the local tabloids, they were gossip fodder for everyone in the scheme. His mum's nerves had been shattered. Her GP had suggested that they approach their housing officer to ask for a re-location. Although Lucas blamed his mother for some of what had gone on, he'd still felt sorry for her and hated to see what she had to put up with on a daily basis at the hands of the community.

Graffiti, and faeces through the letter box were soon followed by very real threats of physical harm. It had been made crystal clear to them that their lives were at risk if they remained living there. His mother had tried to reason with her neighbours, but the community had been unforgiving. They knew exactly the deal she'd made with that particular devil to satisfy her own selfish need for a child. They wouldn't forgive, nor would they forget.

They were relocated across to the East End of the city to Dennistoun, and for a while, things were relatively calm. Even when the news of his father's death reached them, his mother had still been unable to function normally. She had retreated into her shell after the court case, ashamed to show her face and so Lucas ended up taking on the role of her reluctant carer, as she gradually stopped leaving the house.

She became increasingly paranoid, convinced that everyone was looking at them, talking about them. Her demands on Lucas grew, and soon he was doing everything for her. It was a burden he didn't want but had felt he had no other choice. If he left, who would be there to look after her?

It soon became clear that her battle was more than just with her mental health. Physically, she was declining, and rapidly too. Lucas attended to all her personal care needs and he could see she was fading away. The weight was dropping off her despite all his efforts to ensure she ate properly. The house became neglected as Lucas began to drown under the burden of caring for her. She refused to go to her doctor and, by the time he had persuaded her to seek medical attention, it was too late. The doctor had referred her straight to the hospital where she was diagnosed with advanced ovarian cancer. There was nothing they could do. Within a month, she was gone. Lucas knew that she had simply given up.

Lucas had found himself alone in the world. With no other family, he was cast adrift. He hadn't known whether to feel terrified or excited by the opportunities that lay before him. Free from the shackles of his past, he was determined to put it all behind him and reinvent himself. He changed his surname from Campbell to Findlay in order to sever all links to his father.

He began his career volunteering with Space to Grow, at first just doing admin and helping out with the groups until a job came up as a support worker. Encouraged by his manager, Anne Cater, he had applied for it, never believing he stood a chance and the rest was history. But not everything in his earlier life had been consigned to history…

A hand on his shoulder startled him out his reverie and he recoiled, afraid his past had returned to claim him.

'Penny for them,' a familiar voice whispered, and Lucas turned, the smile lighting up his face.

He stood up and wrapped his arms around the woman in front of him. Burying his face into her long blonde hair, he stole a discreet kiss.

'You've no idea how good it is to see you, Nicole,' he breathed.

27

JIM'S SLEEP HAD been fitful, the drink had sent him into oblivion but hadn't stopped the nightmares haunting him. He had got up that morning and drank the dregs of the whisky straight from the bottle to steady his nerves. He had added two takeaway coffees on his way into the office and now, sat at his desk, he felt wired.

Trying to focus, he opened up his emails and quickly scanned his inbox, irritated when he saw there was still no reply from Rebecca. He'd sent the email two days ago and couldn't work out why she was taking so long to reply. This new service should be right up her street. He'd wanted to get her thoughts on it from the potential perspective of the women who used her service.

He contemplated sending another email, then decided the direct approach might work a bit better. Taking a deep breath to steady his nerves, he picked up the phone and dialled the number for Phoenix. Just as he pressed the last digit, Nicole came into the office. Pointedly, he looked at the clock on the wall. It was nine-thirty already. She was late again, and she hadn't returned to the office the previous afternoon. Despite his affection for her as a colleague, her terrible timekeeping and lack of communication was beginning to get on his nerves. She looked back at him, smiled and just shrugged. She gestured to him asking if he wanted a coffee. He nodded just as the phone was answered.

'Good morning, Phoenix. Emma speaking. How can I help you?'

'Hi, Emma, it's Jim Aitken here from Criminal Justice. I'm looking to speak to Rebecca if she's about?'

'Hi, Jim, she's just this minute walked into the office. Give me a minute and I'll transfer you over.'

She wouldn't be able to avoid him now. His stomach churned as he waited for her to answer.

'Rebecca speaking, what can I do for you?' The voice on the other end of the phone sounded clipped.

Christ, I wouldn't want to get on the wrong side of her, he thought, recognising the irritation in her tone.

'Hi, Rebecca. You're a difficult woman to track down.' There was silence at the other end of the line. He carried on, he knew he was getting nervous now and was likely to ramble. 'I was hoping to get a meeting in with you to talk about the new service we're setting up? I did send you an email, but I don't know if you got it. You know what it's like with internal servers, always sending stuff to junk mail.'

There was a short pause at the other end before she replied, 'Yes, I got your email, but things have been really busy here and I haven't had time to get back to you. What sort of information is it you're looking for? I can arrange for one of the team to send you some stuff over if you want?'

'It's more a chat I'm looking for, rather than some leaflets. It would probably be better if we met up?' suggested Jim. 'It's a chance for me to find out a wee bit more about your project, too. I'm still pretty new to this area and I like to get a handle on what's out there, if you know what I mean?' He laughed softly. 'Plus, you work alongside a lot of women who have been affected by the abuse and it would be helpful to have your perspective from that angle.'

Again, a short pause before she replied, 'Well, I'm busy at the moment, I could let Emma catch-up with you and fill you in on things?'

'I'd rather meet with you, Rebecca, if you don't mind. I've heard so much about Phoenix and your passion for the work. I'll not take up too much of your time and anyway, the word on the street is that Anne Cater is keen for some partnership work between the sectors. I know she holds you in high esteem. You've quite the reputation in this area.' Flattery might help break some barriers down here, he thought.

Rebecca sighed on the other end, and Jim knew he'd nailed it by dropping Anne's name into the mix. Rebecca couldn't afford to get on her wrong side. As one of the key players in the strategic partnerships, Anne had a lot of influence when it came to the funding of services, including Rebecca's. He waited for her reply.

'OK then, I'm free tomorrow afternoon at two for an hour, if you want to come over here, we've got plenty of meeting space?' The voice on the other end of the phone now held more than just a hint of irritation.

Jim sensed the reluctance in her response but ignoring it, he said, 'Perfect, I'll see you then.' He put the phone down smiling to himself just as Nicole came back with the coffees.

'Hey, you look like the cat that caught the cream.' She smiled, putting his coffee down and shoving her paperwork out of the way to make room at her desk.

'Aye, something like that. I've finally tracked down the elusive Rebecca Findley. I've set up a meeting with her tomorrow over at their place. I got the distinct impression she was trying to avoid me, though.'

'Oh, I've heard about her but never met her before. The darling of the third sector they call her,' replied Nicole.

'Everyone sings her praises, but there is nobody as perfect as folk make them out to be. She sounds too good to be true if you ask me.'

'Female intuition is a wonderful thing, but I think I'll make my own judgement tomorrow. I'm quite looking forward to it, actually. I'm interested in what she's got to say about the work we're doing. I noticed you were late again today, and you never came back to the office last night. Is everything okay?'

Her face had flushed slightly before she responded, 'Yeah, everything's just fine. I've just had some personal stuff to deal with.'

She drew his attention to a new case that had landed on their desk. Jim knew there must be more than she was letting on. She had a right shifty look about her. But he said nothing. He got the sense that Nicole was the type of woman who wouldn't take too kindly to being interrogated and, at the end of the day, he wasn't her line manager.

Her phone pinged, signalling an incoming message and she answered it quickly, cutting short any further conversation with him. He noticed the smile on her face as she read it.

'Anyone interesting?' he asked.

She just shrugged.

'Aye well, okay then, sorry for being so nosey.'

She didn't reply.

Jim shook his head. Women—he just couldn't work them out. But Nicole was already engrossed in paperwork and had her head down, there was clearly no more to be said here.

ACROSS THE DESK Nicole pretended she was busy doing paperwork, but inside she was seething at Jim's constant prying.

She watched him from under her fringe, his hair greying at the temples and worry lines etched in his face. This job certainly didn't do the ageing process any favours. He was really starting to get on her nerves now. Always wanting to know who she was on the phone to. It was none of his bloody business. She laughed internally. He'd die if he knew who she had been receiving messages from. But this one had been good news, she couldn't help but smile. Everything was finally falling into place.

Pulling out her phone, she punched in a quick message to Lucas. 'I had a great time yesterday, shame it was so short. Hope to spend more time with you VERY soon. XXXX'.

Almost immediately a reply came pinging back.

'Can't wait XXX.'

A small smile turned up the corners of her mouth as her stomach fluttered in anticipation.

28

WALKING INTO THE office the next day, Rebecca was relieved to see that someone had got rid of the flowers, but a deep sense of dread remained in the pit of her stomach. The night before, she had been convinced someone was watching the house—she was sure she had seen a dark shadow in the garden. She'd made Lucas go out to check, but he had been worse than useless. All he had done was pop his head out the back door and have a quick look, too interested in shutting himself away in the spare room on the pretext of catching up on paperwork. She'd spent an hour checking and re-checking the locks on the doors and windows before she went to bed. Lucas hadn't joined her until gone three.

She'd tossed and turned most of the night—the threats of her night time demons scaring sleep away. Samantha had come back with a vengeance, and her voice was a constant chatter inside Rebecca's head, to the point she could hardly think straight.

It had been a long time since she had completely disassociated, and she didn't want it to happen now but keeping up the pretence was becoming increasingly difficult. She was beginning to fear it wouldn't be long before her colleagues noticed something was very wrong with her.

Things had gone from bad to worse when Emma had transferred that call from Jim through to her. Rebecca hadn't wanted to speak to the man before she had mentally prepared herself for it. This was what happened when you started to lose control, she chided herself. Furious at feeling forced into accepting the meeting with Jim, Rebecca feigned a migraine and cried off work at lunchtime, telling Emma she was going home to sleep it off. The streets were quiet as she left the hustle of the main road to walk towards the bus stop. Glancing around nervously, her chest tightened as she searched for the eyes burning into her back. There was nobody there apart from an old man. He was staring at her, concern etched across his face.

'Are you all right, love? You don't look so well.'

'I'm fine,' Rebecca snapped back at him, annoyed at herself for losing control so publicly.

The thought crossed her mind that it might be Lucas, trying to be smart, trying to fight back. But she didn't believe he'd have the balls to do something like that. Reaching the bus stop, for once relieved to see a crowd of people waiting, Rebecca shoved her headphones in her ears, and hunched over her phone to select her playlist for the journey home.

If only she had known her nightmares were just beginning.

29

WHAT SORT OF a freak marries the man who abused her? What sort of sick bitch do you have to be to do that? Does it give you a kick, Rebecca? Maybe you're just as sick and twisted as he is. Maybe it's all a game to you. But I'm warning you, it's not a game to me. You are both going to pay.

You see, it's not just you, Rebecca. I'm watching him too. I know all his dirty little secrets. He's not the man he pretends to be. He's used you just as much as you've used him.

But don't you worry your pretty little head about him. I've got it all under control now. Some mutual friends have been very, very helpful.

You know what, Rebecca? I think I'm actually going to miss you when this is all over. I feel we've grown close. I feel like I know you so well. It's been a lot of fun. Even though I'm not that sure I like your home décor—it's a bit old fashioned, don't you think? Yes. I've been inside, more than once. I know where you sleep, I've smelled the perfume on your sheets, I've smelled you, Rebecca, and do you know what? You smell like fear.

30

LUCAS'S STOMACH LURCHED as he walked through the front door and saw Rebecca's shoes discarded in the hallway. Automatically, he moved them to the shoe rack, his eyes darting around to check everything was where it was meant to be. She's never home this early, he thought.

A mix of terror and frustration washed over him. Rebecca changing her routine was never a good sign and he had planned to use the time alone to call Nicole. He wanted to hear her voice again. It was crazy, he knew it was, but something about her had touched him. For the first time since marrying Rebecca, he had started to think perhaps there was a way out for him.

Opening the living room door quietly, Lucas let out the breath he had been holding when he saw that Rebecca was fast asleep on the sofa, a blanket thrown over her. Watching her sleep, it was difficult to reconcile his feelings for her, she looked so peaceful, so serene. Yet he knew, better than most, what lay underneath that beautiful face. Sitting down across from her, he watched her chest rise and fall with each breath, thinking to himself how easy it would be just to put the cushion over her face and end it all. His thoughts shocked him. This wasn't him... Was it?

Could I really do it? He wondered. Could I cause harm to another human being? Lucas didn't want to think himself capable of murder but thoughts of his past floated around his mind, reminding him exactly what he was capable of.

He shook his head. No. He couldn't kill her. He wasn't brave enough for a start. Just the thought of being caught and ending up in prison made him break out in a cold sweat. He knew what happened to men like him in prison. His only chance of any sort of freedom would be if Rebecca and he were to split up. But Lucas wasn't stupid, he knew there was no chance of that happening unless Rebecca wanted it to happen.

As he watched his wife sleep, he thought back to how quickly she had changed after they had married. The abuse had started as soon as they had returned home. Only at the time, he hadn't given it that name. Lucas had no real experience with women. Other than his mother, he hadn't ever lived with a woman before and had believed Rebecca's behaviour to be normal. Small things at first, like the sly smirk when he got his hair cut, and the look that screamed: 'Are you really wearing that?' when he bought any new clothes. Little digs at the amount he drank, suggesting that perhaps he had a problem, always demanding to check his phone, waking him up as soon as he had fallen asleep for no particular reason, answering the phone to his friends and humiliating him.

Looked at separately, it had seemed childish to complain about such trivial things, but combined, they began to take their toll on him. He felt constantly on edge, terrified of doing or saying the wrong thing. Afraid to challenge or question her. Until the day he had come home from the barbers. He'd been pleased with his new look, but Rebecca had burst out laughing as soon as she walked through the door.

'What the hell do you think you look like?' She'd spat at him. 'You're not a bloody teenager, for Christ's sake.'

Lucas had been hurt by her words. He had plucked up the courage to challenge her, telling her how she'd upset him. She'd stared at him as though he had lost his mind.

'What the hell are you talking about, Lucas? I never said anything of the sort.'

His laugh had died when he saw the look on her face. She clearly didn't think it was funny.

'Rebecca, you did. You told me I looked ridiculous, you laughed at me. You hurt my feelings.' Even as he had said it, he realised how petulant he sounded.

'Honestly, Lucas, I swear you're hearing things. I'd never say anything like that. You know I wouldn't.'

She'd become quite indignant about the whole event, and he'd watched the rage build up behind her eyes. He'd let it go and switched on the TV, willing it to be forgotten. Maybe he had picked her up wrong, he thought, she wouldn't have said anything like that, would she?

But that night as they went to bed, Rebecca had started picking at it all again, like a scab. She would always keep picking at things, almost as though she was giving herself a reason to lose it with him. He'd given in as usual, agreeing with her just to try and stop it all going too far. He'd leaned over to give her a hug.

'Get away from me, you bastard,' she'd hissed. She'd shoved him hard in the chest causing him to topple over and graze his head on the corner of the bedside table.

'Now look what you've done, you clumsy idiot. I suppose you're going to go and tell everyone I hit you now.'

The colour in her face had risen, a warm red flush taking over her cheeks. Her hands had balled up into fists and her breathing had ragged. He had truly believed at that point she might seriously injure him.

'Hey, love, calm down,' he had said, trying to defuse the situation but his words had only seemed to inflame her further.

'Calm down. How fucking dare you? How. Fucking. Dare. You. Tell. Me. To. Calm. Down?' She spat each word out, the vitriol dripping from her mouth. Leaning over the bed to where he was lying on the floor, Rebecca had brought her hand down to his chest and raked her newly manicured nails across his abdomen, breaking the skin and leaving long, tell-tale slashes across his stomach. A mark only he knew was there.

Lucas remembered the feeling of shame. His wife had just lashed out at him. He knew that he should have got up there and then, packed a bag and left. But he was paralysed. How could he? Who would he tell? What would he say? He'd be a laughing stock, a big lump of a man like him battered by a wee slip of a woman. He'd crawled into bed beside her, lying still as he listened to her breathing regulate until she'd fallen into a deep and restful sleep. Lucas had spent the rest of the night staring at the walls, wondering what the hell he had just committed himself to by his silence.

It wasn't just his appearance or things he did at home; she had even started on his work, always keen to point out any mistakes she thought he had made, telling him how she would do things and constantly berating him for a lack of ambition.

But then on the very odd occasion they were out together, she was over the top in her praise of him to others. She would act all coy and shy, almost as though she were in his shadow, always checking with him if it was okay for her to have a drink, or talk to someone. She would constantly make out that she wasn't allowed to do anything without his permission.

He'd see folk looking at him as though he was some kind of control freak. He wanted to tell them it was an act, but he couldn't. He knew nobody would believe him. Everybody thought Rebecca was a saint, he had no chance.

He'd cancel plans to go out with his friends, trying to win her round with romantic meals he had spent hours preparing for her. She would take one look at them and throw them in the bin.

'I'm not eating that muck,' she would spit at him before taking herself off to bed early, making it clear that he was not invited. If he pushed, she'd accuse him of being a predator, talking about women she had worked with who had been raped and abused by their partners, making him ashamed for existing in his own skin. Then she would wake him up the next day only to tell him he wasn't man enough for her, that he couldn't satisfy her.

Slowly she began to isolate him. She'd make excuses for them not to attend events, she demanded to check his phone daily, she would forget to pass on messages from friends, yet swear blind that she had to the point that his friends stopped calling him. Once, she had even called his manager Anne, and told her he was sick when she decided that she didn't want him to go to work.

Lucas knew exactly what she was doing. He wasn't stupid, he knew that there was a term for this: coercive control. He had been on enough training courses about it and he'd seen the impact it had on clients. He knew he should have left her, it's what he would have told anyone else to do, but he didn't know how to.

He couldn't work out exactly what it was she wanted with him, though. It made no sense, she was an intelligent and beautiful woman, so why would she want to be with a man she so clearly despised? He asked her if something had happened in her past, if perhaps an ex had hurt her. She had flown into a rage at that, he still had the scar on his left shoulder where she had burnt him with the iron that night.

When he'd tried to find out more about her family, Rebecca just made vague noises about being an only child and her family living abroad now. He had tried to encourage her to make contact, suggesting that they go visit them on holiday. However, he soon learned the hard way that nobody made Rebecca do anything she didn't want to do. The broken foot was his lesson not to try to make her contact her family. All his injuries were either hidden or easily explained through a series of silly accidents. She knew exactly how to make sure nobody asked awkward questions. Lucas was too ashamed to tell anyone the truth. And so that was their relationship.

Rebecca took the lead. Rebecca took control. It was Rebecca's way or no way. Lucas quickly learned how to keep her happy and not to break her rules.

Lucas suddenly felt the panic rise as he realised that if Rebecca was in before him it meant that he hadn't had time to complete the tasks she expected. He hadn't got the kettle on boil—she liked a cup of tea made when she got in from work—and he hadn't lit the candles. It also meant he hadn't started preparing dinner. His heart was hammering against his chest. Frozen to the spot, he didn't know whether to start the preparations now or wait for her to wake up.

While he sat fretting, the decision was taken out of his hands. Rebecca stirred as she began to wake. She rubbed her eyes sleepily and smiled softly at him. Reassured by her smile, his breathing began to even out a little. She beckoned him over with her finger, kissing him tenderly as he knelt before her.

'Oh, Lucas,' she said. 'I felt so unwell, honey, I had to come home and rest.' Lucas wrapped her in his arms and stroked her hair just the way she liked. She stretched out like a cat almost purring in delight.

'Be a love,' she said. 'Go and stick the kettle on for me please, I'm parched.'

Like an eager puppy, Lucas got to his feet to do as he was told. Relieved she seemed to be in a good mood, he walked into the kitchen and filled the kettle. He was humming to himself as it came to the boil, Rebecca's favourite mug in place with the teabag waiting the boiling water.

He heard her pad softly into the kitchen and make her way over to him, wrapping her arms around his waist from behind. He stiffened but leaned into her embrace as she stretched around him, picked up the kettle and slowly, very deliberately, poured the scalding water down the front of his legs.

She whispered, 'Don't do it again, Lucas.'

He opened his mouth to scream, but no sound came out.

31

REBECCA WATCHED, EXPRESSIONLESS, as Lucas crumpled quietly to the floor, his face twisted in pain. She searched for some feeling, anything, but there was nothing. No remorse, sorrow, anger or joy. Just a great big empty void. She was flat, detached from her surroundings, detached from herself.

Samantha's voice was growing stronger and all the time Rebecca was fading away. Her head was spaced out, everything was foggy. The house didn't seem real, everything was distorted, walls closing in on her, trapping her.

She ran to the bathroom, slamming the door behind her. Her hands clutching onto the sink to hold her up, she looked in the mirror and Samantha screamed back at her. *Good girl, Rebecca, you did good. We're almost there now. Almost done. You know what you need to do right now. Go on, Rebecca. You know it will make you feel better.*

Rebecca reached down into the cupboard under the sink and pulled out a razor blade. Samantha smiled back at her from the mirror. *That's a girl! Go on,* she whispered.

Rebecca ran her finger along the length of the blade, the sharp sting on her finger registering in her mind. Slumping to the floor, she pulled her skirt up over her thighs, her hand dropped, and she let the blade slice. With the first trickle of blood, she felt the numbness subside.

Rebecca came back to herself, sitting on the bathroom floor. Quietly, she fixed her clothing and disposed of the razor blade. Washing her hands, she stared in the mirror and smiled back at herself. Slowly, she made her way back into the kitchen. Lucas was on his feet now, running a towel under the cold tap.

'That looks nasty,' Rebecca's voice was full of concern.

Lucas nodded, his face blank. 'Yeah, it is. I think I might need to go get it seen to?'

She smiled, at least he knew to ask permission.

'No, I think you will be perfectly fine. It was just an accident, easily done and the first aid kit in the bathroom should sort you out. It's not like you're going to die, is it? It's not like any lasting damage has been done, is it?'

She spat the last sentence out at him as she pushed him aside and filled the kettle. 'I'm parched, Lucas. You never did make me that cuppa. I don't know, what sort of husband are you, eh?' Rebecca laughed and walked out the kitchen.

There would be no need for flashing blue lights or others poking their noses in where they weren't wanted. Not on her watch, there wouldn't. No, she always judged her actions perfectly, ensuring that they were a reminder to Lucas of just how far she would go and just how much control she had over him.

'I can't be all that bad,' she muttered to herself, 'If I was really bad, I'd have just killed him, wouldn't I?'

Yeah right, you keep telling yourself that, sweetheart. You've not got the balls to do anything of the sort. That's why you need me so much.

Rebecca put her hands over her ears, she didn't want to hear Samantha right now. Breathing in deeply, ten deep breaths, she clenched her fists tightly, then let it all go.

Slowly, Rebecca made her way up the stairs to the bedroom. She lay down on the bed and waited. He'd come to her. She knew he would.

She watched as the bedroom door nudged open and Lucas stumbled through it. His handsome features masked by the clear fear shining from his eyes. Smirking, she patted the bed beside her, indicating for him to sit. He faltered over towards her, lowering himself gingerly onto the bed, his eyes seeking out her approval.

'Lucas,' she chided, as though talking to a very small child. 'You know that it was your own fault. These things don't happen when you play by the rules, do they?'

He nodded his head in agreement. 'I'm sorry,' he whispered as he lay down on the bed beside her.

She looked at him mockingly. 'Oh, Lucas, not in here, not tonight. You've really disappointed me you know. Go and sleep in the spare room, it will give us both time to think.'

With no argument, he did as he was told, as she knew he always would. She didn't know whether to be pleased with her level of control or disgusted at his lack of self-respect. He had no backbone at all. It was too easy for her to lay the blame of everything that had happened at Lucas's feet. After all, it was his fault.

Technically speaking, she knew that his father was to blame, but he wasn't here to pay the price now, was he? And what was it the Bible said? The sins of the father are to be laid upon the children.

With Lucas out of the way, Rebecca switched off the bedside light, throwing the room into darkness. She tried to settle herself down to sleep. She needed her rest before her meeting with Jim Aitken the next day. She was still furious at herself for agreeing to meet with him, but she knew she had been caught unaware and when he had thrown Anne Cater's name into the mix, she had little choice but to agree.

Sleep wouldn't come, her mind was all over the place. She thought back to her conversation with Kate Noble. The stupid woman really believed that it had been her compliance with statutory services which led to her having her kids returned, but little did she know that Rebecca had played a major role in social work's decision to relax the contact conditions with her kids.

If it hadn't been for Rebecca ensuring Martin had been caught with a large quantity of gear stashed in his car—thanks to one of her street girls—then he'd still have been out of prison and knocking her about. She had heard Martin was out now and indeed her husband dearest had come home blabbing about a referral he had received for him.

She shook her head. She was letting her mind wander again—a sure sign of losing control. She had to rein it in. She had to be careful. She couldn't get caught now, not when she'd come this far.

Her eyelids grew heavy as sleep began to take over. She was sinking deeper into the black of hole of semi-slumber when she sensed a shift in her brain and the beginnings of a rush of air towards her as the darkness gave way to a shadowy figure reaching out towards her. She struggled to get away, but it was no use, she was paralysed and couldn't move. She tried to get her conscious mind to take control, tried to move a finger to free her from the paralysis, to remind her that this wasn't real, that it wasn't happening, but the bony hands of the faceless figure wrapped themselves tightly round her wrist. The sensation of a hundred pairs of tiny hands began to grab and prod at her, poking and pinching and pinning her down, sitting on her chest and stopping her breathing.

She pushed harder in an attempt to free herself and she heard the whispers in her ear, malevolent and threatening, warm against her skin and penetrating deep inside her head becoming louder and louder, turning into an intense tremor inside her brain like an electrical surge. She tried to clasp her head in her hands to halt the vibrations, but something held her back, stopping her from freeing herself from the experience. And then a flash of light, a whooshing sound, and as suddenly as it had started, it stopped. She prised her eyes open to see the dark demons scurry back into the shadows, their fire-red eyes boring into her until the last minute. She was drenched in sweat and her breathing was fast and shallow.

She reached over and turned on the bedside lamp to rid herself of the last of the demons and slowed down her breathing until the room had returned to normal. But this time, the room felt different. Someone had been there, she could sense it. The light from the bathroom seeped through the bedroom door. She was sure Lucas had closed it when he'd left... Hadn't he?

She could have gone and woken Lucas and sought comfort from him. He would have gladly given it to her. But she refused to let him see this vulnerable side of her. She had to keep it hidden. She could never expose this side of herself to anyone. She couldn't be weak, she had to be strong.

She climbed out of bed and looked out of the window onto the streets below where she was convinced that she could see a shadow sinking into the darkness, but not before it lifted its head and looked straight at her. She wasn't alone. Someone was watching her.

32

LUCAS LAY IN bed. He was broken, mentally and physically. His life was a mess, driven by the secrets and lies swallowing him whole. He knew that his love for his wife was dead now. There was nothing left between them. But leaving her wasn't an option. Her threats to destroy him lay heavy on his mind. And it wasn't only Rebecca who could bring him down, there were others out there who knew even darker secrets—who knew who the real Lucas Findlay was.

Not for the first time, he considered ending it all. It would be so simple to take the easy way out, a handful of tablets and a bottle of whisky and it could all be over. But he couldn't even pluck up the courage to do that. He tried to rid himself of the negative thoughts and think about Nicole, the one good thing in his life right now. But if Rebecca was to find out about his relationship with her, he dreaded to think what the consequences would be.

He thought back to his first meeting with Nicole, six months earlier, when they both attended the same case conference for a prisoner. He'd walked into the waiting room and sat down beside her. He remembered the look of concern on her face as he had winced sitting down on the hard, plastic chair, and the questioning look she had given him when he had tried to brush it off as a football injury.

The case conference had been late in starting, so they had got chatting and soon phone numbers were swapped and arrangements for coffee dates arranged. He'd tried to convince himself it was all very innocent, just two colleagues meeting for a coffee, letting off steam about the work they were doing, but he found himself opening up to her in a way he had never done with anyone and before long he had fallen for her big time. And now here he was, head over heels in love with a woman he could never have.

Even if Rebecca wasn't in the picture, there was the other stuff—the things he couldn't share with anyone. Shivering, he wondered what would happen now he'd sent the files. Surely, that was his debt paid now. Surely, they would let him go? He'd said in his email this was the last time, he wouldn't be sending any more files, taking part in any more of their sick games.

But Lucas knew the type of men he was dealing with—you didn't say no to them, they decided when things were over. He wished he had never got involved but he'd been given no choice. In the back of his mind a little voice niggled; 'You enjoyed it too, though, Lucas, didn't you?'

He pulled the covers over his head and tried to ignore his thoughts and the pain he was in. The beatings were getting worse. The boiling water tipped over his legs was a testament to that. It was becoming harder to hide the evidence of her outbursts. Things were escalating rapidly, just a few nights ago she had held a knife to his throat while screaming. She wasn't stupid, she knew exactly what the neighbours could hear and it sure as hell wasn't him.

He turned the bedroom lamp off when he heard footsteps on the landing. He couldn't face the thought of Rebecca coming in and starting again if she thought he was awake. He hadn't listened hard enough, for if he had, he'd have heard the footsteps head back downstairs and the click of the front door as the stranger left their home.

33

I WATCHED YOU sleep last night, Rebecca. I watched your silent struggle as your night time demons took over. The muffled screams as you felt them touch you, caress you with their cold hands.

I bent down and I kissed you gently, a feather brushing across your cheek. You smiled. I slipped out and left you. I could have killed you, Rebecca.

I really should have killed you.

34

ARRIVING AT THE office early, Jim noted Nicole's vacant chair as he slammed the office door behind him. His head was thumping. Reaching into his desk drawer, he pulled out the water bottle he kept for emergencies, his 'special' water—a hair of the dog always helped with the headache and the tremors. He tipped it to his mouth, feeling himself relax as the lukewarm vodka slipped down his throat. Jim wasn't fussy what his tipple was and in work, vodka was easier to disguise.

He looked at the clock again, it was almost ten now and Nicole still wasn't in. His own irritation at her timekeeping was annoying him. It had nothing to do with him, he wasn't her manager. But it frustrated him that she seemed to come and go as she pleased. Maybe she wasn't cut out for this job after all.

He knew he was over reacting. He'd been doing that a lot lately, becoming increasingly irritated over the silliest things. The job was starting to get to him and he was losing his focus, his mind becoming increasingly preoccupied with the past. Pushing away his memories, he tried to concentrate on work, but his hands found their way to his pocket where he clutched the trinket tight in the palm of his hand. His heart hurt at the thought of what he had never fought for.

'Jim,' a voice shunted him back to the present.

'Morning,' he snapped, his eyes darting towards the clock on the wall. The unspoken message was obviously not lost on Nicole.

'Sorry I'm late. Women's troubles…'

Jim turned away, embarrassed by what he saw as Nicole's oversharing. Quickly changing the subject, he acknowledged his anxiety about his forthcoming meeting with Rebecca.

'I just get the feeling she was trying to avoid meeting me.'

'Hmm, she's probably just busy. Listen, is there any chance I can tag along with you? I'd love to know more about the work they do over there. My appointment this afternoon is cancelled anyway, he was nicked last night for attempted murder, so, it looks like that's one less on my books!'

'Aye, okay then, maybe soften her up a wee bit you being there. Sisterhood and all that.' Jim laughed, hiding his annoyance at his meeting with Rebecca being hijacked by Nicole. Although, he thought, it might prevent him blurting out what he actually wanted to say, if Nicole was there.

'Yeah, I guess. Do you want a coffee?'

He indicated he did and settled himself back down to prepare for the meeting.

WHEN NICOLE RETURNED with the drinks, Jim was so engrossed in his thoughts, he didn't even notice her.

'Hey, Jim,' she called across the desk. 'Do you know a guy called Lucas Findlay? He works for Space to Grow?'

'Aye, I know who he is. But I don't know him, I've only spoken to him on the phone once. He's married to that Rebecca we're going to meet later today,' Jim said.

'Oh, right? I've come across him a few times, he really didn't seem like her type. There was something almost human about him.'

She didn't think it was any of Jim's business to know just how long she'd known him for, or exactly how much she did know about his private life.

'Ohhh, you got a wee eye on him, have you?' A look of mock shock on his face

'I have not,' she retorted, a soft blush working its way up from her neck. 'I was just really interested in the work he's involved in over at Space to Grow. I was impressed with his report and his attitude at one of the Integrated Case Management meetings for a prisoner we both work with. The guy had a real compassion and empathy about him. You know that job isn't always easy, working with some right dirt bags. It would be too easy for the support staff to get jaded by it all. He just seemed to approach it with a fresh pair of eyes, and I was impressed that's all. I'm just a bit surprised that Rebecca is his wife. She didn't seem his type from what I've heard of her. It sounds like she is a bit of a control freak.'

Jim frowned. 'You seem to know a lot about her considering you haven't met her before?'

Nicole looked down at the desk, momentarily silenced. 'Eh, it's that female intuition, Jim.'

She laughed, but even to her own ears, the laugh sounded false.

JIM'S MIND WAS ticking, he wondered just how much truth Nicole had actually told him and how much she'd kept buried.

'Word is that she doesn't make a big deal about their marriage publicly. She wants to be known for her own accomplishments and not tied up with those of her husband,' said Jim. 'One of those feminist types.'

He laughed, not noticing that Nicole didn't laugh back. 'But I also heard that she can be a little bit of a control freak, others seem to think that perhaps if you scratch beneath the surface you might see some things you weren't expecting.'

'Oh, listen to you getting all caught up with the office gossip now, Jim. What happened to 'I'll reserve judgement until I meet her'? You've certainly changed your tune now, eh?'

Jim laughed again. 'And reserve my judgement I will. Just because I've repeated the tittle-tattle doesn't mean to say that I believe it.'

Nicole smiled over at him. 'Yeah, yeah, whatever you say, Jim, now how about a top up of my coffee. Don't want folks thinking you're some sort of chauvinist and it's the little lady that's always having to put the kettle on in this office, do we?'

'Aye, okay then. You win. Kettle on it is then. And would ma'am like a chocolate Hob Nob with that?'

'Actually, any chance you can go to the café and get us a takeaway? My shout. I need to mainline some caffeine this morning and that instant crap is not going to hit the spot at all.'

He sighed, but agreed.

SHE SAT BACK as he grabbed his jacket and left the office. What a wimp. He hasn't got the balls to say no. He'd touched a raw nerve when he picked up on her observations about Lucas and Rebecca. She would have to be more careful about what she said.

She grinned as she remembered the look of embarrassment on Jim's face a few minutes ago when she had given her period as an excuse for being late. He had been mortified. What an asshole.

She was exhausted and hoped Jim would bring her an extra shot in her coffee, she had been up late last night and was going to need all the help she could get to stay awake today. And by the stink of the stale booze from her colleague, she thought a shot of caffeine wouldn't do him any harm at all either.

Waiting for Jim to return, she stared into space. Her late night had been nothing to do with women's troubles at all. She had been busy putting the final touches of her plan into motion. That and thinking about Lucas and the future.

She thought back to the first meeting she'd had with Lucas. She flushed slightly as she remembered her first sight of him. He was a good-looking guy and she was embarrassed at the effect he'd had on her. She hadn't been expecting that at all.

They'd both been attending an Integrated Case Management meeting in HMP Lowood. The meeting had started late, as was the usual state of play with these things. They'd been waiting in reception to be called through. She'd noticed straight away that Lucas had winced as he sat down on the hard-cased chairs and she'd asked him if he was okay.

'Been in the wars there, have you?' She'd joked. She'd felt kind of bad when she saw the flush draw up over his neck and onto his face. He clearly had something to hide. She'd been intrigued.

'Aye, something like that. Getting too old for five-a-side, I guess.'

He had sat down and held his hand out towards her. 'Lucas Findlay.' He offered. 'Senior over at Space to Grow.'

She'd smiled at his formality but had taken his hand which felt cold and clammy in the warmth of hers.

'Nicole Holten, Criminal Justice Social Worker. Pleased to meet you.'

Introductions over, they'd sat in awkward silence for a moment.

'So, you're clearly not from Glasgow,' started Lucas at the very same time she'd asked: 'So, where do you play fives?' They'd both laughed.

Lucas had been the perfect gentleman, offering for her to speak first, but she'd wanted to know more about the man in front of her. She could see he was hiding something, and she was eager to uncover his secrets.

'No, you first,' she'd smiled.

Lucas clearly hadn't wanted to offer too much information about his sporting injuries, so she'd quickly filled the silence giving him her own version of her background.

'Wow, no difference from Canada to the East End of Glasgow.'

She'd laughed again. 'Yeah, you could say that, certainly not much chance of seeing a moose or a game of baseball around here, is there? Have you ever been to Canada? I know I'm biased, but it's a great place to visit, and if you like your sports then we have all sorts going on over there. And of course, we have the best coffee in the world at Tim Hortons. That alone is worth the trip.'

Lucas had looked down at his feet. 'No, I'm afraid the furthest I've travelled was a week down to Butlins in Ayr when I was a kid. I'd love to travel though.' He sighed as though he was holding the weight of the world upon his shoulders.

'You should do it.' She'd encouraged. 'There's a whole world out there waiting to be explored.'

Lucas had just smiled sadly. He seemed almost relieved when the door to the conference room opened and they were called in.

After the meeting, she'd suggested the two of them meet up for a coffee sometime, telling him that she would love to hear more about the work that his project carried out. Sensing his reluctance and not wanting to frighten him away, she'd said: 'Hey, it's cool, I'm not trying to jump your bones, you know? Just keen to do some networking in this area, that's all.'

'N-n-no, it's n-n-not that.'

She laughed kindly. 'Hey, sorry, it's okay, no biggie. But we could swap email addresses, keep up to date with case work and stuff that way?'

She had seen the relief in his face as he scribbled down his email address and handed it over to her, almost jumping back as their fingers brushed against one another. She winked at him, smiled, and walked off, leaving him open mouthed in her wake.

Nicole smiled at the memory of her boldness; she wasn't usually quite so forward with guys, but Lucas was different. Hell, yeah, he was different alright, she laughed to herself.

Jim still wasn't back, so she pulled out an old Nokia from her bag and quickly tapped in a message and sent it to the only number she had stored in the phone. A smile washed across her face as at the same time a shadow cast a dark cloud over her eyes.

35

LUCAS HAD CONSIDERED calling in sick this morning, but he knew it wasn't worth the hassle Rebecca would give him for breaking the expected routine. So, he'd come into work and immediately wished he hadn't.

The office was busier than normal, the phones were ringing off the hook and it seemed like everyone around him had turned the volume up. He'd already had three calls looking for urgent appointments, he was behind on his reports and everyone seemed to want everything yesterday. He was really struggling to hold it together.

His brain rattled as he tried to focus on his work while his head was full of Rebecca, Nicole, the letter and the files he had sent. The files were blackmail, there was no other word for it. Yet, he couldn't go to the police about it. He couldn't tell anyone without landing himself in a whole heap of trouble. He just couldn't work out who was behind it all. He found himself scrutinising his colleagues and wondered if any of them were the perpetrator.

A few years before, he had briefly spoken to Anne Cater about the difficulties of his early years. She was so easy to talk to and one day at supervision he just found himself blurting some of it out, but not everything. He couldn't tell anyone the whole truth. He trusted Anne; she was old school, and not the kind of manager to get involved in office gossip. He certainly didn't think she was the type of person who would send anonymous letters or blackmail anyone.

Looking about the office, he considered the others he worked with. Katy Moir was a quiet girl who grew up in Belfast and was unlikely to have any idea who his dad had been. Stephanie Hunter was from Milngavie and Lucas doubted that, until she'd started this job, she would have mixed in the same circles as he had. Besides, she was far too young to have heard about his father's case. Graham Smith though… He was one to watch.

Lucas had often felt that Graham didn't quite trust him and was almost waiting on him making a massive mistake. He'd often find him sniffing around his desk when he walked back into the office, always on the pretext of looking for a stapler or something. Lucas had always assumed he was jealous because of his seniority within the organisation and that he was looking for him to slip up so he could take his place. But maybe he wasn't, maybe he knew about his dad. He was old enough and had been around a while. Lucas constantly found himself looking around the team, his suspicion feeding his paranoia.

He was also feeling anxious about his appointment with his next client, Martin McCrae. He had tried to avoid this case, but the member of staff who had been due to meet him today was off sick and he was going to have to do the assessment. He glanced at his watch just as his phone rang. It was reception; Martin had arrived.

His mouth dry, Lucas took a gulp of water before going out to meet Martin. As soon as he saw him, the hairs on the back of his neck stood to attention and he felt a prickle of fear tingle his scalp. The guy looked cocky, not anxious at the thought of the assessment at all—six-foot, shaved head, full of muscle and covered in prison tattoos. Lucas knew he shouldn't judge but he couldn't help it.

Coughing to clear his throat, Lucas invited Martin through to the assessment room. He had all his paperwork in front of him and was anxious to get it completed and get this guy out the building as soon as possible. But Martin didn't seem to be in any rush, he seemed to be quite happy to chat about his time behind bars.

'You wouldn't believe the type of people you meet inside. All sorts.' He leaned his heavy bulk back in the chair, making himself comfortable. His eyes never left Lucas.

'Quite,' said Lucas, 'Now, I've got some forms for you to fill...'

'Aye, whatever, but as I was saying, there's all sorts in there, not just the usual like me—but nonces and everything. You know what I mean?'

'Yes, I suppose there are, now, these forms...'

'Nonces. Know what I'd do with those bastards?' He cracked his knuckles and Lucas winced; the sound was of bones snapping like twigs.

'I'd fucking cut them up into little pieces and feed them to the pigs. If it was up to me, that's what I'd do. But it's not up to me. I just do what I'm told, eh?'

Lucas just looked at the man in front of him. He had no idea where this was going, but he knew Martin had no intention of leaving until he had his say.

'Anyways, I found out loads of stuff in there. About lots of different people. Got some pictures too.' He winked.

Lucas paled as the man leaned over the coffee table separating them.

'See yer forms pal, you can shove them. Ahm not interested, write what you want in them. I'm just here to give you a message. Those files were not the end of it. Just the start.' He sat back.

Lucas sat still, his jaw slack.

'I-I-I think y-y-you better leave,' he stuttered.

Martin pushed back the chair and stood, towering above a pale Lucas.

'Aye, I'm going. And another thing, say hello to that missus of yours. Bitch that she is.' And with that he sauntered through the door not looking back at all.

Lucas's head dropped to the table. There was no way out now. He was trapped.

36

REBECCA HAD BEEN awake most of the night. After seeing the shadowy figure stare up at her window, she had paced around the house, checking and rechecking that the doors and windows were locked. Her nerves were shot. The glimpse of the figure last night had convinced her she hadn't been imagining that she was being followed.

She'd waited until Lucas had left for work before getting herself ready—she just couldn't face him this morning. She had already sent Emma a text telling her she wouldn't be in until just before her meeting with Jim. She had done some digging into his background and her gut instinct had been proven correct. He was the same Jim Aitken. She had considered cancelling the meeting or asking Emma to stand in for her, but she knew she might as well get it over with, their paths were bound to meet at some point. At least this way, she was prepared for it.

The landline rang just as she was about to leave. Automatically, she picked it up, then cursed herself, thinking it would be one of those nuisance telesales call. She wasn't paying too much attention, until she realised nobody had replied to her greeting. She was about to put the phone back down when a voice growled: 'Bitch, you're going to pay.'

'Who is this?'

There was no reply, just a heavy panting before the phone was slammed down. Staring at the handset, the colour drained from her face; the photograph of her and Lucas on their wedding day seemed to stare back mockingly at her. She clenched her fists and took ten deep breaths.

'I'm okay… There is nobody here… It's just kids,' she tried to convince herself. But convincing herself was getting harder by the day. Grabbing her mobile from her bag, she went to punch in the number for her therapist. She hadn't seen him in almost a year, things had been going that well. Maybe she should make an appointment soon.

No point, Rebecca, they will lock you away… They will say you are crazy… Let me take care of you… NO… LET ME… Fuck off all of you, I'm the only one looking out for her… Why do you want to look out for her? Bitch that she is… A fucking dirty bitch… Everyone knows your secret, Rebecca…

On and on they went, the voices clamouring to be heard, demanding to be the one in control. But it was Samantha's voice that came through loud and clear, and Rebecca didn't know if she was ready to let her take over.

'No!' she screamed. 'Leave me the fuck alone! All of you. Fuck off and leave me alone! I'm sorting this now, FUCK OFF!' She threw her phone down on the floor, the call to the therapist would not be happening. Rebecca couldn't risk it, she couldn't risk being hospitalised again. She had to keep strong, she had to finish what she started, only then would she be able to begin to heal herself.

Almost as though her outburst had frightened the voices, they retreated back into silence, but she knew Samantha wouldn't be silent forever. She knew it wouldn't be long until she returned for good.

Grabbing her jacket and bag, she brushed herself down and checked her face in the mirror. She was good to go. Stuffing her earphones in, her head down, she marched along the path. She never saw the man in the bushes. She didn't see him watch to make sure she had left. She never noticed him sidle up the side of the house and let himself in. Rebecca didn't see a thing.

On the bus, she thought back to how easy it had been to get Lucas to go along with whatever she had said. Rebecca hadn't wanted to stay in Glasgow when she married him, she needed to be away from the city and the schemes and the memories of her childhood. Trouble was Lucas was a Glasgow boy through and through. He was at home in the city, he had friends there, he was part of a community and she needed him away from that support network if she was going to bring him down.

She'd had her sights set on moving back to Kirkintilloch. Her time there with the Nikolics had been as close to happiness as she could remember. She liked its proximity to the city, but also its rural setting. She had worked on him, finally wearing him down. Rebecca had even found the perfect home for them; a small end cottage in a row of ten terraced houses on Waterside Road. Perfect for a family, she'd told him, ignoring the look of horror on his face at the mention of children. Rebecca had no intentions of starting a family with Lucas, or with any man. Arguments had ensued but she had finally got her way, an offer was put in and accepted and so their new life had begun.

Her neighbours were perfect too, keeping to themselves most of the time. Mary Picken, who lived next door, had turned out to be her perfect ally. In her late fifties, Mary lived alone and, with her grown up children living in Australia, she was ripe for befriending.

Mary loved nothing better than a good chinwag and was always happy to spend time with Rebecca. She also knew everyone who was anyone in the local community and quickly took Rebecca on as her new pet project. Encouraged by Samantha, Rebecca played into Mary's perception of her as a quiet young woman who lived in fear of her husband. Mary had quickly introduced Rebecca to a number of other women and took great delight in taking her along to the community events she was a part of. It really was the perfect opportunity for her to ramp up the picture of herself as an abused wife.

She would gleefully feed the other women little snippets of the life she wanted them to believe she led. 'Lucas was stressed,' explaining away the bruises on her face. 'He suffers from anxiety.' 'He can't help his temper.' It was amazing what some clever make up could do. Of course, Rebecca was well aware that in a small town like this, people loved to gossip and she knew the town gossips would gather and piece all her little asides together and come up with the picture of Lucas she wanted them to see.

This, combined with her ability to portray herself as downtrodden and submissive, helped them colour that picture in for themselves. Rebecca was a chameleon, able to blend into any situation and give exactly what her chosen audience were looking for. She adored the power that gave her. If others were happy enough to make assumptions based on the image portrayed, then she was more than happy to use it to her advantage.

Obviously, she made excuses for his behaviour.

'He's not well. He's unstable,' she'd whisper. 'It's not his fault, honestly. Underneath it all, he is so kind,' she'd plead on his behalf.

She watched their eyes glaze over with a knowing pity. She never invited Lucas along to these events and would explain his absences as a result of his painful shyness.

'His family told him he was a freak, they belittled him, and he has no self-confidence.' They would nod, understandingly, of course. Then they would converge into their little groups, their whispers and glances confirming that her plan was working. She would make her excuses to leave events early, her obvious fear of returning home late clear in her eyes. The whispers would grow louder.

'Poor, Rebecca.' She heard them say. 'That poor girl.'

The bus slowing down pulled her out of her thoughts. She yawned; she was exhausted. Trying to exist as so many different people was wearing her down. She felt torn. Something inside her hurting at the pain she was causing. These feelings confused her. Rebecca wasn't used to feeling guilt—it made her anxious. It sent her back to a place in her childhood she never wanted to go again. The nightmares were becoming worse, her episodes of self-harm more frequent. Constantly questioning herself, in a perpetual state of conflict, it would be much easier just to give in to Samantha and let her take over.

But no. Not now. Not yet. The bus had stopped. It was time to get off.

Focus, Rebecca. You need to stop being so weak or you will leave me with no choice but to step in… Samantha's voice whispered harshly. Rebecca shivered as she tried to drown it out.

37

REBECCA WATCHED THE two visitors approach from the safety of one of the centre's meeting rooms. She was both intrigued and anxious—the silent phone call this morning, her nightmares and the memory of the unwanted bouquet of flowers had left her shaken. More than that, it was beginning to leave her feeling as though she were unravelling.

She kept experiencing short black outs. They were not quite as bad as when she was younger, but she was aware of passages of time passing without her being aware of what had happened. She was terrified one of her colleagues would notice something soon. Terrified to seek professional help for fear of being hospitalised again, she had let it continue but she knew she had to end this game sooner rather than later. It was taking its toll on her. Perhaps I should just leave Lucas, she thought, after all, I've destroyed him now, he's a mess.

Coward… Stupid bitch can't even sort it out… No wonder she needs us… NO SHE ONLY NEEDS ME…

The voices were becoming relentless, Samantha always at the forefront, but the others creeping back in, arguing amongst themselves, talking about her, talking to her. Her head felt as though it were about to explode… Placing her feet firmly on the floor and breathing in deeply, she clenched her fists in a bid to calm herself.

She had to maintain control. She had to remember she was her, she was not them. She would take back control. She had to.

You can't do anything without me. You don't have the guts, Rebecca. You need me... Me... Me.

The centre was busy that day and, focusing her attention on her visitors, she watched as the man and woman pushed through the front door, clearly desperate to get out of the hard needles of the Glasgow rain. She smiled as they tried to avoid the avalanche of women in Lycra aiming for the door they'd just come through. The running club were certainly committed. Rebecca shuddered—she could imagine nothing worse than running, never mind running in weather as miserable as this.

Shaking the rain from their clothes, the new visitors looked around them. It was a real hive of activity in here and Rebecca knew they would be impressed. Most folk came along to Phoenix thinking it was some kind of needle exchange or counselling service.

Rebecca knew immediately it was Jim Aitken; they weren't expecting any other visitors today. She wondered who the woman was, she didn't recognise her.

As the noise levels dropped, she heard the woman say, 'This place is awesome. It has a real energy about it.'

Rebecca grimaced. God, she's American, she cringed. She hoped she wasn't overly gushy. Rebecca couldn't stand gushy women at all, especially gushy American women.

Rebecca slid up silently behind them. As much as she had been dreading this moment, she could also feel a small bubble of excitement rise in her stomach. She couldn't help wondering if he would remember her and if he did, how he would react. Would he be surprised at the success she had made of her life? Would he be impressed? While she didn't want him disclosing her past to anyone else, part of her craved the recognition for all she had achieved.

She took a moment to take in his appearance. He had aged, and not particularly well, but there was no mistaking that this was the same Jim Aitken who had turned up at the house that fateful day. The same Jim who had removed her from her mother's dead body. The same Jim who had finally abandoned her in that hospital, when she'd needed him most. Rebecca's insides were churning, her palms sweaty and the desire to turn and run was almost overpowering.

Breathe, she told herself. She'd spent the whole night convincing herself that he wouldn't recognise her. Her hair was a different colour, she'd grown into her once gaunt face, and only her bright blue eyes might be a giveaway. Still, Rebecca had made some extra effort with her hair and make-up that morning, trying a look that was a bit more dramatic than she usually went for. She'd been pleased by the result; the heavy eyeliner had changed the appearance of her eyes and her severe hairstyle scraped back in a facelift inducing bun had resulted in a complete transformation.

She gave a sharp cough and had to hold in a snigger when it made Jim Aitken startle. She watched him turn around and held her breath as she caught sight of him properly. The memories he triggered fought for space in her head. She dug her nails into her palms, willing them to leave. The scars on the tops of her legs were throbbing now. God, she would give anything to run to the toilet and open them up. She felt Samantha's presence offer her reassurance. *It's okay, Rebecca, I've got you.*

'Hi, we're here to see Rebecca Findlay,' he said. 'I'm Jim Aitken and this is my colleague, Nicole Holten. We have an appointment with her at two.'

Rebecca relaxed. He clearly didn't know who she was, and she hoped he didn't remember who she'd been in the past.

'I'm Rebecca,' she replied shortly, shaking his hand.

Turning to Nicole, she tried to feign interest in the woman 'Whereabouts in America are you from?'

'I'm Canadian,' she retorted. But Rebecca had already turned back to Jim and missed the flash of rage cross the other woman's face. She didn't need to see it; she knew her mistake would have irritated her. *Good.*

She smiled and indicated they follow her into the office. She'd taken time to ensure her desk and surroundings were pristine, not a paper out of place. This was her territory; this was where she was in control and she was not going to lose it here. He still hadn't shown any signs of remembering her. She felt confident that her appearance had fooled him, she had changed beyond all recognition. Rebecca was not the same girl she'd been on the day of the incident, or in the terrible years that had followed.

Smoothing down her skirt gave her chance to wipe her hands which were still clammy with sweat. She sat down, inviting them to join her. Under the table her fists clenched slowly. Ten times. Her breathing slowed down as she mentally prepared for the next hour. The mask firmly in place, she began.

SITTING ACROSS FROM Rebecca at her desk, Jim was taken aback by the woman in front of him—she had changed beyond all recognition. Gone was the straggly hair and the waif-like child, and in her place was this self-assured, confident young woman. He felt proud, then guilty, as he realised he had nothing to be proud of. Nothing at all. He had abandoned her, he had let her down, walking out on her like he had. If anything, he thought, he should feel even guiltier. He prayed she didn't recognise him.

Despite her outward appearance of composure, Jim could sense a nervousness coming from her. She clearly hadn't noticed that he'd seen her hands clench tightly as she'd sat down, or the soft sheen of sweat across her brow. Jim was pretty good at reading people and he definitely saw Rebecca was hiding something from them. That made two of them. He shivered as though someone had walked over his grave and had to give himself a small shake before starting off the meeting.

He desperately wanted to reach across the desk, take her hand and tell her who he really was, to say sorry for the way he had treated her. But he couldn't. He had to remember that his colleague, Nicole, was there with him. She'd sat quietly taking in the scene in front of her. There was an almost puzzled look on her face as though she were trying to work out what was going on.

'Thanks for seeing us at such short notice,' began Jim, his words faltering in a way that was completely out of character for him. 'I know you're a busy woman, so we won't take up too much of your time, but I think that this is a project that both services have a part to play in developing.' Jim looked towards Nicole, almost as though he were seeking approval.

With Nicole making no sign she recognised Jim's need for her support and Rebecca staring at him waiting for him to speak, he continued hesitantly.

'We're setting up a new service for domestic abuse perpetrators…' He ran a finger under his damp collar.

Rebecca nodded but said nothing, looking straight at Jim. He could feel himself wilt under her gaze and wished Nicole would step in and take the heat off him a little, but Rebecca had pretty much ignored Nicole since they'd moved through to the office. Realising his colleague was going to offer no support at all, Jim went on, 'Well, w-we thought it pertinent to come and speak to you, as one of the main service providers working with women who have been subjected to abuse.' He realised he sounded totally unsure of himself.

He wondered if Nicole would be taken aback by his change in demeanour. Jim had always tried to present himself as a bit of a cheeky chappy, always ready with a bit of banter. She'd never have seen him so nervous. She must be thinking he was losing his touch, or terrified of the woman before them. She never said a word, yet out of the corner of his eye he could see a small smirk play across her lips. He ran his fingers under his shirt collar again.

'So, how do you think we can help you?' Rebecca asked, raising one eyebrow.

'Y-y-you know that if any programme for offenders is going to work then we need to take into account the views of the victims. We need to know what the triggers were, what impact the violence had, and to hear their suggestions for changing offending behaviour. It's not the whole picture, I know, there's a whole lot of other stuff that comes into play in these programmes. The voices of the victims have to be a key driver in their delivery.' As he went on, he grew in confidence, clearly at ease talking about his work.

'And what if our clients don't want to help? You are aware that some of the women who come here have lived through some of the most traumatic abuse; many have lost their kids, their families, their homes. What makes you think they want to do something to let these animals off the hook now?'

'I hope they would see that if they can make a difference to one man's behaviour then that's one less woman at risk of abuse when he enters into a new relationship. That's got to be worth something, surely?'

Rebecca stared at him, a long cold glare as though appraising him from the inside out. 'I'll tell you what I think, shall I?' She spat. 'I think you've been told by Anne Cater that you need to involve us, and you don't have the balls to stand up for yourself to say what you really think or want.'

SITTING NEXT TO Jim, Nicole had been enjoying watching the power struggle play out. She knew Jim had been angling for her support as he floundered, but she'd been quite happy to sit back and watch him squirm. She sensed Rebecca was toying with her colleague and seemed to be relishing whatever game it was she was playing.

Despite her dislike of the woman across the desk from her, Nicole had a fleeting moment of admiration for her. Damn, she was good. Shame the two of them couldn't join forces. She imagined Rebecca's reaction if she were to find out who she really was and why she was here.

Turning her attention back to the meeting, Nicole smirked as she watched Jim's face flush. She knew that Rebecca had a point. Jim hadn't really wanted to join forces with Phoenix. Anne had probably pushed him into it and Rebecca was smart enough to realise that. And if Rebecca knew it, then she'd bet her last dollar that most of the women who used this centre would pick up on it too. These women weren't stupid. They might have put up with some shit in their lives but they'd also worked hard to pull themselves up and if she knew the type of women they were, they wouldn't be too happy about letting some social worker use them to make a name for himself while playing the hero. Jim had no clue how to sell this project at all.

Watching Rebecca, Nicole almost felt guilty for hooking up with Lucas, but not quite. Again, she wondered if she should have perhaps joined forces with Rebecca instead. But then she remembered everything that had happened, and the guilt left her along with any ideas of forming an alliance with that woman.

Nicole noticed Rebecca's foot tapping underneath her desk—a nervous tap, rather than an impatient one. 'Oh, you're not quite as in control as you like to think you are lady, are you?' she thought.

She decided it was time for her to jump in and rescue Jim who looked as though he were about to burst into tears.

'Rebecca, you have a point about the women who use your service and we certainly didn't come here intending to play lip service to their involvement in the setting up of this new project.'

Out of the corner of her eye she could see a look of relief spread over Jim's face. She carried on, 'We recognise that Phoenix is the local leader in services for these women, and as such we are really keen to take that expertise and help it shape the service we're trying to deliver. Without your involvement, there's no way this service is going to get up and running successfully.'

She sensed that she had Rebecca's attention now. Playing to her ego, Nicole continued, 'You're right in saying we've been told by those up above to work alongside you, but please don't think that's the only reason we've come. Without your buy-in, we aren't going to be able to get the women to open up and engage with us; and without them engaging, we aren't going to be able to design and deliver a programme that's going to make any real difference. I guess what I'm saying is that you're right, we have no choice but to work with you, but Jim and I are totally committed to making this programme a success. We are not just doing this because we've been told to. We've been working on this for a long time—before anyone up there decided it was worthy of funding. We're committed to getting it off the ground, but only if we can do it properly—only if it's meaningful and is going to make a difference. We want to work with the perpetrators to challenge the offending behaviour, and we want to work with the women to help us understand exactly what the impact of that behaviour is. We can't do it without them, and without your support, it's not going to get off the ground.'

She sat back with a sigh and carefully watched for Rebecca's reaction.

REBECCA LOOKED AT Nicole, her attention now fully focused on the Canadian. There was something intriguing about her. Something that made her sit up and listen. She was also impressed by her boldness and her ability to take charge in a situation that old Jim had clearly lost all control over. If she were to admit it, Rebecca found herself slightly in awe.

She realised she'd been wrong to dismiss her as unworthy of her attention. She was someone she would need to watch, someone who may be able to see underneath her skin. Rebecca gave a little shiver, not quite sure if it was admiration or fear that she felt.

Smiling, Rebecca leaned forward. 'OK, Nicole, you've impressed me there. Let's talk some more.' She looked over at Jim who was now just sitting slack jawed as he watched the strange dance of power play out before him.

'Jim, do you want a coffee or something? You're looking a bit overwhelmed.' Rebecca laughed as the colour came back to his cheeks and he nodded.

Rebecca rang through and asked Emma to sort them out some coffees as she turned her attention to the project in hand.

Oblivious to Jim, the two women discussed the practicalities of setting up some sessions for the clients of Phoenix to take part in.

JIM SAT BACK and watched them, fascinated. He had just witnessed a different side to Nicole. She'd taken control of a situation that he had quickly found himself floundering in. He felt unsettled, this was not how he usually reacted. He was usually on the ball, able to build up a rapport with most people and get them on side right away.

Yet with Rebecca, his confidence had deserted him as his guilty conscience had come to the fore. He wished he had the guts to apologise for abandoning her, for letting her down when she needed him. He thought about trying to get her on her own, to explain things to her properly. But she hadn't shown any signs of recognising him and why would she? She had just been a kid back then.

God, I need a drink, he thought. His hands trembled, and to hide the shaking he put them in his pockets, feeling for the lucky charm he always carried around with him. He rubbed it between his fingers as he watched Rebecca and Nicole. A strange feeling of unease and a very real sense that something was about to go terribly wrong washed over him. Whatever it was, he felt powerless to stop it.

Finally, the meeting was over. Nicole had smoothed the waters between Jim and Rebecca and left the two of them chatting. She had made her excuses to leave. Once outside the project and safely away from prying eyes, Nicole took out her mobile, she punched in a number and held it to her ear.

'Come on, hurry up, you asshole.'

On what seemed like the hundredth ring, the phone was picked up.

'It's me, where the hell were you? What took you so long to answer?'

'Fuck off, lady. You don't own me.'

'Oh, you think not? You better believe I own you, I control what happens in your miserable little life now, so don't you forget it, or you know exactly what will happen.'

'All right, fer fuck sake, keep yer hair on.'

'Well, did you sort it this morning?'

'Yep, easy as pie, in and out.'

'And are you sure nobody saw you?'

'Yip.'

'And the rest of it? You did go to that appointment, didn't you?'

'Yes, for Christ's sake, I went to the appointment. So you can get off my case now.'

'I decide when I'm on your case, don't you forget it. It's me who holds all the cards here, alright?'

She heard a grunt in response.

'Okay, well I'll have another job for you soon, so next time answer the phone faster, asshole.'

'Aye, whitever.' And the phone was hung up.

Nicole ignored the rage building inside her. That little shit would pay for that later. Right now, she had other stuff to take care of. Taking out her work mobile, she typed in an email, 'Hey Lucas…'

38

STILL TENSE FOLLOWING his meeting with Martin, Lucas tried to settle down and check through his emails. His face went scarlet as he noticed Nicole's name pop up in his senders list. He glanced around the office to make sure that nobody had noticed his blush and that no one could see his screen. He smiled as he read the message.

'Hey, Lucas, it was great to meet up with you again. I'm really enjoying our time together. I hope you don't mind me saying, but I feel a real connection between us. It's been difficult to make friends up here; your company means so much to me. Hope to catch up soon. N x.'

His thoughts flipped back to their last encounter just a few days ago. He enjoyed his time with her and although they hadn't slept together, he didn't feel any need to rush things just yet. Just being with her was enough for him, but he didn't know how long he could hold off from showing his true feelings. He knew she was the woman he wanted to spend the rest of his life with. She could be the woman to change him.

Lucas and Rebecca's sex life had dwindled away to nothing, not that it had been that spectacular to begin with, he thought. She had always been lukewarm towards him in the bedroom department. He knew she'd pretended to be asleep on more than one occasion to avoid his advances. If he was to be completely honest with himself, the lack of any sex life hadn't bothered him—sex hadn't been high on his agenda for a long time.

Despite his reputation for being a bit of a ladies' man, it was mostly all show, a front to hide his true leanings. A front to hide the real Lucas Findlay, his father's son. But Nicole had changed all that. For the first time in as long as he could remember, Lucas wanted to be with a woman in a way he had seldom felt before.

Lucas and Nicole had been very careful to keep their developing relationship hidden and indeed, to the casual observer, they would only ever appear to be two people who knew each other professionally. But Lucas knew they had something more, something much deeper than just a professional relationship.

He felt a small shiver; she'd signed off with a kiss. Maybe she wants the same as me, he thought. But then maybe she was just being friendly. She probably signed all her emails off with a kiss, it was probably a Canadian thing. But he still felt a warm glow as his fingers hovered over his keyboard considering his response. Lucas remembered that Rebecca had said she was going to be working late that night; he had been due to play football with some of the guys but that wasn't until six-thirty. He could... Hell, he was going to go for it. His fingers punched out the words before he lost his nerve.

'Hi, Nicole, was lovely to catch-up with you too. I'd love a coffee. I don't suppose you're free at about five this evening? We could meet up in the café on Tollcross Road, at the entrance to the park? Let me know what you think. L.'

He pressed send before he changed his mind. He agonised over putting a kiss but refrained in case she thought he was a weirdo. After all, her kiss may have just been a girl thing that she did with everyone. He laughed at that thought, thinking of

Rebecca. She certainly wouldn't be signing emails off with kisses, no matter who she sent them to.

He felt his private mobile vibrate in his trouser pocket. He pulled it out slowly, frightened to look. But he couldn't ignore it. He daren't, not after Martin's visit.

"So, you received your message? Glad to know you are still on board. Speak soon, mate.'

The phone fell through his fingers, there was no point in replying. He already knew he was trapped. He would have no choice but to go through with whatever they wanted him to do. God, he hoped he wasn't going to have to be the one filming again.

His panicked thoughts were interrupted by a ping alerting him to an incoming email. Glancing down he saw the sender was Nicole.

That was quick, he thought. She must be keen. Or maybe she'd changed her mind, thinking that he was too desperate after replying so quickly. Hands trembling, he opened up the mail and saw her response was positive.

'Sounds perfect, I can't wait. Mine's a skinny latte if you're there before me xx.'

Two kisses this time. His heart gave a small jump as the phone on his desk rang.

'Hi, Lucas speaking.' He smiled as thoughts of the evening's meeting settled at the front of his mind.

'Hi, Lucas, it's Jim Aitken here. I just wanted to pick your brain, if that's okay?'

39

SO, LUCAS, YOU didn't really think I was going to let you off with this too, did you? You deserve this as much as your darling wife. If not more.

You got my little message today then? Bet you're all in a panic now, eh? Wondering what you are going to have to do next?

You can't tell anyone though, can you? You might not know who I am, but you do know I've got pictures, lots of them. Folk are really helpful, you know? Always happy to give me what I'm looking for.

Anyway, must dash, I've lots to do. Time is running out now. For both of you. It's been a blast. Really, it has.

40

SEEING JIM AITKEN again had really thrown Rebecca. She was sure he hadn't recognised her, but just seeing him had sent her back to a place and time that she didn't know quite how to deal with. She had managed to hold it together throughout their meeting... Just. And she had Samantha to thank for that. She'd had to give in to her just to get her through the meeting. But back in the office now, she was in turmoil. She could feel the control slipping through her fingers and there was nothing she could do to prevent it.

She sat for a while, trying to ground herself and calm the chattering in her head. It wasn't just Samantha, they were all there, telling her what to do, what to think. Digging her nails into the palms of her hands, she breathed in deeply, but it was no use. She could feel herself floating out of her body, losing it. She had to move, she had to get out of here.

Forcing herself to stand, she took a deep breath and, deliberately placing one foot in front of the other, made her way through the office, convinced all eyes were on her. But nobody said a word—heads down, they all appeared to be getting on with their work.

Emma sat with her back to the room, engrossed in paperwork. Rebecca felt an irrational flash of anger as she stared at her colleague's back. She was so calm and in control. She was everything that Rebecca wanted to be. She would bet Emma didn't spend every day and night battling her demons. Yet at the same time, she also felt a stir of compassion for her.

Rebecca thought back to the way she had treated her colleague at times—cruel and overly harsh, using her for her own means without giving any thought to how that might affect her. She felt something strange, something that she wasn't used to feeling. It was creeping up inside of her, threatening to pull away at her façade. Guilt. She started to shake, her hands trembling and her mouth dry. Tears formed in her steely blue eyes as she struggled to compose herself. She couldn't let this happen. Please, she thought, not here. Not now.

As though she could sense Rebecca staring at her, Emma turned around. Her mouth formed a perfect O of surprise as she looked at her. Pushing herself roughly out of the chair, she jumped up, rushing over to Rebecca.

'Are you okay, love?' She asked, placing her hand gently on Rebecca's arm. 'You don't look yourself at all.'

Rebecca just stared at her blankly, speechless, unable to stop the tears falling down her face. Inside, she was crumbling, horrified at what was happening to her. Terrified she would be revealed.

Emma gently led her back into the small office where she'd just met with Jim and Nicole. She sat her down on the seat and crouched down beside her.

'Shh,' she murmured, gently. 'Just take some deep breaths.' She breathed deeply herself, urging Rebecca with her eyes to mimic her.

Slowly Rebecca's breathing began to return to normal, the trembling subsided, and she slumped back in her seat, drained. Emma looked worried.

'God, you gave me such a fright.' She pulled out a bottle of water from the drawer at the desk, opened it, and handed it to Rebecca.

Grateful, Rebecca slowly sipped, allowing her heart rate to return to its natural rhythm. She didn't know what to say to Emma, she didn't know how to explain what had just happened. She said nothing.

Emma knelt before her, murmuring reassurances like a parent comforting a distraught child. She simply sat and held her hand. She let Rebecca compose herself before asking, 'Is everything okay at home, Rebecca? Is everything alright between you and Lucas?'

Rebecca recognised an opportunity to rationalise her behaviour to her colleague. Her head bowed; she shook her head slowly.

'Not really,' she whispered softly, so Emma had to come a little closer to hear her. 'We've had a bad few weeks. Work has been really stressful for Lucas and I think he's blaming me for not falling pregnant.'

She looked out of her hooded eyes to see Emma's mouth drop open in shock.

'I never realised you guys were trying for a family.'

Rebecca just nodded.

'But, even if he is stressed about work or about a baby, you know it's not right that he should do anything to hurt you, love, don't you?'

Rebecca could see her surreptitiously checking all exposed areas of skin for any signs of bruising or violence. There were none. Rebecca wasn't stupid enough to allow any visible signs of what went on at home to show. That would have risked too much interference from others. Implied abuse was much stronger in her eyes. It gave a certain quality of authenticity too as it was a well-known fact that domestic abuse was not always about physical violence and there was a growing recognition of just how severe the impact of psychological abuse could be.

She lowered her head allowing the tears to fall freely. She could feel herself returning to normal, her strength coming back and her breathing settling again. It suited her perfectly for Emma to believe that Lucas was behind this irrational behaviour. She allowed Emma to comfort her, relaxing as she realised that her colleague had bought her story hook, line and sinker.

'Thanks, Emma. Look, don't think badly of Lucas. It's just been a tough couple of weeks. We've had a few arguments, but nothing to worry about really. Honestly, I'll be fine. I'm probably just a bit hormonal.'

Emma didn't look too convinced, but Rebecca knew she wouldn't push her. They'd all been through the same counselling course and had been well taught to allow women to open up in their own time. Really, her job was such a bonus. Development opportunities weren't just for work, she thought wryly.

'Well, if you're sure. But you know where I am if you need to talk, don't you?'

Rebecca nodded. 'Thanks, Emma, I really appreciate it. Listen, I'm going to nip home and freshen up a little. I'll be back in time for the group tonight, though.'

'You don't need to come back, I can manage. Why don't you go home and chill out for the night?'

'Nah, it's okay, I need to get some paperwork done anyway and sometimes getting out of the house is all the relaxation I need.' She smiled weakly, hoping that Emma would just take the hint and leave it.

'Okay,' said Emma. 'But just go and take your time.'

She gave Rebecca a hug. Rebecca hoped she hadn't noticed her stiffen as they made contact. She hated this compulsion people had of hugging and pawing at everyone. There was just no need.

She grabbed her bag and left. She had no intention of going home to freshen up, she was going home to pack her bags while Lucas was at work. She had made her decision; she couldn't do this anymore—it was destroying her. She was leaving him. She had to get away from here, while she still could.

REBECCA OPENED THE front door, calling out just in case Lucas had come home. She knew it was unlikely as his car wasn't outside, but her paranoia was getting the better of her now. The house responded with silence. There was nobody there. She closed the door behind her and sunk to the floor. The tears flowed freely as her body trembled. She was unravelling.

Then something caught her eye. The photograph of her and Lucas on their wedding day had been placed face down. She knew it wasn't her doing and the frame was too heavy and sturdy to topple over by itself. Someone had been in here. *They're watching you, Rebecca... Watching and waiting... Let me protect you... ME... No, me... ME, ME, ME...*

'Shut the fuck up... all of you!' Her hands rained slaps to the side of her head in an attempt to close down the voices. But they wouldn't let up. Her heart was about to burst out of her chest, her hands clammy, as the voices became louder and louder. It was unbearable.

Forcing herself to her feet, she stumbled into the living room. There, in the middle of the table, lay a photograph. It was yellowing and curled at the corners. She knew it wasn't one of hers or Lucas's. Cautiously, she picked it up. She turned it over and retched. Staring back at her was herself as a child, in her bedroom, with a man standing with his back to the photographer. In the picture, she was screaming.

Backing out of the living room as if expecting to see the man return her stare, she stumbled upstairs. She burst into her bedroom and began pulling her things from the wardrobe. Piles of shoes and bags were pulled out in a frenzy, she didn't care about the mess she was making. Right at the back where she'd hidden it was the memory box—the only thing she had left from her childhood.

Collapsing in a heap on top of her discarded clothes and shoes, she clutched it in her hands. By now, she was almost hysterical. She snapped open the lid and her past flew out to greet her. Her eyes filled with tears as the flashbacks came fast and furious, poking and prodding at her brain, reminding her of times gone by. Events, people, and places rushed by as she watched the years of her life play out before her like some bizarre and twisted horror movie. A small bunch of photos lay on top, happier memories mocking her along with the voices, growing louder and louder.

Next to the photos was the letter, crumpled and yellowing with age. She smoothed over the paper, drinking in the words as she played with the necklace in her hand. The cheap chain had turned green with age but the half heart still shone and the inscription was clear: 'Side by side or miles apart'... She'd googled the image a few years ago and worked out that the other half of the necklace said: 'We are always connected at the heart'. She had no idea where the other half was, only that whoever had it was her father. *Your daddy didn't want you, Rebecca... Nobody wanted Rebecca... Not even her mummy. Only the bad men wanted Rebecca... Dirty little Rebecca...Nobody loves you.*

Her others were frantic now. She grabbed the side of the bed, trying to slow her breathing. Her eyes darted around the room, willing her to fix on something real, something solid to cling onto, anything to ground herself. But it was useless, she felt as though she was floating under water. Everything was blurry, unfocused, the voices in her head muffled but all demanding to be heard. She couldn't stop it. She couldn't stop them. She lay down on the floor and let it wash over her.

She didn't know how long she'd lain there but she was dragged back to the present by the sound of the phone ringing downstairs. Leaving the box on the bed, she ran down to answer. When she picked it up and heard the caller speak, she wished she'd not come home at all.

'Bitch, I know who you are. I'm watching you now. Step outside and see,' the distorted voice rasped. Rebecca dropped the receiver and she ran, slamming the door behind her. She ran as though she were being pursued by the devil himself. And perhaps she was.

41

'SOUNDS INTRIGUING.' Lucas laughed, glad of the distraction. 'But I don't know how useful my brain is for picking these days, Jim.'

'Oh, it's nothing too taxing. I'm just trying to set up a footy team for some of the lads here. You know the score, something to keep them out of mischief. The thing is, I'm doing it off my own back, no funding for any extras. So I'm on the scrounge. I was talking to your wife earlier and she was saying you were a keen footballer and ran a few five-a-side groups. I don't suppose you've any spare kit I can borrow, do you?'

'Thank God, an easy question,' Lucas said, trying to ignore the mention of his wife. He wondered why she had been meeting Jim, she hadn't told him anything about it.

'Actually, I do have some kit. It's back at the house though. I've not ran any groups for a while now and we have nowhere to store anything here, so I took it back for safekeeping. I could bring it in for you tomorrow if you want?'

'Well, you'd be doing me a huge favour if I could swing by and get it today? I've got a group of lads coming in tomorrow. I thought since it was the weekend and the forecast is good, I'd take them down to the park for a quick game. I know none of them are likely to have any kit of their own. Nicole was supposed to be coming in to do some group therapy with them but she's buggered off home unwell.'

Lucas hesitated as a plan began to form in his mind. If Nicole wasn't in the office, he could drop her an email and try to catch-up with her earlier than they had arranged. He hoped she wasn't too sick to meet up with him. Rebecca had already told him not to expect her home early, so he had time to nip to the house and grab a shower first. He had no other appointments for the afternoon and the rest of the team would never notice he had gone. Plus, he had some time owing to him. 'Okay, I tell you what, do you want to drop by in about an hour?'

'Brilliant,' said Jim. 'I'm going out on a visit round about then, so I could swing by on my way if it's on the road there.'

Lucas gave him the address.

'Perfect,' Jim replied. 'My next client is out at HMP Lowood in Bishopbriggs, so it's not that far away from you. Catch you soon. You're a star, son.'

Replacing the receiver, Lucas felt a little frisson of excitement bubbling up inside. The thought of seeing Nicole was chasing away his anxiety after this morning's meeting. She's definitely good for me, he thought.

Whistling, he picked up his jacket and keys, gave a cursory explanation to his colleagues and made his way out of the office with a spring in his step that he hadn't felt for a long time.

Pulling up at the house, Lucas was surprised to see the front door slightly ajar. A feeling of panic settled in his chest as he slowly pushed it open, shouting tentatively, 'Hello, Rebecca? Are you there?'

There was no reply and the house was blanketed in silence. Lucas slowly made his way through the downstairs room, relieved to see no sign of Rebecca or indeed any disturbance. He stopped to right their wedding photo which had fallen over. It wouldn't do to give her an excuse to start on him tonight. He made his way up the stairs, grabbing the umbrella lying at the bottom of the stairs.

Not that it'll protect me.

Glancing in the rooms, he noticed the mess of the bedroom. It looked like a bomb had hit it. What the hell had gone on here? Walking over to have a look, his thoughts were interrupted as he heard Jim Aitken's voice making its way up the stairs.

'Hello, anyone in?'

Heading back to the top of the stairs, Lucas put the umbrella down, feeling a bit embarrassed at his reaction. She probably didn't close the door over properly this morning, he thought as he padded down the stairs to invite Jim in.

He watched as his visitor looked around the house, whistling his appreciation. Lucas took in what the man in front of him would see. A home that wouldn't look out of place in one of those fancy magazines. He had to give it to Rebecca, she had a great eye for detail and knew exactly how she wanted everything to look. Memories of the consequences of things being out of place flashed through Lucas's mind, the pain still fresh.

He laughed. 'The missus. You know what women are like once they've got an idea in their heads, eh?'

Jim winked conspiratorially. 'Aye, true, son, but mind you, it's not a problem I've got these days. Just me and the dog. Less hassle, you know? So, am guessing there's no wee Findlays running about the gaff yet, given there's not a thing out of place in here?'

Lucas shook his head, his eyes betraying the lightness of the words that left his mouth.

'Nah, not yet. We're having fun trying though.' He winked, hiding the nausea he felt at the very thought of it. 'What about you? Any kids, grandkids?'

'Aye, enjoy the making of them, son, because it's all hard work after that. Or so my mates tell me. Nah, no kids here. The missus wasn't the maternal type, or that's what she said before she ran off with the man down the road and next I hear, she's shooting out her own football team.'

Lucas tried not to stare at Jim. He could see the man was clearly upset about his wife leaving him despite his attempts at humour. Also, he felt slightly uncomfortable with the conversation turning a bit too personal for his liking and was glad when Jim steered it back onto neutral territory.

'So, the kit, son? Is it about? And any chance of a cuppa before I head off? I'm gasping. Ran out of milk in the office, as usual.'

Lucas nodded. 'Aye, no bother.'

He liked Jim, something made him warm to the man. He guessed he must be about the same age as his father would have been, and he found himself wishing, not for the first time, that he'd had a proper dad. Someone to confide in, someone to chew the fat with. Instead, all Lucas was left with were the bitter memories of a childhood from hell.

The two men sat chatting companionably until Jim looked at his watch.

'Jesus, is that the time, son? I'm going to be bloody late again and us social workers have a bad enough reputation for being late as it is. Can I use your loo before I go? At my age, I don't think I'll make the journey to the prison.'

Lucas showed him where the toilet was before going back to clean up the cups. He couldn't risk Rebecca realising he had been home in the afternoon. Ensuring the cups were in the right cupboard with the handles facing the right way, he gave the worktops a quick wiping down before firing off an email to Nicole. Like all statutory workers, her emails went to her phone and a buzz of pleasure ran through him when she responded almost immediately.

'Cool, would love to meet up earlier. I'll be at home this afternoon. I wasn't feeling too great, so I came home. So just come round and we can have a coffee here if you want. xx.'

She gave him the address and asked if he could be there in the next hour. Lucas sent back an immediate yes, knowing he wouldn't have time to shower and clean up after himself. He would just have to go as he was. He shouted up to Jim that he was just going to get the kit out of the garage, and that he'd see him at the car.

Jim came outside a few minutes later, looking chalk white.

'You seen a ghost mate?' Lucas laughed.

Jim just stared at him, shaking his head. 'No, son, just came over a bit dizzy there. Think I'm forgetting my age at times. Thanks for this,' he said, grabbing the kit and throwing it into the back of his car. Waving to Lucas, he promised to return the kit and catch-up with him soon.

AS SOON AS he had driven out of sight, Jim pulled over and lay back in his seat. His breathing shallow and tight as he struggled to come to terms with what he had just seen. The bedroom door had been open, he'd only popped his head in for a quick nosey. His ex-missus had been right that he was like an old sweetie wife at times. This time he wished he hadn't looked at all.

It was the glint of the chain that had caught his eye. He had gone closer to see what it was and had almost collapsed when he saw what he was looking at. Sitting in the car, he put his hand in his pocket and pulled out his own pendant. He had just found the other half of the pendant. Reaching back into his pocket, he pulled out the crumpled-up photograph that had been lying next to the pendant, and opening it up, he looked at it again. He closed his eyes and wept.

It was a sign, it had to be a sign. She was looking for him. It was time he came clean, it was time he made it up to her. It was time he finally became the father he should have been all those years ago.

42

LUCAS SHOOK HIS head as he watched Jim drive away. Something had clearly spooked the man. But he didn't have time to think about it now. He was eager to get to Nicole's. He felt a real connection with her and, for the first time in years, he could see some light at the end of the tunnel. Perhaps Nicole would give him the strength he needed to face up to Rebecca. Maybe if he told her the truth about what life with Rebecca was really like, she would believe him. After all, she must have seen all sorts in her time in probation. Surely, she would be a little more open-minded? He hoped so.

Nicole would understand. His imagination began to run away with him—he was fantasising all sorts now: Nicole helping him access supports... Reporting Rebecca to the police... Pressing charges... Divorcing her... Setting up home with Nicole... Starting a family. He laughed to himself.

For God's sake, Lucas, you're only invited around for a coffee, it's not a marriage proposal!

Giving himself the once over in the rear-view mirror, he switched on Pharrell Williams' *Happy* and reversed out of the drive, the smile wide across his face.

Pulling up at the flat on Duke Street, in the heart of Glasgow's East End, a sudden feeling of anxiety gripped his stomach. He popped a mint in his mouth and quickly crunched on it. This was a bit close to home, just minutes from where they both worked. What if Rebecca saw his car?

He shook away the doubts; he knew that Rebecca didn't have much cause to leave the office. Besides, she had told him that she was working late with one of her groups tonight. None of the other staff knew his car since she would never let him take her to work. If by any chance anyone was to see him, he could always say he was doing a home visit. None of his colleagues knew that Nicole lived here… He hoped.

He was caught unaware as Nicole opened the door before he'd even had the chance to knock. It was almost as though she'd been watching for him.

NICOLE STOOD AT her window, she'd been watching for Lucas, and smiled to herself as she saw him fix his hair and smooth down his clothes as he got out of the car. She even caught him popping a mint into his mouth.

Opening the door just as he raised his hand to knock, they both laughed.

'Hey, did you hear me click on the kettle?' she joked.

'Yeah, that's me, I can hear a cup of tea brewing from a hundred paces.'

'You Scottish guys and your tea… What is it they call you? Tea Jennies? Give me a freshly brewed coffee any day.'

'I'll remember that when it's my turn to put the kettle on.' He winked, feeling unusually bold in his approach. Gone was the tongue-tied nervousness he had experienced around women ever since he'd got involved with Rebecca.

Nicole was so easy to talk to. He followed her down the brightly decorated hall into the living room. Lucas nodded his approval as he took in his surroundings. The high ceilings were set off with pale lemon and grey striped wallpaper, a grey sofa, and cream chaise longue making the space feel welcoming. Little knick-knacks placed discreetly around created a warm, extremely well-thought-out and fashionable room. It looked perfect, but not in a cold clinical way like his own home, where Rebecca's strict regime set out exactly how each room should look at all times of the day. This room looked lived in, homely and, most of all, welcoming.

'Wow, a woman of many talents. You never said you were into interior design too.'

He watched her face light up with pleasure. 'Oh, I try, you know? Nothing like having a nice place to come home and relax in after some of the cases we deal with. It's important to me. Hey, it's not too sterile though, do you think?'

'No, not at all...' Shaking his head as he looked around 'It's perfect.'

'Phew, thank goodness! The last thing I want is for my house not to look like a home. Come on, sit down and relax, I'll fix you that tea.'

She watched him from the kitchen as he looked around. She knew that she'd got it just right when she'd picked this flat. She couldn't give a monkey's about interior design and, as far as she was concerned, this stuff sucked. She would have much preferred deep, luxurious purples and reds, dark colours to match her dark moods. But when she'd viewed the flat, she had known right away that it would appeal to Lucas.

After all, she'd seen inside his house. She knew the exacting standards Rebecca insisted on and she wanted something similar to make him feel comfortable, but with the little touches to make it look like a home and not just a copy of the latest celebrity home and garden magazine. By the look on his face, she'd got it just right.

Nicole came back in with a tray, tea, milk and sugar and what looked suspiciously like home-made scones.

'I didn't know what you took in your tea, so I just brought it all through for you to sort yourself,' she offered.

'Did you bake these yourself?' Lucas asked as he picked up a scone, still warm to the touch.

'Yeah, but don't be telling everyone. I don't want to be ruining my reputation as a ball-breaking social worker, right?' She laughed. And inside, she really was laughing.

God, he was lapping this all up. A tray, a jug of milk and stick some shop bought scones in the oven and this guy was hers for the taking.

She sat down and tucked her legs underneath her, then watched him try not to drop any crumbs.

'It's okay, no standing on ceremony here, Lucas. I *have* got a vacuum cleaner, you know. I'll get any crumbs later. Just relax. So, what will we talk about?'

'Tell me a bit more about yourself, your family in Canada. I'd love to get to know you a bit more.'

'Jeez, you don't want to hear all that boring stuff, do you?' She moved closer to him, her perfume wafting under his nose. 'I'd love to hear more about you.' She almost purred as she ensured her thigh rested gently against his. She sensed his body tense up as she drew closer. She pulled back a little, gazing at him, her eyes curious.

'Hey, I'm sorry, Lucas.' Moving closer again, she laid a hand over his thigh. 'It's just... Oh, I don't know... There's something about you that makes me feel relaxed. I feel I can be myself with you. Do you know what I mean?'

She didn't wait for a reply as she brought her face closer to his, gently touching her lips to his. She was glad she could taste the mint as it quashed the nausea she felt.

This time, she didn't feel him tense as she used her tongue to part his lips and began kissing him... Gently at first, before moving in for the kill. It was then that he jerked back, pulling abruptly away from her.

Shit, she thought, maybe I've gone too far.

LUCAS STARED AT her, unsure about what to make of her. He was attracted to her, that was not in question, but he hadn't expected her to make a move so fast.

'Wow, I wasn't expecting that. Not that I didn't like it. I mean, I do find you attractive, but you know I'm married, right?' His words tumbled out.

'Yeah, I know. You said. But I also know that despite not knowing you long, you're definitely not in the *happily* married camp, that's for sure. In fact, I'd go as far as to say that you're more like your wife's personal punchbag the way she treats you.'

Lucas looked down, ashamed of the truth. He clearly hadn't hidden things as well as he'd thought.

'You're right. I'm not happily married. I don't even know how you would describe our relationship.' The tears formed in his eyes as he faced Nicole straight on, fearing the contempt he would find in her face. But it wasn't contempt he found, it was compassion.

Taking a deep breath, he continued, 'I'm in such a mess, Nicole. I don't know what to do. I'm terrified. Where is this all going to end. Her behaviour is getting worse and the violence is escalating to the point that I'm in fear for my life.' He let the tears go now, struggling to keep them silent.

Gently taking his hand, she moved closer, this time with no sexual overtones but only those of comfort.

'Lucas, look at me. You know that none of this is your fault. You know what she's doing is wrong. She's abusing you.'

There, the words were out, in the open, hanging like a flashing beacon in front of him.

Abuse.

He knew that *was* what it was. He hadn't wanted to admit it. Didn't want to say it out loud in fear of making it even more real than it already was. But Nicole had released the word, she'd brought it out into the open. It was going to be all right. She believed him, she hadn't laughed or turned away in disgust.

He moved closer to her, his head falling onto her shoulder, his tears soaking through her T-shirt. He felt himself calming as she stroked his hair, whispering words of reassurance, holding him, just being there. He held onto her like a drowning man holding on to a lifebelt.

'Sshh,' Nicole whispered softly, holding him just a little bit tighter.

43

JIM WIPED THE tears from his eyes as the full reality of the situation hit him. His suspicions had been true. The different surname had thrown him at first but when he'd seen photographs of her speaking at events, he'd recognised her immediately, despite the efforts she had made to change her appearance.

It had taken all his resolve not to dive straight in, pick up the phone and admit who he was, to apologise for abandoning her, not only as her social worker but when she was a baby too. Instead Jim had played the long game, wanting to see her first, without any relationship complications getting in the way.

Rebecca really *was* his daughter—the pendant had confirmed that. He had always suspected it but had never been able to bring himself to admit it. Yet, that wasn't what had broken him.

It was that photograph—his little girl terrified—while that monster stood over her. That bastard. Jim wished Duncan Campbell wasn't dead because right this moment, he wanted to go and strangle the life out of him, himself. But there was another person standing in the corner, almost out the frame but not quite. Jim held the photograph up and squinted. He knew that face, he knew exactly who it was: the man he had just left. Lucas. That bastard.

He called the office and told them he had taken unwell and to cancel all his appointments for the next few days. He needed some time. Time to speak to Rebecca, to make her see he was sorry for leaving her, to make her see he was ready to be her father. He had to tell her the truth about the man she was married to. He could finally help her. She would understand, he told himself over and over again.

Bowing his head, his shoulders trembled, and the tears flowed. He felt such deep shame. He'd barely given her a thought all of these years, he'd abandoned her, and not just once. He'd abandoned her twice and the second time was worse because, deep down, he had already known who she was, but he had been too embarrassed to admit it.

'You selfish bastard!' he shouted at himself. He knew it had all been down to his fear that his career would be destroyed along with nervousness about her condition. He couldn't cope with it, with her, and so he had walked away and never looked back.

He remembered reading Dr Sullivan's case notes and Rebecca's detailed account of her other selves. They'd discussed it as a team with her psychiatrist, suggesting that Rebecca was most likely adopting her alternative personalities to cope with the trauma she'd endured.

Long buried feelings of guilt from his past flooded him. He had spent his whole life suppressing them and in some ways, trying to make up for what he had done through his work. He had abandoned her as a baby and had fooled himself that he was helping her as a child. But when she'd been detained in hospital, he had chosen to up sticks and relocate to another department just so he didn't need to see her anymore.

He knew his actions had been questionable, to say the least. He should have fought harder for her from the beginning, but instead, he had taken the easy way out. He had left nothing of himself behind apart from a hastily scribbled note, and one of those pendants where one person had one half of the heart and gave the other part to someone significant in their life.

He remembered thinking it had been a cheesy thing to do back then, but felt he had to do something. At least her mother had passed it on if nothing else. That must have counted for something. She must have recognised something father-like in him. He wished things could have worked out so differently, he wished she had grown up knowing him as her father.

That day when they found her lying next to the lifeless body of her mother, he could have stepped up to the plate and admitted who he was, who she was. She could have had a chance then; she could have been a part of a real family. She wouldn't have had to endure the horror that was the care system back then.

But he hadn't.

Instead, he had stood back, remaining silent, covering his own back, his own career. He knew he had a chance of making it and didn't want the dirty reminder of his past to spoil that. He didn't want to be associated with the terrible life that was evident before them. No, Jim Aitken had kept quiet and gone home every night to his own home, his own wife, and his own life.

Rebecca could have been a part of this life; he and his wife may have still been together with a child to unite them. But no, Jim knew he had been nothing but selfish, and his actions had led to the mess he found himself in now. And the mess Rebecca's life had become.

He had to put it right. He had no choice. This was all his fault. He could have stopped this.

What sort of father was he?

44

REBECCA RAN UNTIL she couldn't breathe. Leaning forward, she clutched her sides, not caring about passers-by staring at her. The caller's words rang through her head as she drew breath deep into her lungs.

'They know who I am... How can they know? I am Rebecca... I am Rebecca. I'm in control. They don't know.'

She repeated it over and over like a mantra, trying to slow her heart rate. Trying to retain control. Trying to keep herself to the fore. She looked around her and realised that she'd run to the edge of the woods behind her house. The stillness of the trees beckoned her, offering her a place to hide.

The deeper into the trees she walked, the calmer she felt. She looked up and saw the sky peeking through the treetops, the cold winter sun promising light ahead. She felt strangely comforted surrounded by nature—safe somehow—as though she belonged there. Sinking to the ground, she huddled against a giant oak tree, wrapping her arms around her knees, her head bowed, and she cried.

She cried like she'd never cried before. A strange peace came over her as she sat and let her emotions drain from her body. She felt different somehow. She didn't know whether to be scared or relieved. She wished she could stay there, beneath the trees, hidden away from the world.

She could hear Samantha's voice whispering inside her head, her soft words caressing, soothing and calming.

Sshh, Rebecca. It's going to be all right. Just let go and relax. I'm here with you, I've always been here.

Her voice made Rebecca cry again, softer this time. An acceptance drawing over her. She knew, as she'd always known, that this would come to an end. Her plans, her revenge, her sense of control.

Standing up slowly, Rebecca looked around her, expecting to see someone staring back at her. But there was nobody there, only Rebecca and the trees. Quiet, still and waiting.

With purpose, she made her way out of the woods. Walking back home, she knew that whoever had been on the other end of the phone couldn't hurt her. They couldn't reach her. She wouldn't let them. She would finish what she'd set out to do and then she would leave.

Reaching the front door, she was relieved to see that the house looked just the same. Nobody was around. All the neighbours would be out at work, and there was no sign of Lucas's car. She went inside.

The door was closed. Rebecca guessed the wind had caught it and blown it shut. She let herself in. The house didn't speak; it was as silent as she'd left it. Looking at the phone, she felt a small frisson of fear, but tucked it away. She wouldn't let it stop her. She wouldn't let it take control. Upstairs, she shoved everything lying on the bed and floor back into her wardrobe. She would sort it later when she'd pack. She had to finish this now.

Rebecca changed into her jeans and T-shirt, fixed her hair, and touched up her make-up. Her mask was complete. She would go back to work. She would end this once and for all, and then she would leave Lucas. She took ten deep breaths, clenched her fists, and left.

45

YOU THINK YOU'RE smart, Rebecca, don't you? You think you have everything all sewn up, don't you? Everyone thinks you are wonderful, but they don't know the truth. Not like me.

I know what you do to him behind closed doors. Maybe he deserves it, but nobody else knows that, do they? They all think you are the one being harmed, don't they?

'Poor Rebecca,' they say. 'Poor, poor Rebecca.' My heart bleeds for you... Not.

Watching you crumble, watching you slowly fall apart, I wonder how long it will take before you are completely lost again, suffocated by your others. Poor dead Rebecca... You might as well be dead.

46

HIS SOBBING SUBSIDING, Lucas pulled back. His mouth opened, and the whole story came tumbling out. His meeting Rebecca, their whirlwind romance, and the insidious evil that crept into their relationship, stripping away his confidence before her harsh words had turned to beatings. Right up to the present time and the letter that had sent him into turmoil.

All the time he spewed out the misery that was his marriage, Nicole didn't say a word. She just sat and listened to him, offering a soft touch and an understanding nod every now and again. She just let him get it all out.

'Lucas, you're so brave to have finally told someone about what you've been going through. You do know that, don't you?'

He nodded, unsure of himself but wanting to believe the reassurance she was offering. Inside, he was still waiting for the behaviour he had come to expect from Rebecca. But Nicole seemed different. Really different. She was laying out his options for him. Helping him sort it all out logically in his mind. He recognised this way of working. This is what they did with their clients. Breaking a big thing into small manageable chunks. Nothing too overwhelming but enough to let the client know that they had it in their power to take back control.

'So, this letter? What did it say?' Nicole asked.

'It said: I know what you did,' he offered quietly.

'What does that mean? Do you have any idea? Any clue as to who might have sent it?'

He hesitated; should he really tell her? If he told her about his father, about his own actions, then surely even someone as open-minded as she was would be bound to be disgusted.

She sensed his hesitation. 'Lucas, if you want me to help you, you need to be honest. There is nothing you can tell me that will disgust me. Nothing will put me off. I know this isn't the right time, but you do know that I've got feelings for you, right? I know we haven't known each other long and nothing has really happened between us yet, but surely you can feel the connection between us. It's more than just a common interest in work. There's a spark. But we can leave that to the side at the moment. The most important thing is to make sure you're safe and to find out who sent this letter and why.'

He put his face in his hands, as though hiding his face would lessen the shock of what he was about to admit.

'My dad was Duncan Campbell.'

He looked up to gauge her reaction but there was nothing. No sharp intake of breath, no pushing him away in disgust.

'The Duncan Campbell? The one that was murdered weeks into his conviction?'

'Yep, that one.' A watery smile as he tried to work out how to say the next part.

'Well, you know you can't help who your father was, don't you? It's not your fault he was a paedophile. You're not your father, you know?'

'There's more,' he whispered. His heart raced. He thought he was going to be sick.

She left space for him to talk, stroking his hand, her eyes promising acceptance.

'I used to follow him. I saw what he did. He caught me watching one day. I thought he was going to be mad, I thought he was going to beat me. I wish he had; I so wish that he had beaten me within an inch of my life. Anything would have been better than what happened next.'

'Go on. You're doing well,' she encouraged

'He threatened me, I had no choice. He said if I didn't do what he said, then he'd give me to his friends who liked young boys.' His voice was getting lower and lower, his shame silencing him.

Nicole squeezed his hand. 'It's okay.'

He looked up briefly and saw only compassion in her eyes. He looked back down and continued. If he had kept on looking at her, he would have seen her true feelings staring out, ready to gouge his very heart out.

'He made me join in with his abuse of the wee lassie. The one who was found with her mum's dead body. She was just a kid. The neighbours all said she was weird; she used to talk to herself all the time, as though there was someone else with her. But even if she was weird, she didn't deserve what that bastard did to her... What we did to her.' His voice broke as the sobbing engulfed him.

'Was there anything else, Lucas?'

'He made me get the lassie next door—he made me get her to come, he wanted her to join in too.' As the words tumbled from his mouth he completely broke down, his body heaving as he sobbed uncontrollably.

Nicole wrapped her arms around him, drew him close, stroking his head as though he were a child.

'Shh. It's okay, Lucas, it's over now. I'm here now, and everything is going to be okay.'

He didn't know whether to feel relieved or terrified that he had told Nicole everything. While she had appeared to accept his confession without judgement, Lucas could sense a shift in the atmosphere, almost as though something dark had been released. He shivered as he glanced at his watch. Rebecca would be home soon; he didn't need to rush as she thought that he was playing fives with his mates. But something was telling him to leave, to get home. He made to stand up.

'Hey, where are you going? Sit down and chill. It's okay, you know?' Nicole reached up, pulling him back down on the sofa beside her. 'You've not fazed me with what you told me. I don't blame you, Lucas. The only one to blame is your dad. Not you— you were only a kid yourself.'

'I know, but I could have done something to stop it all. I could have told. I'll never forgive myself for those two wee lassies and what they went through. Their faces will haunt me forever.'

'YEAH RIGHT,' THOUGHT Nicole, you don't even know who we are when we're both sitting right in front of you. Out loud she said: 'You need to stop that. You were a victim in all of this too. And that letter, I mean, it could be anybody. A disgruntled client? One of their family? It's one of the downsides of the job, folks taking umbrage at us when things don't work out their way.'

'But how did they know where I live? What if they come back? What if they tell Rebecca?'

Nicole watched as Lucas started to crumble again. She wanted to fist pump the air and laugh in his face but she had to hold it in for just a while longer. She felt her stomach heave when he moved in as though to kiss her.

She put her hand out on his chest, stopping him just before his lips met hers.

'Hey, you're right about one thing. We need to sort the Rebecca thing out before anything can happen between us. I don't want to be the cause of anymore guilt for you, Lucas. We both know there's something between us, but there is also something—or rather someone—standing in our way. We need to deal with this before we go any further.'

She watched as his face fell. Trying to hide her true feelings, she reached out and took his hands in hers. 'It's okay,' she whispered. He leaned in and kissed her gently on the cheek.

She manoeuvred him back towards the couch and pulled him down beside her. Nicole let him wrap his arms around her and together they sat in silence, lost in their own thoughts.

Nicole broke the silence a little later. 'You probably need to be getting a move on soon. I'll call you tomorrow. Let me have a think about what we can do. In the meantime, don't worry about that letter. It will be something and nothing. Put it through the shredder tomorrow and forget all about it.'

They lingered at the doorway and he tried again to kiss her. She let him once and smiled as she pushed him away playfully. 'We have our whole lives for this. Go home and start to put things right.'

'But what should I do? Tell Rebecca about us? About the letter? You don't know her, she'll go ballistic.'

'You will know the right thing to do at the right time,' she whispered mysteriously. 'Now go.' She gave him a smile as she closed the door behind him and rubbed her lips to take away the taste of him. She stripped off her clothes where she stood. She needed a shower, the stink of that man was making her sick.

LATHERING THE SOAP deep into her skin, removing all traces of his scent, she grinned, knowing she had Lucas exactly where she wanted him. It was like taking candy from a baby.

She had used all her willpower not to tell him everything back then, to tell him exactly who she was and why she was so interested in him. She had wanted to, so badly. Watching him drink his tea, she'd had a sudden urge to pick up a knife and stab him in the heart.

What a sucker, she thought. It was pretty ironic that both herself and Rebecca had used their charm to get him right where they need him. He deserved everything that was coming to him.

'And, so do you, Rebecca. You're not so innocent in all of this either, are you, you little bitch?' She spat the words out and began humming her happy tunes. Nicole had watched Rebecca as a child. She knew exactly who this woman was, and she most definitely wasn't who she led everyone else to believe. She remembered her as well as she remembered Lucas. She would never forget them or forgive them. Neither of them.

She had lived her life immersed in anger, planning her revenge. After a car crash had wiped her family out in Toronto when she was thirteen, she'd been sent back to Scotland to live with a distant aunt from her father's side. She had never even met the woman before and the family life she had known and loved had been taken away from her. It was then she'd vowed her revenge. If it hadn't been for Rebecca and Lucas, she would never have had to leave Scotland. They would never have had to flee to Canada where nobody knew what had happened to her in that house. Her parents and her brother would still be alive.

She'd left her aunt's loveless home as soon as she was seventeen, hightailed it down south and made a new life for herself. She worked hard to maintain her Canadian accent, knowing that she needed something to help her keep up her new persona. She couldn't risk anyone working out her Scottish connections.

She'd put herself through college and university, working three jobs to make her way. Her hard work paid off when she gained her degree with distinction and it wasn't long before she worked her way up the parole service to a senior role. With her experience under her belt, she started her search for employment in Scotland.

Moving back to Scotland had always been her plan but the job in Glasgow had been an added bonus as it brought her closer to her prey. Initially, she had planned to kill Lucas and destroy Rebecca, but she had soon come to realise that she would be the only one who would pay for that. She wasn't clever enough to get away with murder. However, she was clever enough to fuck with people's minds. She couldn't wait for the final showdown with them both.

Discovering that Lucas and Rebecca were married had made things even easier for her. Having both of them living under one roof gave her the perfect opportunity to play some great mind games.

She knew exactly where they worked and everything about them. They thought they were smart when it came to online activity, but neither was as smart as she was. Her contacts through work, not always legitimate, had helped her find her way around the loopholes and she had kept her eye on them from a distance until the time was right to strike.

Watching Rebecca had been fun. She'd sat back and observed her as her outer shell began to crack, bit by bit revealing the true person underneath. Each little push she gave drove her closer to the edge, and it had been fun to watch her unravel while she tried to maintain a façade of respectability and control. Sneaking into her house and moving things around had been easy, the guys she worked with had no qualms about helping her break and enter. Especially Martin. He was furious at Rebecca for what he saw as interference in his life. He blamed her for him losing Kate and the kids and for his prison sentence.

Oh, Rebecca may have thought she was smart, but she was nowhere near Nicole's level. The stupid bitch was so self-obsessed she didn't even notice Nicole watching her. She was that absorbed in her own life she couldn't even recognise the danger she was in.

Nicole looked back on the meeting she'd had with Rebecca and Jim earlier. She'd wanted so much to stand up and announce who she was and why she was there. Rebecca hadn't even looked at her at first. She was too focused on Jim and Nicole knew exactly why.

It had been sheer luck that she ended up employed on Jim's team, she couldn't have planned that if she'd tried. She remembered him from that day. She had seen him, following the broken girl out of the house in front of the silent watchers. Burt none of them had noticed her hiding behind her father's legs. Nobody had cared about the damage that had been done to her in that house. In front of Rebecca. Nicole had felt like the invisible child and, if it hadn't been for her brother stumbling across the depraved playtime one day, she too might have been carried out of that house of horrors in the arms of the social services. Jim, of course, had never recognised her.

Another one too self-obsessed. Nicole had seen it the day the child had been removed from the house. She'd seen the way he'd looked at Rebecca, his protectiveness radiating out of him. Nicole had watched and taken it all in. None of them had paid any attention to her at the time. If only they had, they might have saved themselves a lot of grief.

Her thoughts turning to Lucas, she grimaced. He was pathetic, really; he could have stood up to his bitch wife if he'd tried. He could have stood up to his monster father. What sort of man was he?

Martin had unearthed the evidence of Lucas's other life, the one he was trying to pretend was in his past, but prisons were full of people with stories to tell and currency to trade. Martin had struck gold when he'd discovered the double life Lucas had been leading all along. He might have reinvented himself as this all-round good guy, but she knew exactly what lay beneath, and she had no qualms about bringing him down. He was his father's son.

They weren't the only ones who could reinvent themselves. She'd taken her former self and turned her into someone new. Someone strong, who would make them all pay.

She picked up the phone and called Martin. This time, he answered right away. He was learning. She smiled.

'It's me. Is everything ready? Do you have the pictures and videos for me?'

'Aye, they're all here. Ahm telling ye, I better get seeing ma kids after all this.'

She ignored his last statement: 'Have you seen Rebecca?'

'Aye,' he laughed. 'She bolted out that house like a bat out of hell after I made the call. Now, my report, my kids, when am I going to see them?'

'Oh, for Christ's sake, you will see them, quit whinging. You did check the videos he sent you to make sure they're not duds? I don't want that bastard getting away with anything.'

'Aye, I checked them. You told me to, didn't you? Near made me sick, so they did. He's a fucking pervert, didn't have to persuade him that hard to make the first one. It was only when he realised what we were using them for he started to freak out. Like father, like son, that yin.'

Nicole's stomach churned. The thought of what Lucas had been up to in the intervening years made her want to throw up. Nobody had been forcing him then.

'I'll meet you tomorrow, usual place. Don't be late.'

'Aye and mind my report, I want to see what you've written.'

Nicole hung up. He could sing for his report. Martin deserved everything he was going to get too. She'd make sure his involvement with Lucas and the paedophile ring he was a part of would be exposed. Martin McCrae would be back inside in no time. He wouldn't see his kids or his wife again, not ever, not if she had anything to do with it.

47

STRIDING BACK INTO the office, Rebecca marched over to her desk, trying hard to remain focused. She had to hold it together just a little longer, she told herself. The office was quiet, most of the team were out on visits or had finished for the day. Only Emma was still there waiting for her group to start.

'You okay?' she asked, concern etched across her face.

Rebecca nodded, not quite trusting herself to speak. She knew she looked calm on the outside, but inside she was falling apart. Samantha's voice echoed inside her head, relentless and sharp, scraping the inside of her brain. She was terrified to open her mouth in case it was Samantha's voice that came out.

She put her head down, pretending to lose herself in the paperwork scattered across her desk. She could see nothing but a blur, the words could have been written in a foreign language for all the sense they made to her. She tried to use her own voice to shout Samantha down. She was frightened of what she might do. Flashbacks of her mother's dead body lying in the kitchen, the knife by her side, the knife Samantha had taken and used to murder her mother. She couldn't let it happen again. This wasn't what she wanted. She had wanted to destroy Lucas, not kill him.

'Shut up, shut up, shut up!' she screamed inside, but Samantha's voice kept getting louder and more forceful, more insistent. It jarred in her brain, malicious then gentle, petulant then contemptuous, all trying to win her over, to convince her to relinquish control. The noise inside her head was excruciating, an uproar of sound, the confusion growing. Her heart was pounding, a sheen of cold sweat covered her body, the tremors in her hands were becoming increasingly difficult to hide.

She could feel Emma's eyes boring into her, but she was too frightened to look up. Too frightened to think what or who Emma might see. Scraping her chair back roughly, she staggered out of the room to the ladies.

Locking herself in a cubicle, she fell to the floor, clutching the pan as she dry heaved, trying to expel the demons she knew were inside her.

Frantic knocking and the sound of Emma calling her name snapped her out of her trance. Her sobs subsided, and she wiped at her face roughly. She couldn't stay here, she had to get a grip. She had to stand up. Pulling herself up, she steadied herself against the cubicle door.

'I'm okay,' she croaked. 'I'll be alright, just go back in.'

'No, Rebecca, I can't leave you like this. I'm worried about you. Please open the door.'

Deep breaths steadying her turmoil, Rebecca slowly began to return to herself. Samantha's voice was getting quieter now.

She watched her hands struggle against the door as she pulled it open a fraction.

Emma's jaw dropped. 'God, Rebecca, what the actual fuck?'

Rebecca fell out of the cubicle, righting herself against the sinks.

She looked in the mirror. She didn't recognise the woman staring back at her. Eyes puffy, streaks of mascara like a black stream down her face, hair wild as though she'd been trying to pull it out.

'I-I-I'm fine,' she stuttered. 'It's just some food poisoning. I had eggs for breakfast, and I knew they hadn't tasted right. I'll be okay.' Thrusting her hands under the cold water, she began to splash her face as though that small act was going to make it all better.

Emma didn't look convinced; she just stared at Rebecca. 'Has Lucas done something to you, Rebecca? You need to tell me. Please. I can help you.'

Rebecca glared at her in the mirror. 'No,' she spat. 'I told you. It's food poisoning. I'll be fine. Stop fussing, for Christ's sake.'

Emma looked hurt. 'I'm only trying to help.'

'Help? You want to help? Well, why don't you get your finger out and get the bloody paperwork done. Save me having to drag myself out of my sick bed to cover for your ineptitude. That would help!'

Rebecca smiled back at Emma in the mirror. She knew it wasn't her voice. She knew it was too late now, she was losing it.

Good girl, Rebecca. Everything's going to be alright now. Just you wait and see.

Emma said nothing. She just stared at Rebecca before storming out and slamming the toilet door behind her as she left.

Shrugging, Rebecca turned back to the mirror. She tried to tame her hair using her fingers and splashed more water on her face, trying to take away as much of the puffiness as she could. She felt herself return to normal.

Samantha was silent now. It was just her again. For now. It wouldn't last much longer though.

48

SOMEHOW, JIM MADE his way home. He was on autopilot, with no idea how he had made it back to his house. His thoughts were racing. He had to get everything ready: himself and the place, for his girl. She was coming home. He was going to be a father and this time he wouldn't let her go.

As soon as he opened the door, Cooper jumped up, paws on his shoulders, licking his face enthusiastically as though sensing his exhilaration.

'Calm down, boy,' he laughed, pushing him down. 'We're going to have some company, Cooper. Yep, guess what? Daddy here isn't just your daddy. I've found my little girl and she's coming home. Everything's going to be okay now, wait and see.'

The dog's ears pricked up and he bounded over to the table where his lead was kept, looking expectantly between the lead and Jim.

'No, sorry boy, got too much to do. Later, eh?'

Jim couldn't stand still. He rushed from room to room trying to work out where would be best for Rebecca to stay, muttering to himself and wringing his hands. The dog, sensing his erratic behaviour, tucked his tail between his legs and sloped off to his safe space, brown eyes fixed on his master.

Ignoring Cooper, Jim pulled a glass from the sink full of unwashed dishes. His hands trembled as he poured himself a whisky. 'Think, Jim, stop and think, man. You need to get this right.' Pacing the house, swilling back his drink, he muttered to himself, answering the questions his brain was firing at him.

Slamming down the glass suddenly, he yelled: 'Perfect, that's where she can go, it's perfect!'

He ran downstairs to his basement, his unfinished project. Now he had a reason to finish it. He was going to make it a room fit for a princess, his princess.

Jim couldn't see how grim the room actually was, with the small single bed pushed up against the wall, bare plastered walls and an unfinished floor. In his mind, it was perfect. All it needed now was Rebecca.

He lay on the bed, suddenly exhausted. Memories of the day she had been found with her dead mother flooded back. Anger and shame washed over him as he remembered how he'd found her, his little girl, covered in her mother's blood.

Jim felt the guilt engulf him. He had tried his best. He had followed her from each placement, crossing professional boundaries to ensure that he remained her caseworker and could keep checking up on her. But deep inside, he knew he'd failed her.

The incident with the Reids played heavily on his mind. That man had been a nasty piece of work. Jim knew that it hadn't been Rebecca's fault the placement broke down. Yet, he had been instrumental in covering it up. He had falsified the files citing Rebecca's behaviour as the cause. He hadn't wanted anybody to find out what had happened to her in the Reid's home. It would have looked bad on him since he had been visiting on a regular basis. He should have picked up on the signals, but he hadn't. He had let Rebecca down from the very beginning, and every single step of the way.

All these years he had blamed Stella, telling himself she had stopped him from building a relationship with Rebecca. While she hadn't been exactly welcoming towards him, he couldn't really blame her, given the way he had unceremoniously dumped her as soon has he'd found out she was pregnant.

But while she didn't want anything to do with him, she had never come out and said he couldn't see Rebecca, she hadn't stopped him. That was all down to him. The truth of the matter was that Jim had slunk off into the darkness quite happily. He hadn't wanted the burden of a child. He hadn't felt ready to be a father. He didn't want the responsibility, nor had he wanted a child to cramp his lifestyle. He had pressed a drunkenly penned note and a cheap necklace into her hand and walked away without another thought for the woman or the child he was leaving behind.

Until the day he'd turned up at the house to find Stella brutally murdered and Rebecca sobbing over her body, he hadn't given them a second thought. But he *had* kept the other half of the pendant. He had carried it with him everywhere, as if he had known that one day, he would have the opportunity to match it up. One day he would be ready.

Jim pulled the pendant out of his pocket, clutching it close to his own heart. He rocked back and forth on the bed, staring into the distance but seeing nothing but his past flash before his eyes. He was falling apart, Rebecca floating in front of him like some crazy hallucination. He could almost hear her calling: 'Daddy, help me. Help ME!'

He was her dad, she was his little girl, and it was his duty to protect her, to look after her, to take care of her, like he should have done all along. He had to make amends and he knew exactly what he had to do to save her.

Roused from his thoughts by the bleep of his phone signalling an incoming text message, Jim tried to clear his head. He couldn't lose it now, not after all these years of guilt.

Stuffing the pendant back into his pocket, he grabbed his phone. The message was from Nicole.

'Hey, Jim. My dad's had a massive stroke and I'm having to catch the first available flight home. Management know, but I wanted to give you a heads up that I'll not be around for a while. Take care and catch you later. Nx'

He briefly considered replying, before batting that thought away. He wasn't in the right frame of mind to be offering sympathies to his colleague and he didn't actually care about anyone other than Rebecca anymore.

It was almost time for him to start making up for the sins of his past. It was time to bring her home.

49

MAKING HER WAY out of the office, Rebecca ignored the pointed stares and whispers of her colleagues. Emma had no doubt gone out whining to them about the way she'd spoken to her. Rebecca didn't care. She didn't give a toss about what any of them thought about her now. They didn't matter to her at all. They'd simply been a means to an end; a part of her act. A role she'd been given to play. And I played it damn well, she thought. Every one of them had fallen for it hook, line, and sinker.

She'd already penned her resignation and left it in her manager's pigeonhole. She'd cited personal reasons; a breakup with her husband, and the need to get away. She'd played them all. They all believed Lucas had been controlling her, abusing her. She knew her manager would be sympathetic to her, she would be able to wangle her way out of working her notice. It wouldn't be too difficult; one final day of role playing and she would put on the performance of a lifetime, telling them she had to leave, that she was in fear of her life. She had the email ready to send to Lucas's boss, disclosing all the abuse she'd suffered under his hands. Even if he didn't lose his job, he'd have to leave, the gossips would make sure of that. His reputation would be in tatters.

Pathetic, Rebecca, whispered Samantha. *To just lose his job after everything he's done. He deserves more than that. Let me help, Rebecca. I can fix it for you. I fixed your mummy for you, didn't I? I fixed Annie Reilly for you.*

Rebecca ignored her. She couldn't let her take over, she had to get home and get out of there. She'd decided.

She ran out of the office and into the pouring rain. It had been coming down in sheets all day, typical freezing Scottish rain, the type that not only soaks you to the skin but stabs you like a knife. She welcomed the cold. It was a distraction from the voices wheedling inside her head.

She was walking to the bus stop when a car pulled over next to her. Peering into the passenger window, she realised it was Nicole. She pretended she didn't recognise her and walked on, but Nicole was persistent. She wound down the window and crawled along beside her.

'Hey, Rebecca, it's me, Nicole? We met the other day with Jim Aitken?'

Shit, thought Rebecca. Nicole was not going to give up.

She bent her head forward, painting on her best smile. Leaning into the car, she noted that Nicole was looking a little flushed, almost flustered really. Something about her behaviour triggered an alarm inside Rebecca's head. She might not know this woman well, but Rebecca was an expert at getting the measure of people on a first meeting, and Nicole hadn't seemed the type to get flustered easily.

'Can I give you a lift? Get you out of this rain? It's wild out there.' Her smile seemed just as wild.

Rebecca knew that it would look churlish if she were to refuse. Especially in this weather. Her hair was clinging to her face and her feet were sodden.

'Yeah, that would be great, if you don't mind?' She plastered on her best smile as she jumped into the warmth of the car.

'God, this rain is awful, I just can't get used to this Scottish weather, all that four-seasons-in-one-day nonsense,' Nicole said, slipping into that age-old tradition of talking about the weather when you weren't quite sure what to say.

'Yeah, I suppose it's a bit weird. Though you must be used to some rough winters, being Canadian?'

'Too right, I miss the snow, though. Crazy, eh?'

Rebecca's eyes narrowed slightly; something about this woman was bugging her. She couldn't put her finger on it. 'So how long have you lived over here then? You must miss your family.'

Nicole looked straight ahead, concentrating on the poor driving conditions.

'Oh, a while. Feel like I'm almost a native.' She gave a nervous laugh.

Rebecca watched her from the corner of her eye. She felt like she knew this woman, but she just couldn't place her at all. She knew it wasn't on a professional level and it was definitely not through any social circle, with Rebecca preferring to keep that very small indeed.

'You have a pretty strong Scottish accent, are you sure you even lived in Canada?' Rebecca laughed as though it was a joke, but it wasn't—not really. There was something that Nicole wasn't telling anyone. Something she was hiding. Rebecca didn't like other people having secrets. She liked to be the only one to have secrets. Her hands clenched tightly by her sides as she watched Nicole closely.

She's dangerous Rebecca, watch her.

Nicole seemed to shift uncomfortably under her gaze.

'Yeah, of course I did. I'm as Canadian as they come. Hell, I've got Tim Horton's coffee running through my veins instead of blood, you know.'

She pulled the car over to the side of the road. 'Looks like we're home now, Rebecca. Was great chatting to you. I'd really like for us to meet up for a coffee or a drink sometime? I'd like us to get to know each other better, I'm sure we have a lot in common.'

Rebecca stared at her before muttering noncommittally: 'Yeah, I suppose.'

Whatever it was about Nicole that was unnerving her, she couldn't worry about it now. She could feel herself starting to break down, she had to get out of here now.

Saying a hasty goodbye, she got out of the car and stood watching as Nicole drove off into the rain.

Something wasn't right. Rebecca could feel a change coming and it frightened her. The cracks were definitely showing. She could feel herself becoming increasingly detached. She felt as though she were floating above, looking down at herself. Her mask had slipped, her panic levels were rising. She had to finish this soon, before it was too late.

Wrapping her arms around herself as though she was trying to keep herself whole, she shivered as she turned to go inside. And then it hit her: She hadn't given Nicole an address when she'd got into the car. So, how the hell did that woman know where she lived?

50

LUCAS HAD LEFT Nicole's flat and driven out to an industrial estate. He had been sitting in the car for the last couple of hours, trying to compose himself. He knew he was going to be late home, but he didn't care anymore. He didn't even know if he would go back home. He was shaking with a mixture of emotions; fear, guilt and desire, all milling about inside.

Nicole had certainly got his head in a spin and he wasn't quite sure how he should be feeling now. He had disclosed so much to a woman he hardly knew. It was almost as though she'd hypnotised him into telling her his story. He just hoped it hadn't been a mistake, that it wouldn't lead to him being publicly exposed.

His thoughts drifted back to the letter. Someone out there knew already, though. What were they intending to do with that information? His hands trembled as the reality of his situation became clear. Rebecca would never let him go; he had to find a way to escape her. Nicole was a potential escape route, but just how much could he trust her? He hadn't known her that long and yet he'd told her everything. And with someone else out there who knew his true identity, how long could he continue to hide this? Lucas felt himself begin to spiral into a panic.

His hands gripping the steering wheel, he crunched the car into gear and sped off, deciding to stop back at the office first. The thought of going home filled him with terror right now. Something was warning him to stay away.

All was quiet in the office. Everyone had finished, most of them would be out in the pub for Friday night drinks. Only the cleaner was in. She smiled at him as he came in. She had headphones on and was bobbing away to the music, so thankfully didn't try to engage in any conversation.

He sat down at his desk to plan his next steps. He had to get rid of those files on his laptop and destroy all the evidence connecting him to the men he had grown up with, the men who he had continued his journey with long after his father's death.

Someone must have told Martin about him when he was in prison. He didn't know why they were blackmailing him, or even who was behind it all. Martin was just the messenger, and it wasn't even as though he had any money they could get out of him. But they could destroy his life.

Waiting for the cleaner to finish, he went through to the kitchen to grab a coffee. Passing the staff mailbox, he noticed an envelope sitting in his pigeonhole. His name was typed on the front, along with the words PRIVATE AND CONFIDENTIAL across the top of the envelope. Nothing unusual there, they often got Child Protection minutes via internal mail.

The mailbox was situated in a narrow corridor on the way into the offices. Security was relatively lax and, to be honest, anyone could have made their way in and picked up anything they wanted. Feeling calmer now, Lucas recognised his paranoia for what it was, and laughed to himself. Carrying his coffee and the letter back to the desk, he settled down to read.

He took a sip of his coffee and tore open the envelope before dropping it in horror when its contents spilled out. A single white sheet with the words: I'M COMING TO GET YOU. BE READY in bold capitals, shouting at him off the page.

Far more worrying than the letter was the stack of photographs that fell out alongside the single sheet of paper. Old and grainy, from a long time ago. The first one showed Lucas and his dad, arms around each other and Lucas didn't look as though he were being forced to spend any time in this man's company.

And the others didn't look as though Lucas was being forced to do anything.

Now, his past was really catching up with him. And his present was about to be exposed.

The photographs had dislodged his memories, bringing them to the forefront of his mind.

He was glad his mother was dead, he wouldn't have wanted her to learn about this. It would have broken her heart. He could no longer bring himself to blame her for getting in tow with Duncan Campbell. He knew that she'd only wanted a child. She hadn't counted on any of this happening.

His father had been an evil bastard. Lucas had been terrified of him. But he knew he had spent his life painting his own sanitised version of the story and burying the dirty truth deep within. Now that truth was about to be unearthed and he didn't think he had the strength to stop it.

Someone, somewhere, knew everything and had the evidence to prove it. Lucas too knew what he really was. He was no better than his father had been. He hadn't been an unwilling participant at all. He cried as he remembered the day he had become an instigator. And still, his tears were not for the atrocities he had committed, his tears were for the life that was about to come crumbling down around him. He was a fool if he thought he could keep it hidden forever. Everyone was bound to find out the truth.

He wished he had the courage to end it all.

The office door slammed as the cleaner left. He pulled out his laptop from the drawer and began to smash it repeatedly over the desk.

51

SO WHY YOU, Rebecca? Why have I chosen you? I'll answer that with my own question—Why me, Rebecca? Why was I the chosen one? What did I ever do to you? Did you send them to me? Why did you sit back and let it happen?

It's all your fault. Okay, so you didn't do that stuff to me, but you might as well have. You could have stopped it. You could have told someone, anyone. You could have stopped it all.

I'm tired now, Rebecca. I've almost broken you and he's just about to get his comeuppance. But I feel sorry for you. You don't even know who you are anymore. You are just a shell. I did that. I should feel good, but I don't really. I feel drained and empty. Revenge doesn't taste as good as it sounds. But it's too late now. I've got to finish it once and for all. I'm sorry. I *am* really sorry. I just don't have any choice. Probably just as you didn't all those years ago.

It's almost over now, Rebecca. Have you guessed yet? No, probably not. You didn't see me then and I don't suppose you see me now. I'm that little girl, Rebecca, the little girl next door. The one you let them destroy while you sat in the corner talking to yourself.

Lucas is going to jail now, Rebecca. Where he belongs. He is paying for his sins and the sins of his father.

I'm outside now, I'm coming to visit you. To put an end to it all. I'll tell you the truth, Rebecca, the whole truth and nothing but the truth. But it's too late for you now. Maybe you didn't deserve all this, maybe you were a victim too. Poor mad Rebecca. I don't care, though. Because of you, I lost everything and now you are going to know exactly how that feels.

52

NICOLE WATCHED IN her rear-view mirror as Rebecca turned into a tiny dot in the distance, disappearing into nothingness which was exactly what Nicole wanted. She wanted this woman out of her way. She wanted her to disappear and she was going to make it happen. She kicked herself as she suddenly realised that she'd dropped Rebecca off without having asked her for an address.

'Shit,' she admonished herself. 'You stupid bitch, Nicole. Slip ups like that will cost you, you know? You need to focus, woman.'

Parking up in a quiet street, she gave Rebecca plenty of time to get into the house and get settled, before she made her final move.

Nicole found her mind jumping all over the place, from her journey with Rebecca to the afternoon with Lucas. God, these two had it coming, she thought. They ruined my fucking life.

The stalking and the letters had just been for starters, and Nicole was hungry to deliver the mains. But she knew she had to be careful. Lucas might be easy to manipulate, but Rebecca was a different kettle of fish. She was just as manipulative as Nicole.

Pushing her grudging respect aside, she steeled herself. That bitch had to pay for the part she'd played in the mess that had become Nicole's life.

Her thoughts wandering to Lucas, she wondered if he'd gone back to the office. If he had, he would have seen the letter and photographs by now. Nobody had noticed her slipping them into his mailbox and even if they had, it would have been simple to explain away. She'd come armed with leaflets about training opportunities via their team and put them all in everyone's mailbox. It had been all too easy to slip the letter into Lucas's box. She grinned as she imagined the look of sheer terror on his face as he opened the envelope and saw the photographs.

Her contacts through work hadn't always been legitimate, some of the pictures Duncan Campbell had taken had been passed into various grubby hands over the years and there was always somebody willing to give something up to get a positive report from their probation officer.

It had been a piece of cake to find them both. They had hardly hidden themselves. She could remember Rebecca clearly. She'd always been a little weirdo, sitting in the corners whispering to herself. It was like she was having a conversation with someone else half the time. When Nicole had been taken into the flat by Lucas and his father, she had watched Rebecca sit in the corner, pulling faces and giggling manically to herself. Nicole now recognised it for what it was, but it made no difference to her. Rebecca still had it coming to her.

Nicole's thought process was becoming increasingly erratic as the memories of her childhood came flooding back. Lucas may have tried to convince himself that he had been an innocent party in it all, and that his beast of a father had forced him to do what he had done. But Nicole knew what she'd seen; she knew what she'd experienced. Lucas may have initially been coerced into joining in with his father's depravity but by the time he had started to groom her, he was more than enjoying it. Lucas was as much of a beast as his father was.

And now it was time for the bastard to pay.

She slowly drove back to their house, rage building inside her. Parking up, she sat for a couple of minutes to steady her nerves.

This was crazy. She had wanted to destroy them both. Following Rebecca, sneaking into her house while she was at work, making her feel watched—it had all been designed to break her down mentally. And it had worked, she was falling apart at the seams.

Lucas had been different though, she really wanted to screw with his mind and destroy him. She couldn't afford to mess things up now. She had to stay focused.

It looked like Rebecca had had the same idea as her. Only she'd got her claws into Lucas first. Nicole briefly considered coming clean to her, telling her who she really was and why she was here. But she couldn't—she didn't trust the woman at all. And it was clear she was not in full control of herself.

Nicole couldn't trust which version of Rebecca she would get if she told her. It was a real shame. Together, they could have really taught Lucas a lesson, one that he would never have forgotten.

Pressing send on the text she'd just composed, she stepped out of the car into the driving rain. Wiping the drops from her eyes, she stepped forward and rang the bell.

INSIDE THE HOUSE, Rebecca slumped against the wall. She couldn't do this anymore. The pretence was exhausting. Perhaps she really *should* just pack up and go. Save herself. Move away, somewhere different. She could reinvent herself again. She could become Samantha. Samantha was already growing stronger inside of her. She could feel her eating away at what was left of Rebecca, devouring her strength and using it to build up her own. Samantha was getting ready to return and, when she came back, there would be nothing Rebecca could do to stop her.

She was dog-tired. Perhaps she should just give in. Stop fighting. She could just let Samantha out.

The doorbell rang. Rebecca pulled herself up from the floor. Glancing at herself in the mirror, she was shocked by the changes she saw. Her confident gaze had deserted her and staring back at her was a face from the past. That little girl who couldn't say boo to a goose. Fear was written across her face.

She put her eye up to the spyhole and her stomach clenched as she recognised the woman standing in the pouring rain at her front door. Nicole had come back, and she looked wild.

Rebecca opened the door an inch, feeling vulnerable despite the safety chain blocking entry.

'Rebecca, I need to talk to you,' said Nicole. 'Let me in, will you?'

'Rebecca isn't here. She doesn't want to talk to you. Go away.'

'I don't care which one of you is there right now, we all need to talk.'

Rebecca made to close the door but Nicole was having none of it. The weather had made sure there was no one around to see her kick the door. It flew open, the safety chain clattering to the floor. Rebecca scuttled backwards, feeling Samantha rising in her defence.

Nicole slammed the door behind her and turned to face Rebecca. Rebecca sank to the floor, her exhausted body shuddering.

Let me take care of her, Rebecca.

'I'm not Rebecca,' she muttered, over and over again.

Nicole stood over her, casting a threatening shadow. She leaned down, moving closer until her mouth was right up at Rebecca's ear. 'I don't care what your name is. I know exactly who you are, you stupid bitch. I know everything about you.'

Stunned, she stared at Nicole, her mouth hanging open, the unspoken words hovering on her tongue, afraid to take the final step forward.

'I'll bet you thought you'd never see me again, didn't you?' Nicole sneered.

'I-I-I don't know who y-y-you are. Just leave me alone. Don't hurt me.'

'Don't hurt me,' mimicked Nicole. 'Hurt you? Have you any idea what you did to me? Hurt you? I'm going to kill you, bitch!' She spat the words out as Rebecca cowered before her. 'You and your bastard of a husband forced me into a room with those animals. You forced me to see things I can never un-see. To do things I will never forget. It's because of you my dad moved us across the world to Canada. It's because of you my family were wiped out in a car crash and I'm left on my own with nothing.' The words seemed to deflate her as she slumped down the wall beside Rebecca.

'I don't know who you are... I don't understand...'

'I'll tell you a little story, shall I?' Whispered Nicole. The fight had gone out of her now and she seemed to be sinking into the woodwork as she began her tale.

'I was six years old when Lucas lured me into your sick little house of horrors. Six years old when you introduced me to the local beast. Six years old when Lucas held me down and made me watch. Six years old when you begged that beast to use me instead of you. Six years old when my life was uprooted, and we moved away. I was thirteen years old when my life changed forever. I have nothing and I have no one. I've spent my life hunting you both down and what do I find? You two cosied up and happily married. Only, Rebecca, you forget that I know all your secrets. I've been the one who has been watching you. I'm the one who has been calling you, watching you fall apart. ME!'

Rebecca turned to face her, seeing a maniacal grin spread across Nicole's face.

'I've also been fucking with your husband's head. Poor little Lucas, all beaten up by big bad Rebecca, eh? Hiding his bruises and his embarrassment. I've been watching you both. Your husband nearly wet himself when he got the letter I sent him. Terrified that his secret will come out. Lucas doesn't want anyone to know who his daddy was, he doesn't want anyone to know just how much of a daddy's boy he really is, and he doesn't want anyone to know that his fucking wife beats the living daylights out of him. Lucas doesn't want anyone to know who he was and who he still fucking is. I want you both to pay for what you did to me. Not only have I fucked with your darling husband's head, he actually thinks I'm about to invite him into my bed too. Can you believe it? Your wimp of a husband is about to leave you. Then you're going to know how it feels to be left with nobody and nothing in your life. Not only will your husband desert you, but your professional life is about to come tumbling around your ears. In the next few days, flyers will be posted through all your neighbours' doors, telling them what a bitch you really are. I have photos and evidence to prove it all. Your next-door neighbour, Mary? Yeah, Mary Picken, isn't it? She's a lovely woman, really. Invited me in for a cup of tea, she did. Of course, I had to tell her that I was investigating claims of domestic abuse. She immediately jumped to your side, but I have to say she was horrified when I showed her the pictures of Lucas's injuries. I was watching you both, you see. Well, Mary's sure to be telling all the others, now isn't she? I did tell her it was all highly confidential, but you know what she's like, don't you?'

OUT OF NOWHERE, something dark seemed to snap inside Nicole; she curled her right hand into a fist and aimed it straight for Rebecca's nose, the feel of the bone breaking fed her rage. She couldn't tell if the red mist was her anger or the blood splatter blinding her as she aimed punch after punch at the woman crouched before her. Each punch was accompanied by a torrent of vitriol as she purged herself of the memories that had tormented her all her life.

Grabbing a fistful of hair, she pulled Rebecca's bloodied face close to her own. She spat the words out as she crawled until she was almost on top of her. 'You fucking little weirdo. I was always going to find you. I could fucking kill you right now if I wanted to, you little bitch.'

Rebecca offered no resistance as Nicole cracked her head off the wall behind her. Nicole seized her by the throat, squeezing tighter, harder, until her eyes began to bulge. 'This is all your fucking fault. YOU made me do this. You fucking deserve to die.'

The light began to fade from Rebecca's eyes. She was giving up. But as her eyes glazed over, something made Nicole stop. Rebecca's face had changed, and all Nicole could see now was a child—a small child, as vulnerable as she herself had been. She dropped her hands from Rebecca's neck and slumped back against the wall, her own fight escaping along with the last scraps of venom she felt.

REBECCA STARED BACK at Nicole, unable to defend herself against this crazed woman. Those eyes. There was something so familiar about those eyes. The flashbacks were coming fast and furious now. A child, standing behind the safety of her daddy, protected. Protected from the evil she'd had to endure every day. Safe in her little house with her perfect family, and yet she had been subjected to the horrors that no child should ever face.

The memories threatened to drown Rebecca. Those same eyes watching when Rebecca had been carried from her home, smeared in blood from her mother's body. Her mother's body laid out on the floor, the blood pooling around her dirty hair. Her hand taking the knife from the kitchen cupboard and plunging it into her over and over and over again.

Who was she?

Something inside her shifted, Samantha had come back.

Wiping her bloody mouth, she stared back at Nicole. 'So, what are you going to do?'

Nicole looked down, confused by her self-assured tone.

'I'll tell you exactly what I'm going to do. I'm going to text your husband and tell him I love him. I'm going to beg him to leave you, and believe me, he will when he sees what I've got to offer. And then I am going to destroy him in a way that you never could.'

Nicole smiled, but the venom seemed to falter in her glare.. 'As for you—' she sighed '—you know what, there's nothing more for me to do really, is there? Looking at the mess of you, I reckon that's punishment enough. I came here to kill you Rebecca. I really wanted to kill you. But I can't. Despite everything that happened to me, I know you were a victim too. You were only a kid. Lucas and his father were the beasts, you didn't really have a choice.'

The tears streamed down Nicole's face as the truth of what had really happened to both of them as children hit.

Rebecca pulled herself up into a sitting position. She watched as Nicole's heart broke. She felt nothing for her. No sympathy, no empathy. But she did sense an opportunity. Nicole was clearly hell bent on ensuring Lucas paid for the past.

By letting her take the risk, Rebecca would be able to safely slip away, she could start again. She could be gone well before Nicole told everyone who she really was and what had gone on.

The reality was that the fight had already left her. She was done. The voices in her head were confusing her, she no longer knew who she was.

'Do what you need to do to him,' whispered Rebecca. 'I don't care anymore.'

SITTING UP, NICOLE wiped away her tears. She had to see this through, she couldn't live the rest of her life haunted by what had happened. She pulled herself backwards, drew back her arm and threw it round to land a sideswipe to Rebecca's jaw.

She smiled as Rebecca's head snapped to the side and she slumped to the floor, unconscious.

'Sorry, sweetheart. I need to do this my way. I can't risk you telling Lucas. By the time you wake up… If you wake up… The damage will be done. Enjoy the rest of your life, sweetie.'

And with that, she was gone, slipping out of the house like a thief into the night.

53

LUCAS'S PHONE PINGED. He grabbed at it, sure that it was Rebecca wanting to know where he was. It wasn't her. It was Nicole.

'Hey, Lucas. I can't stop thinking about you. Come over to mine. We need to talk now. It's important. You don't need to worry about Rebecca. I saw her going into the Prince Charlie pub with some of her team. Come over. N xx'

What could be so important that she had to speak to him again so soon? He tried calling the number but it just rang out. He sent a text in reply.

'I'll be there.'

XX was the reply a minute later.

Charging through the rain, Lucas ran to the car, soaked to the skin before he even reached the driver's door. Shaking with cold, he turned the engine and blasted up the heating to warm the chill in his bones.

The drive to Nicole's flat didn't take long, the roads were dead. In weather like this, most sensible folks were curled up inside with their loved ones.

Loved ones. The thought pinged in his head and it was Nicole he pictured, not Rebecca. He'd give it all up for her, everything. He felt a connection with her that he had never felt with anyone before. He knew that she felt the same. He had felt her desire for him that afternoon in the flat.

Maybe with Nicole by his side, he'd have the strength to leave this life behind. To move forward. A new life. A new start. Away from the anonymous hate mail, away from the abuse. A new life with a new woman. A new love.

His heart was buoyed as he pulled up outside Nicole's flat. Remarkably, he managed to get a parking space almost immediately, not a common occurrence in this area, but he wasn't complaining.

Peering at her flat, he wondered if she was watching for him. What was she thinking? Was her heart pounding like his? Was she looking for the same thing as he was? Only one way to find out, he thought, as he bounded up the stairs like an overexcited schoolboy on his first date.

NICOLE SMILED. She placed the phone down on the coffee table, sat back in her chair, and waited for Lucas. He would be here any minute.

When the doorbell rang, she jumped up to answer it. He was standing at the door, soaked to the skin with a huge grin plastered across his stupid face.

'Come on in. It looks like it's finally you and me, honey. On our own at last, and boy do I have a surprise for you.'

She smiled as she saw the reflection of flashing blue lights bounce off the walls of the closet. She closed the door, locked it, and pocketed the key before turning to Lucas.

'Do you remember me yet, Lucas? It's time for you to pay.'

54

AS THE WORLD around her began to regain focus, the face in front of her became clearer. Jim Aitken stood in front of her, as he had the night he'd taken her from her mother's house. Only this time, his eyes were red rimmed with tears and he had a stoop to his shoulders. He was a broken man.

Despite his outward appearance, there was something about him that was scaring her. His body language might be that of a broken man, but his eyes were burning with a determination she couldn't fathom. Her shoulders slumped and any last vestiges of rage ebbed out of her. Deflated, she hauled herself to her feet, while trying to maintain a defiant glare.

'How did you get here?'

Jim shook his head. 'Why, Rebecca?'

Her head whipped up at the sound of his voice. Trying to draw herself taller she hissed, 'I'm not Rebecca, I'm Samantha.'

Jim moved towards her holding his hand out reassuringly.

'Rebecca, Samantha doesn't exist. She isn't real, sweetheart, none of your others are real,' he whispered softly.

Her scream pierced the air, a howl of anguish escaping her lips, 'I am Samantha... I am fucking SAMANTHA!'

He moved closer to her, drawing his arm around her. Patting her softly, murmuring reassurances.

She recoiled from his touch with a childish scream, 'Get off me, you pervert! Mummy, help me please, please... Get off me! MUMMY, HELP ME!'

Her hands flew towards him, nails raking his face. Jim grabbed her by the wrists, pulling her close, but her struggles were too much for him and he let her go.

Collapsing back to the floor, her sobs intensified—her grief consuming her. Her shoulders shook, and she whispered over and over again: 'I am Samantha.'

JIM LOOKED AT her, feeling that familiar mix of guilt and dread. Rebecca was his daughter. This Samantha that possessed her was a devil. As he watched Rebecca struggle to find herself again, a realisation dawned on him. There was nobody there, nobody to see him, or her. The door to her house was closed. The wind and rain were wild enough to keep most people indoors.

Lucas would believe she had left him, wouldn't he? And Jim would think of something to explain her absence from work. Right now, he just knew he had to save her. The way he should have done all those years ago.

Nobody knew his connection to Rebecca. He could end her pain now. Nobody would ever know.

Picking up a scarf, he moved forward, reassuring, soothing, and caring. She watched him approach, her eyes narrowed in suspicion. Sitting down beside her, he wrapped the scarf gently round her neck.

'To keep you warm,' he whispered, stroking her arm.

DESPERATE FOR THE human contact—the acknowledgement of who she really was and why she was the way she was— Rebecca fought Samantha back down and leaned into his embrace. She allowed herself to sink into his arms.

She reached up to stroke his face, like a lover, thinking she could play him like most men.

'Rebecca, please, you can't do that. You can't touch me like that. I'm your father.'

She looked up at him, confused, just as he drew up his other hand from his pocket to slip a handkerchief over her face. A sickly smell filled her nostrils. The light faded as she felt herself slump forward. Her father?

'I'M SORRY, SWEETHEART. I didn't want to have to do this to you, but I need you to come home now. Come home where you can be safe.'

Jim worked quickly. The streets might be deserted but he couldn't take any unnecessary risks. Not when he'd come this far. Picking her up, he carried her back to the car. He gently laid her across the back seat. Covering her with the dog's blanket, he stroked her head gently.

'It's time to come home to Daddy, Rebecca. Home where you belong.'

55

FOR A FLEETING moment, Rebecca thought she was at home in her own bed. As she stretched out her arms, her hands brushed against something rough. It was cold, it didn't feel like home. Her nose wrinkling, she sniffed, the smell of damp clogging her nostrils. It's a nightmare, she thought. Her eyes tightly closed, she waited for the familiar feeling of the rush of air, the feeling of demons on her chest. There was nothing. Just cold, deadly silence.

She opened her eyes and blinked as she adjusted to the light from the bare bulb swinging from the ceiling.

'Where the fuck am I?' she thought. Her head was thumping, and her mouth was parched. She lifted her head and took in her surroundings. Looking down, she could see she was lying on top of a bed, but it wasn't hers. Her hands brushed against the cold bare plaster walls. She lowered her eyes to the floor and stifled a scream when she saw concrete instead of her plush bedroom carpet. Pulling herself up, she took it all in. It looked like a basement, there were no windows and a heavy wooden door lay slightly ajar.

'Hello?' She whispered. 'Is there anyone here?'

There was no response. Lowering her feet to the floor, she shuffled round on the bed. She winced in pain as the movement caused her head to spin and a feeling of nausea rose in her throat.

'Hello? I-is anyone there?' She shouted this time, desperate for someone—anyone—to respond.

The door inched forward slowly, a snuffling noise coming from behind it. She pushed herself back onto the bed. Her eyes wide with terror, she watched the door move forward again. She closed her eyes tightly, afraid to look. She could hear a gentle panting and the padding of something coming closer. It began to move faster, coming towards her. It jumped up on the bed and she almost laughed in relief when she opened her eyes to see a golden Labrador sprawled out on top of the bed, pushing its nose up against her hand.

'Hello, boy,' she said, a sense of relief washing over her at this sudden appearance of something so normal. The dog nuzzled into her as though to reassure her.

'So, you're awake then, and I see you've met Cooper.'

She looked up, startled. Standing at the door with a huge, slightly wild grin on his face was Jim Aitken. He was holding a tray in his hands.

'I've brought you some dinner, you must be starving, sleepyhead. You've been asleep for almost twenty-four hours.'

'What the fuck?' she spat.

She watched as he walked towards her, the twisted smile on his face scaring her.

He placed the tray at the bottom of her bed and her stomach grumbled at the sight of the roast dinner. She was ravenous, but there was no way she could eat. Her mind was slipping away from her. She didn't know who she was anymore. Whimpering, she drew herself back onto the bed, one hand on the dog, seeking comfort.

'Rebecca, it's me. Your dad. Remember?'

She shook her head in denial, moving back on the bed, away from him. Trembling, she looked around wildly, muttering to herself.

Jim edged closer, slowly, reaching out his hand in a gesture of reassurance.

She pushed her back against the wall and began screaming.

'Shh, hen, it's me, I'm your dad. I'm not going to hurt you.'

She jumped back as though scalded—her eyes on fire, her breath rasping, her head shaking.

'N-n-n-ooooooo.' She began rocking back and forward, sobs wracking her body.

'Aw, hen,' Jim murmured as he moved the tray onto the floor. He sat down next to her and pulled something out of his pocket, handing it over to her. She was watching him through her heavy fringe.

The fight seemed to leave her, and her crying subsided. Putting her hand out, she closed it over the gift offered in Jim's. Clutching it to her, she took a deep breath and opened her fist, revealing the matching half of the pendant she'd kept with her since childhood. He was telling the truth.

She stared at him, her jaw dropping. 'Y-y-you are my dad?' She stuttered.

Jim nodded as he placed his hand over hers and began to cry.

She recoiled from his touch, not caring at the hurt in his eyes at her rejection, as the full weight of his admission registered. He had abandoned her. Her own father had been right there, able to help, and he had left her alone.

Nobody wants you, Rebecca. Not your mummy. Not your Daddy. Nobody loves you. Except me.

'Rebecca, love, you need to understand.'

She slumped back on the pillows, her eyes dead.

'I don't need to understand anything. I'm not Rebecca. She doesn't want to speak to you right now.'

'Love, you are Rebecca. I told you, the others… They aren't real. Remember, I know everything, love. It's going to be okay. You're here with me now.'

Sitting beside her and clutching her hand to his face, his tears spilled down her fingers. She pushed herself back further on the bed, trying desperately to get away from him. He held on tighter.

'Rebecca, please listen to me. I know everything and I know who Lucas is.'

The mention of her husband's name startled her. 'What do you mean, you know who he is?'

Jim's shoulder's slumped as he reached into his pocket and pulled out the crumpled photograph.

'W-w-where did you get that?'

'It doesn't matter where I got it love. What matters is that the man you married is part of the reason you are so messed up inside here,' his finger pointed to her head.

'Do you think we're stupid?' She spat. 'We know who he is. We know what he did. Samantha and I were dealing with it and now you've ruined everything.'

Jim crumpled, the sobs wracking his body.

Rebecca stared at the man in front of her, a mixture of fear, loathing and disgust on her face. *Let me fix it*, whispered Samantha. She ignored her. Prodding Jim sharply, she asked: 'But why? Why this?' She gestured around the room.

'I'm sorry, Rebecca,' he cried. 'I just wanted to make it up to you. I wanted to be with you, to be your dad, to be everything I should have been. I felt so guilty when I realised who you really were. I was too frightened to come out and tell you, hen. I was scared you would reject me. I didn't know what else to do.'

'How did you find out?' She snapped. Inside, her blood was running cold. She was fading again. She was leaving. She wanted to lie down and let her others take over, but she couldn't. This man in front of her was her father. Her dad… She had dreamed of this moment forever.

'I've always known, love, ever since the day you were born. The day I turned up to find you next to Stella's body… Oh, hen.'

She listened as he told her that he'd tried so hard to protect through her years in care. He told her of his shame of being unable to admit who he really was when he had turned up at the house all those years ago, and how he had gone out of his way to follow her through the care system.

'And Nicole?' she asked, memories of her visit to the house filtering through her brain. 'Did you try to save her too, or were you both in on this? What, did you both decide to bring me here, to get me out the way? Is that what happened… Daddy?'

Jim looked at her confused. 'What's Nicole got to do with it?'

'Don't pretend you don't know,' she spat.

'I don't know. What are you talking about? What's Nicole got to do with any of this?'

Something about the tone of his voice told her he was telling the truth. Crying, she told him about Nicole's visit to her house, her plan to get Lucas locked up and how she had spent months stalking and terrorising her.

'That bitch,' Jim growled.

Rebecca laughed mirthlessly. 'Yeah, but I guess she has reasons to be, doesn't she? We both do.'

Rebecca could feel herself shutting down. She couldn't cope with this; she couldn't deal with it. A thousand memories flooded her brain; the men, the abuse, the blood, the deaths… All of it had been his fault. This man had stood by and let it all happen to her. It was his fault. She closed her eyes, curled into a foetal position and rocked herself to sleep.

When she woke up, she felt different. She felt calm. She wasn't scared anymore. She was with her daddy. There was nothing to be scared of, was there? Daddy would look after her. She was home. Everything was going to be alright now.

56

AFTER RECEIVING NO reply to her text, Nicole had called Jim on the phone. He wasn't picking up. She contemplated just leaving without telling him she was going. But she wanted to explain the stuff about Lucas. It would soon be out in the open and she didn't want him finding out about it through office gossip.

Despite all his faults, he'd been okay to work with, one of the good guys. She rang a few times over the weekend but there was nothing, no text or emails. On the Monday morning, she called into the office only to be told Jim was off sick and they weren't sure when he'd be back in.

She knew where he lived, she could pack her car and pop round on her way back down South. Say a proper goodbye.

It was just after dinner time and getting dark when she drew up at the cottage Jim lived in. Lucky guy, she thought, living in such a quiet area, no nosey neighbours and just endless views of fields and hills. His car was parked up outside. At least he was in. She hoped he was okay, she was beginning to get a bit worried at the lack of communication from him. It wasn't like him at all.

When there was no answer at the door, she made her way around to the back of the house. The garden was overgrown, and furniture strewn everywhere. She peered in the kitchen window but saw no sign of him. Feeling anxious now, she looked through the dining room window, but he wasn't there, only the dog lying forlornly on the rug.

That wasn't right at all. She was just about to try the door when she heard a scream. She stopped and listened. It seemed to be coming from the side of the house. She remembered Jim talking about his retirement project, a small basement he was doing up.

Picking her way through the debris, she was careful not to make a sound. Maybe someone had broken in and Jim was being attacked. She felt for her mobile and pulled it out, checking she had a signal.

Edging her way closer to the side of the house, she stopped at the sound of raised voices.

'No Daddy. I fucking hate you!' a woman's voice screamed. The voice sounded familiar.

A man's voice muttered something quietly before the woman screamed again.

'Rebecca, please love, stop screaming. I'm trying to help you. I'm trying to make it up to you.' The voice was louder now. It was Jim's.

Nicole crouched down, intrigued. What the hell was going on here? Looking around, she noticed a small vent at the bottom of the side wall. She crawled closer and listened carefully.

'Come on, love, I'm your dad. You have to trust me.'

Now, isn't that just the perfect ending to this twisted fairy-tale, she thought.

57

IT BEGAN THE same way as always—a sense that something was lurking in the room, a black shape casting its malevolent shadow over her; the feeling of dark beady eyes feasting on her, sharp fingers pinching gently at first then becoming faster, more furious. Their claws dug into her skin, tearing at her muscles until she was sure they would be ripped apart.

In a bid to escape, she bit down hard on the unknown creatures, feeling their small bones crunch against her teeth but her bites didn't register. They didn't stop the relentless grabbing, crawling over her, touching her body, making her squirm, crawling up onto her chest until her breath almost left her.

Struggling against them, she fought to break free with every nerve in her body, pushing until she felt herself being propelled forward—faster, more furious—the wind sounding a mighty roar, escalating to hurricane force, its violence pulling the skin back from her face as she tried desperately to soar to freedom. The vibrations pounded her head, increasing until the point she felt that every bone in her face would shatter, but still the creatures chased, grabbing at their prize and unwilling to let go.

Her heart pumped so hard in her chest, it felt as though it was about to break free. She was sure she was going to have a heart attack or a stroke right here, right now, until finally she forced herself to stretch out her index finger, pushing it forward, screaming to escape and whoosh, it was gone.

Just like that.

The storm had ended and, as she watched the small black hands still grabbing, they slowly faded away; dimmed in their ferocity. It was quiet again.

Still.

Forcing her eyes to open fully, she reached out and grabbed the torch lying next to her. In the safety of the light, her breathing slowed and she became aware of her surroundings.

She remembered; Rebecca must not be forgotten. She remembered; she *was* Rebecca.

Her nightmare was real.

Putting her hand to her throat, she felt the chain, the half heart burning into her skin. The dog lay at her feet at the bottom of the bed, whimpering softly.

Using the torch, she cast the light around the room. The tray lay on the floor with the uneaten dinner congealing on the plate. To the side, the man's body lay motionless. She eased herself slowly from the bed and shuffled across the floor. She touched him gently. He didn't move.

'Daddy?' She whispered. There was no reply.

She laid her hand across his; he was freezing. Something glinted and caught her eye.

She looked up.

The fork was sticking out his neck.

She screamed.

But nobody heard.

Epilogue

1ST FEBRUARY 2019. BBC Scotland Breaking News. Today at Glasgow High Court, forty-one-year-old Lucas Findlay was sentenced to ten years in custody after pleading guilty to a series of historical sexual abuses and to the possession and distribution of indecent images. Findlay was found guilty of the abuse of six-year-old Nicole Holten between 1994 and 1995. Further charges of sexual abuse against another child were dropped due to lack of evidence.

Findlay is the son of notorious paedophile, Duncan Campbell, who was found murdered in Highmoss Prison in the early 1990s. Findlay had initially pled not guilty but made a last-minute change of plea following the admission of additional evidence. Judge Anthony Mann branded him a 'wicked and despicable man', recommending that he remain on the sex offenders register indefinitely following his eventual release.

Key witness in the trial, Ms Nicole Holten, waived her right to anonymity. In a brief statement read by her solicitor, Ms Holten said: 'Today, justice has been done, not only for me, but for all victims of Lucas Findlay and his father.'

Neighbours and colleagues of Findlay expressed their shock and disgust at the man whom they'd known to be a 'bit of a loner.' A source also hinted that Findlay had been abusing his wife for years. No charges have been brought in relation to these allegations and at this time, our reporters are unable to obtain a statement from his wife, who is currently receiving intensive medical care for an undisclosed condition.

Beechtree Secure Care Centre, Glasgow
15th February 2019

NICOLE TURNED OFF the ignition and stared at the building in front of her. Grey, miserable and depressing. Just like its inhabitants, she thought. Checking her reflection in the mirror, she smiled. She already looked better, more relaxed. That's what justice did for you.

Her mind drifted to Lucas and she wondered what he would see when he looked in the mirror. She hoped the monster he was would be staring right back at him. His sentence might not have been as severe as she had hoped, but she knew he wouldn't get an easy ride inside. She knew exactly what happened to prisoners like Lucas. He deserved everything that was coming to him. And she still had her friends on the inside to make sure he got exactly what he deserved. But now it was time to add the final piece in the jigsaw.

The gravel crunched under her feet as she made her way to reception. Set in its own grounds, Beechtree Secure Care Unit sat isolated from the rest of the hospital buildings. The court had decided Rebecca was unfit to stand trial for Jim's murder and she had been detained here for further treatment while they examined the facts of the case.

Nicole knew she could be stuck there for as long as the courts decided, and she had no right of appeal. Rebecca deserved it too, thought Nicole, but inside she felt conflicted. She knew Rebecca was a victim, like her. She knew she hadn't really been to blame for what had happened to them both as children. But she had lost everything because of her. If only

Rebecca had told someone before they'd started on her, then none of this would have happened.

A little voice inside admonished her for victim blaming but she couldn't help herself, her compassion and empathy had died a long time ago.

Her visit had already been authorised by hospital staff. The nurse who met her at Reception was a dead ringer for Uncle Fester from the Adams family. He led her through a maze of stark white corridors, punctuated by bright splashes of artwork from patients until they reached a room at the end. He asked Nicole to wait outside before knocking gently and asking Rebecca if she was up for visitors.

Appearances can be deceptive, thought Nicole. The man was a gentle giant. She didn't think she could have afforded Rebecca the same compassion he was.

After a minute, he came out and ushered her in.

'Do you want me to sit in with you?' he offered.

'No, it's okay, I'm fine. If I need you, I'll call.'

He smiled. 'You'll be fine with her, she's no bother at all, she's a docile wee thing. It's a shame really…'

Nicole cut him off before he could launch into a bleeding hearts speech.

'Yeah, I know, poor Rebecca. That's why I want to see her before I head back to Canada. I won't be long, I've not got a lot of time, my flight leaves this evening.' She hoped he got the hint that she just wanted to get on with this visit.

Nodding, he closed the door softly behind him as he left.

Nicole stared at the figure lying in the bed. She was shocked. Gone was the strong confident woman who had the third sector wrapped around her little finger. In her place was this small and pitiful creature, just lying there, staring at the ceiling. Her lips were moving, a string of unintelligible words whispering out.

'Rebecca?' She whispered. There was no response.

'Rebecca?' A little louder this time. Nothing.

'Rebecca, listen to me.' Her voice was stern.

The creature on the bed jumped. 'Rebecca isn't here just now, she can't speak to you.'

'Don't be so fucking stupid, it's you. I know you're in there.'

'Rebecca isn't available just now. You can speak to Samantha if you want.'

Nicole sighed. 'Okay, if that's the way you want to play it. I don't care what you call yourself. I'm just here to say my goodbyes.'

The woman stared blankly at her.

'Jesus, you really are fucking crazy, aren't you? Well, Rebecca, or Samantha, or whoever you are. Do you know why you are here? Because you murdered your daddy, isn't that right, murdering, crazy little bitch?'

Rebecca twitched a little.

'Only, I've got a wee confession to make,' Nicole giggled. 'You see, Rebecca. I know things have been difficult for you lately. I know you've been feeling that someone has been following you—the strange phone calls, flowers, things moved around the house… Thought you were going crazy again, didn't you?'

Rebecca's eyes widened.

'Guess what, bitch? You weren't going crazy after all. You *were* being followed. You *were* being watched. I've been watching you for months. It was so easy to get close to your husband and snatch his house key to make a copy. The idiot never even noticed. And that house, Rebecca, you didn't deserve to live in that type of comfort. You deserved to be back in this nut house, where you belong.'

Rebecca let out a whimper and Nicole laughed.

'That's not all, it wasn't just me Rebecca. Oh no. I've got friends in high places, you know? Friends who were a bit pissed off at you for all your interfering in their life. Remember Martin? Martin McCrae? It was down to you that his girlfriend grassed him to the police and he ended up in jail. It was all your fault he lost access to his kids. He was only too happy to help me, Rebecca, in return for a good probation report. He was quite happy to follow you, send you little gifts. So, you see, you weren't going crazy after all.'

A tear rolled down Rebecca's cheek.

'And you really should be grateful to him. It was Martin who found out just what Lucas was up to. You see, he didn't stop his ways after us, Rebecca. Yes, that's right… Us… You remember me, don't you? The wee girl next door. The girl you let take your place. Do you remember now?'

Rebecca seemed to shrink, pulling her covers tight around her.

'Yeah, thought you might start to remember. Well, thanks to you, I lost everything: my home, my family and my life.'

'And guess what, Rebecca? That night at Jim's house? You and your daddy weren't the only ones there. When Jim disappeared from work, I was suspicious. I managed to get his address from the files and thought I'd pay him a little visit, just to make sure he was okay. You know, me being a good colleague and all that.

I have to say I was a little taken aback when I saw you there, Rebecca. And then I heard him tell you who he really was. Your daddy. Imagine that? All those years and there was your daddy back to rescue you. Well, weren't you the lucky little bitch, eh?'

'I-I-I'm n-n-not Rebecca.'

'Oh, shut up. Too late now. I don't care what you have to say now. Just listen to me. When I realised who Jim really was,

I knew it was too good an opportunity to pass up on. He was losing his shit—batshit crazy must run in the family, huh? He wasn't going to let you go. Mind you, you didn't look like you wanted to leave him anyway. Cosy wee set up, families reunited and all that shit. So I waited, Rebecca. I waited until you were both asleep and I broke in. It wasn't hard, Jim wasn't the most security conscious. I thought about helping you escape, taking you away and helping you. But then I remembered what it was like for me to lose my daddy—my family, and that's when I decided. It was time for you to know exactly how I felt, Rebecca. It was time for you to know what it was like to lose everything. You didn't kill your daddy, Rebecca. It was me. I killed him and left you to take the blame.'

Nicole slumped back on her chair, spent. The woman in front of her said nothing. Her face was blank, her eyes were dead. There was nobody there.

'And now it's time for me to go, to start my life over again. As for you, there's no point in you even telling anyone what I've told you. Who's going to believe the crazy girl, eh? So, this is goodbye, Rebecca. Hope you have a nice life, whoever you are.'

She leaned over the bed and lightly kissed her on the cheek. Rebecca recoiled at the touch but still said nothing.

March 2019

JANICE KIRK WAS the Ward Sister on Ailsa Ward in Beechtree Secure Care Centre in Glasgow. She'd just finished the morning medication round. As part of her checks, she'd popped her head round the door of room seven, the patient was still resistant to all therapeutic interventions and was refusing to engage with any of the specialist mental health services on site. She largely remained isolated in her room.

Janice watched as the woman rocked back and forward on the bed, muttering to herself and pulling at her hair. She refused to look Janice in the eye and drew the covers over her head as soon as she realised she was being observed.

'Come on, pet,' Janice had said gently. 'Why not get up for a while today. We could go along to the day room and have a wee chat if you want. Just me and you? Eh?'

'My name is fucking Samantha... i am not fucking Rebecca Findlay!' The woman had screamed at her.

Shaking her head, Janice had gently closed the door and made her way back to the duty room to write up the morning's patient records.

Janice thought back to Rebecca's admission almost eight months ago. She'd been found next to the body of a social worker called Jim Aitken. The alert had been raised by concerned colleagues when Jim hadn't turned up for work after an extended period of leave and all attempts to contact him had failed.

Police had been dispatched to follow up on the missing person's report and had found Jim Aitken dead. Postmortem results had ruled a fatal stabbing.

Rebecca had been found emaciated, next to his body, along with a dog. Nobody knew how she'd got there, or what she was doing with Jim. She was the only suspect for his murder. However, a psychiatric assessment had found her unfit to stand trial and she had been sent to Beechtree for treatment.

She had no known family or friends. The only person who had come to visit her was about a month ago. It was the same woman that Janice had seen on BBC news the night before she visited. Nicole Holten, yeah that was her, she smiled recalling the chatty blonde Canadian. Nicole hadn't spoken to Rebecca for very long, but she'd been keen to talk to staff.

Nicole had told them that she'd already spoken to the police about the case. She had informed them that Jim Aitken had been her colleague, but it was her view that he'd always been a bit strange, a bit obsessive in his behaviour. She told the nursing staff that Jim had been obsessed by Rebecca after their paths had crossed through work.

'He talked about her constantly; he creeped me out a little, if I'm totally honest,' she'd confessed. 'But I'd never have thought he would kidnap her. She must have been terrified to have done what she did,' she said, tears filling her eyes. 'You hear about this stuff all the time, stalking and stuff, but I'd never have guessed he would have taken it that far.'

She'd gone on to say that she hadn't mentioned anything about Jim's behaviour before, as she'd just assumed he'd taken some time off to deal with his mental health and had been handling his issues.

'Things are pretty stressful in our line of work,' she'd admitted, as though offering an excuse for his behaviour. Nicole had said she'd thought Rebecca had handed in her notice and left the area and with her own court case coming up, she hadn't been able to face talking about her concerns with anyone until it was all over.

It was after Nicole's brief visit that Rebecca had made another suicide attempt. Janice shook her head as she thought about the waste of the poor lassie's life. She knew that her time in hospital wasn't going to be short. This one needed a lot of treatment.

MEANWHILE, IN ROOM seven, the woman rocked back and forward clutching her knees close into her chest.

I don't like that bitch, Nicole. She giggled. *And you know what happens to people I don't like, don't you?*

The woman in the bed, sat up, a spark bringing her eyes to life. She giggled.

'We're not going to let her get away with it, are we Samantha?'

ACKNOWLEDGEMENTS

Writing a book isn't a solitary occupation; so many people have played their part in getting me to this point in my journey. I've been spectacularly lucky in the support I've been given. I always wanted to write but thought writing books was for other people. And then I found the book community and my life changed. So many people supported and encouraged me to believe in my dreams and in myself.

I just know I'm going to miss someone out, apologies if I do, but you are all in my thoughts.

Noelle Holten, my #Twinnie blogger and partner in crime, you have been my inspiration from the beginning. Your determination and passion for what you do is phenomenal and thank you for giving me the confidence and courage to sit my ass down on that chair and start writing.

Graham Smith and all the Crime and Publishment gang; I was like a rabbit in headlights that first weekend but your support sent me home determined to finish what I had started. And a special thanks to Chris Simmons for being my partner in crime in the naughty corner that weekend and becoming a friend for life.

To Jackie McLean who made me so welcome at the Glasgow writing group and made me realise writers are just ordinary people.

To Alan Jones for all your support and laughs throughout the years.

My beta readers, Claire Knight, Kate Eveleigh, Sarah Hardy and Emma Mitchell along with Noelle and Graham made me believe that maybe I could actually do something with my words.

Emma Mitchell of Creating Perfection edited the first draft of Sins of the Father and helped me get it ready for submission. She made the whole process painless.

To Karen Sullivan of Orenda who met me in Edinburgh and talked me through the publishing process and helped me really focus on what I wanted to achieve. You are a star.

To Theresa Talbot and Heleen Kist for being such kick ass women and making me believe I had every right to follow my dreams.

To Susie Lynes, whose quiet wisdom and words of support have spurred me on. I love you hen.

To Mary Picken and Anne Cater, two true friends for life who I can't imagine not knowing.

To Angela Martin, Katie Berrie & Eileen McCullagh for being my Harrogate and book buddies and keeping my feet firmly on the floor.

To my best friend Susan Bonner, LL - you didn't think I'd leave you out- for always believing in me, even though I'm super scary.

To Team Ceartas for keeping me grounded and reminding me of what matters most.

And to Sean and all the team at Red Dog who took a chance on me, thank you for making my dream come true and giving me a place in the kennels.

Thank you to everyone who has been on this journey with me, thanks to everyone who has picked up this book and read it. I hope you enjoyed it.

But last and most definitely not least to all of my family, way too many to mention. I have to say thanks to my older cousin, Jim Aitken, sorry if you're not the character you wanted to be! But thanks for letting me steal your name!

And to my mammy, my sister, brother in law; my nieces, nephews, the millions of you out there.

To Greg, even though we're not together and we do each other's heads in, thanks for all the support over the years.

To my dad, I hope you're up there looking down and proud of me, Dad, thank you for giving me my love of books and my stubborn nature!

Last but not least my kids, Anton and Jess, hope your maw has made you proud because I'm proud of you two every single day of my life.

ABOUT THE AUTHOR

By day Sharon Bairden is the Services Manager in a small, local independent advocacy service and has a passion for human rights; by night she has a passion for all things criminal.

She blogs at Chapterinmylife and is delighted to be crossing over to the other side of the fence to become a writer.

Sharon lives on the outskirts of Glasgow, has two grown up children, a grandson, a Golden Labrador and a cat. She spends most of her spare time doing all things bookish, from reading to attending as many book festivals and launches as she can.

She has been known to step out of her comfort zone on the odd occasion and has walked over burning coals and broken glass – but not at the same time!